THE KILLING POINT

(An Alexa Chase Suspense Thriller—Book 4)

Kate Bold

Kate Bold

Bestselling author Kate Bold is author of the ALEXA CHASE SUSPENSE THRILLER series, comprising six books (and counting); the ASHLEY HOPE SUSPENSE THRILLER series, comprising six books (and counting); and the CAMILLE GRACE FBI SUSPENSE THRILLER series, comprising three books (and counting).

An avid reader and lifelong fan of the mystery and thriller genres, Kate loves to hear from you, so please feel free to visit www.kateboldauthor.com to learn more and stay in touch.

ISBN: 978-1-0943-9455-8

BOOKS BY KATE BOLD

ALEXA CHASE SUSPENSE THRILLER
THE KILLING GAME (Book #1)
THE KILLING TIDE (Book #2)
THE KILLING HOUR (Book #3)
THE KILLING POINT (Book #4)
THE KILLING FOG (Book #5)
THE KILLING PLACE (Book #6)

ASHLEY HOPE SUSPENSE THRILLER
LET ME GO (Book #1)
LET ME OUT (Book #2)
LET ME LIVE (Book #3)
LET ME BREATHE (Book #4)
LET ME FORGET (Book #5)
LET ME ESCAPE (Book #6)

CAMILLE GRACE FBI SUSPENSE THRILLER
NOT ME (Book #1)
NOT NOW (Book #2)
NOT WELL (Book #3)

CHAPTER ONE

A+ Storage, Maricopa Freeway, just south of Phoenix, Arizona
11 p.m.

The thing that U.S. Deputy Marshal Alexa Chase hated the most about gunfights was the waiting.

Once the bullets started flying, adrenaline and a laser-sharp focus kept you from thinking; but in those long minutes before it all kicked off, minutes that seemed to stretch for days, you couldn't help but think about everything that could go wrong.

Because it had all gone wrong so many times before.

Alexa crouched behind a small prefab warehouse, sweat trickling beneath her Kevlar helmet and vest in the warm Arizona night. In her hands she gripped her Glock 9mm. Next to her, in similar attire and representing the FBI on this raid, crouched her partner Special Agent Stuart Barrett. He held an M4 assault rifle like most other members of the team. Behind them were half a dozen SWAT team members. Just ten yards ahead, crouching behind another warehouse, were another six SWAT team members.

They had formed up in a large complex of warehouses, rented to various small businesses and trucking companies, or anyone else who was willing to pay good money for convenient storage and no oversight. The owner claimed no knowledge of what was being stored in Warehouse Eight just a couple of buildings away from where Alexa and her colleagues had assembled.

But of course he would. It was in his best interest not to know what happened in his storage facility, and even if he did, it was certainly in his best interest not to tell. Otherwise, he'd end up staked out in the middle of the desert with his eyes and tongue gouged out.

Because Warehouse Eight was rented by the Mexican drug gang Los Diablos Auténticos, "The Real Devils," as opposed to the older, mostly white motorcycle gang called Los Diablos. The two gangs attacked each other on sight.

Los Diablos Auténticos ran most of the crystal meth and heroin in central Arizona. Warehouse Eight was where they stored it under the name of a fake delivery company, and tonight was the night when their regional dealers came to pick up their packets for the month.

There were at least ten guys in there, all armed and most of them having probably killed before. There had been a string of unsolved murders in the state that investigators had linked to the gang. Los Diablos Auténticos would not go down quietly.

Alexa looked over to the SWAT team leader at the corner of the warehouse opposite. He held up three fingers of his gloved hand.

Three.

Two.

One.

They moved out, silent save for the crunch of boots on hardpack soil and the soft rustle of equipment. Most of the SWAT team members carried shotguns or assault rifles. She'd been offered one as well, but she felt more comfortable with her Glock, and, this close, a 9mm would do just as well as a shotgun blast.

She hoped it wouldn't come to that, but of course it would.

Stuart ran just by her side, an assault rifle in his easy grip. Two tours of duty in Iraq made him better with that weapon than anyone else on the raid.

He moved well too, keeping his place on point with a precision that looked casual but was anything but.

Up ahead she saw the warehouse with a large number eight painted on the gable. A double-wide garage door was closed and padlocked. A smaller office door stood next to it, no doubt locked too. Beyond the warehouse, the other wing of the SWAT raid emerged from the darkness. She saw no one else. Los Diablos Auténticos hadn't posted a guard. Cocky and stupid, like most drug gangs.

Of course, no one but law enforcement would be cocky and stupid enough to come breaking in on their distribution meeting.

A hulking member of the SWAT team came up to the door carrying a red steel cylinder the guys affectionately called "the big red key." A battering ram. Several of his team members covered him. Alexa got into her position, just to the left of the door. She let out a long, slow breath.

Almost there.

The captain of the SWAT team, up close to the guy with the battering ram, held up three fingers.

Three.

Two.

One.

The officer swung back the battering ram and hit the door, right next to the lock. There was a loud bang, and the door flew open.

"POLICE! GET FACE DOWN ON THE FLOOR WITH YOUR HANDS BEHIND YOUR HEAD!"

The SWAT team rushed in.

Just as Alexa crossed the threshold, the first shots rang out.

Beyond the door was a small office. One civilian lay face down on the floor, a SWAT team member with a knee on his back and already cuffing him. Alexa only saw that for an instant as the SWAT team poured past and into a large warehouse area.

She ducked low and to the left as more shots rang through the large interior, echoing loudly off the metal ceiling.

Her first good look at the scene was one of utter confusion. Rows of wooden crates stood neatly stacked on pallets, obscuring the view of most of the warehouse interior. At the front of the warehouse, near the door to the office, was a large folding metal table covered in shrink-wrapped packets.

The SWAT team fanned out on either side of the office doorway, shouting and advancing on the gang. Some of the young men had obeyed orders and gotten down on the floor. Some ran for a back door that, if they had been thinking clearly, they should have known was already guarded.

Several more were firing back from behind the crates.

A gang member blared away with an UZI. A cop fell. Stuart took him out with a single shot to the head.

Alexa aimed at another young tough firing a Glock much like hers. She hit him in the shoulder. A flurry of bullets from her fellow officers made him duck out of sight.

The SWAT team advanced. Keep up the momentum. Keep them retreating when they had nowhere to retreat.

The natural response would be to flee back to the safety of the office and fire at the gang from there, but that would lead to a standoff that could last hours, and the wall between the office and the warehouse was probably cheap drywall that wouldn't provide cover anyway. The safest way was forward.

She darted across the open space in front of the table, a few yards that felt like ten miles. SWAT team members rushed alongside to her left and right. Stuart was close, but she didn't keep track of where. She focused only on the opening between two stacks of crates where she had seen the wounded gang member disappear. She kept her pistol leveled at that spot.

The gunfire continued as the SWAT team cleared the other aisles. She looped around the table and made it the last few steps to her target.

She got behind the crate, splintered by her and her companions' shots, ducked low, and swung around.

No one. Just a trail of blood leading away and then around another stack of crates.

The pallets of crates were not stacked in solid lines, but set apart from one another in uneven clusters. Alexa had entered a maze.

Cursing to herself, she paced forward, a guy from the SWAT team just to her left. Side by side, they barely had enough room to maneuver.

They got to the next set of pallets. He swung left, Alexa right.

No one. Shots and shouts echoed all around. Some of Los Diablos Auténticos had decided to make a last stand.

She swung left around the next stack of crates. A bullet snapped into the wood next to her head. Alexa didn't see where from, because right in front of her was one of the gang members, blasting away at an unseen opponent to his left with an UZI.

Alexa raised her gun to fire.

Just then the gang member's UZI clicked empty, and the man turned.

Alexa recognized Jeronimo Cortez, the leader of Los Diablos Auténticos.

His face registered shock.

"FREEZE!" she shouted over a flurry of gunfire.

If he didn't drop that gun immediately, she would fire. She didn't have time for negotiations.

Something in her eyes must have signaled that, because one of the most dangerous gang members in the Southwest dropped his gun and raised his hands.

"DOWN ON THE FLOOR. YOU KNOW THE ROUTINE."

The guy had a rap sheet so long that Alexa had stopped reading halfway through.

He got face down on the floor with his hands behind his head like a pro.

The firing started to die down, moving more distant as the gang members retreated to the back of the warehouse. There was a flurry of gunfire right at the back for a second, cutting off short. Alexa figured they must have opened the back door and gotten the police's little surprise.

No more shots came. Now all she could hear through the ringing in her ears were groans and shouted commands.

Alexa checked the coast was clear, put a knee on the small of Jeronimo Cortez's back and zip tied his wrists.

"Jeronimo Cortez, I am arresting you on suspicion of conspiracy to distribute narcotics, possession of narcotics, possession of an illegal firearm, first degree—"

"Let's make a deal," he said, cutting off her long list of charges.

"Make it with the judge."

"No time."

The man sounded desperate, and about more than his current situation.

A shot rang out. A flurry of shots replied. A man screamed something in Spanish.

"What do you mean there's no time?"

"You want me for a murder rap, right? Jorge Cantinflas. Jim Yonker. Juan Garcia. Weston Oak."

"And probably a few more."

"Plenty more you don't know about. I can lead you to the bodies."

Alexa glanced around again to check she was safe. All she saw was a SWAT team member hauling off a gang member. Someone shouted, "All clear!"

Alexa looked down at the gang leader, who craned his neck to look up at her.

"You're leading me to bodies we don't know about? Why would you do that?" she asked.

"Because I didn't kill none of them. But I can help you catch the guy who did."

His voice wavered as he spoke, at odds with his demeanor a moment before.

"Tell it to the judge," Alexa grumbled, hauling him to his feet. She'd heard a lot of bull from prisoners. They all tried to pull something.

"Orlando Fuerte. You'll find him just off of mile 48 of State Road 78 near Bouse. Shot through the head two days ago. If you've been watching me like I'm sure you have, you know I was here in Phoenix. Haven't been out of the city in two weeks. Go find him, and then we'll talk."

Alexa stared at him. She had never seen such openness in a detainee before.

Or such desperation.

His eyes widened further, and his voice shook. "Go find him. Please. I got more to tell you."

Please?

Her partner Stuart came jogging up.

"Thank God you're safe!" Alexa said.

He grinned. "Same to you." He looked at Cortez. "Wow! Looks like you caught the big fish."

"No," she muttered. "No, I don't think we've caught the big fish at all."

CHAPTER TWO

Across town, that same night

Brianna Silverman needed it, needed it so badly she'd do anything to get it. All her usual sources weren't holding or weren't answering. She hadn't had any since yesterday morning, when she'd shot up in her private bathroom while Daddy had a big senate meeting in D.C. and Mother went off to do whatever the hell she did all day.

As Brianna drove her BMW convertible through a working-class neighborhood in Phoenix, she thought about that last time. She had taken the tiny little glob of beautiful black tar, cooked up, and eased the needle in between her toes. The arm was better, but even her clueless parents might notice the track marks. She had to be careful. The heroin had rushed into her veins and filled her with an untouchable sense of well-being. She had sat there on the toilet, nodding off for two hours.

But that had been yesterday morning, and now the first stages of withdrawal warned her of imminent torture. The tenseness in her muscles that would soon turn to cramps and spasms. The irritation in her skin that within another hour would become unbearable itching. The thirst that would soon parch her throat and make her voice come out in an old woman's gasp.

She needed to get some. She'd have plenty of privacy tonight. Daddy wouldn't be back for a week. Rosie had done the cleaning and cooking and had left. And Mother? Well, Mother wasn't ever really there.

As she drove deeper into the neighborhood, Brianna barely heard the thudding music of the block party on the next street over or saw the run-down look of the houses she passed, or the curious and hungry stares her expensive car got. It was late in a bad neighborhood, and Brianna knew she shouldn't be here.

But she could take care of herself. She had street smarts, and more importantly, she finally had a connection.

After a whole day of calling and visiting dumpy neighborhoods like this one, she had finally gotten a lead. A dealer who she had met at a party one night, a friend of a friend of her usual source, had told her about another house where you could get heroin. He had told her as "a favor." She had to do him a favor in return.

She tried not to think about that.

Finally! Brianna saw the house up ahead. The porch light was on, but no one was outside. Light shone dimly from behind dark curtains.

Brianna's hands shook a little as she parked, and a shudder ran through her body. Almost there. The symptoms always got worse when you were almost there.

Her contact had called to tell them she was coming, so she shouldn't have any trouble. Within an hour, she'd be back in her room with the one thing in life she really needed.

She parked, and in her rush forgot to look around her and forgot even to lock her car. Instead, she jogged through the barren dirt yard and up the three warped wooden stairs to the front door.

Brianna pounded on it, desperate now, the first cramps wracking her body. She heard movement inside. The peephole darkened.

"Who are you?"

"Santiago's friend," Brianna replied through clenched teeth.

Pause.

Come on. Come on.

She heard a latch click open. Brianna almost sobbed in relief.

The door opened. A muscular Hispanic man with a shaved head and a tattoo of some Spanish words across the front of his neck studied her.

"I'm Santiago's friend," she said.

He looked beyond her, taking in the car, the street. He gave a quick nod and stepped aside. Brianna rushed in. The guy closed and locked the door behind her.

Brianna found herself in a dingy living room. Empty beer bottles covered a battered coffee table. Three other guys lounged in armchairs, staring at her. In the air hung the smell of marijuana.

"Santiago told me you were coming," Neck Tattoo said. "What you looking for?"

"H."

She said this with no nervousness, no hesitation. She knew she was in the right place. Five years of experimentation, ever since she was fourteen, and two years of hard addiction, had made her an expert.

He nodded toward a back room. Brianna followed.

It was a bedroom, probably his bedroom considering the ease in which he moved through it, pulling open a sock drawer and pulling out a small wooden box. He opened it and showed her the contents. Inside were a hundred little plastic bags with black tar.

Brianna laughed. Too loud. Almost a cackle.

"How much you want?" the dealer asked.

"A gram."

"Two hundred and fifty."

Expensive, and this stuff was probably cut. She didn't argue. She pulled out her wallet, fumbled it, caught it before it landed on the floor, and hurriedly pulled out some money, not even bothering to count it properly.

Neck Tattoo did. He snickered and handed her back her change.

Brianna was too desperate to feel embarrassed. She just fidgeted, moving back and forth from one foot to the other as the dealer pulled out ten little bags.

She grabbed them and stuffed them in her pocket. Another cramp gripped her body, making it impossible to scratch the all-body itch that made her want to scream.

Neck Tattoo studied her for a second.

"You look pretty bad off. You can shoot up here if you want to."

And wake up on that bed naked and pregnant? No thanks.

"Gotta go," she husked, and turned for the door. She hoped she had enough self-control to get home without crashing.

The sound of a door being kicked open in the front room made her yelp and jump back.

Shouts from the guys in the living room, cut off short by three quick shots. Brianna looked around for a place to hide, saw a bathroom at the far side of the bedroom, and ran for it. Neck Tattoo yanked open the drawer on a bedside table and pulled out an automatic pistol. He flicked off the safety, turned to the bedroom door, and fell back with a bullet through his skull. Blood spattered on Brianna, rooting her in place at the doorway to the bathroom.

For the first time all day, she had stopped thinking of her withdrawal symptoms. No, she had something much, much worse to fear.

A man she hadn't seen before strolled into the room. The first thing Brianna noticed was the huge pistol in his left hand. Thankfully it wasn't pointing at her. Then she looked more carefully at the man carrying it. He looked Mexican, dressed in expensive black slacks and matching dress shirt. On his feet were cowboy boots of finely tooled black leather. He had a lean, graceful body and a confident way of moving that told her this wasn't the first time he had killed someone.

And it wouldn't be the last.

Brianna struggled to speak. "D-don't kill me. My dad's Senator Silverman."

The man stood there, not responding, a curiously blank look on his face.

"Senator Silverman. You know? Republican for Arizona? He's rich. He … he can pay. Whatever you want."

The man smiled and stepped toward her, raising his gun.

CHAPTER THREE

Alexa should have felt surprised that Jeronimo Cortez turned out to be telling the truth, but after the look he gave her the previous night, her gut told her they'd find the body.

Phoenix P.D. got the call early the next morning after the La Paz County Sheriff's Office went out to investigate. They found the dead gang member's body exactly where Cortez said it would be, and the initial report from the coroner's office put the time of death by gunshot wound to the back of the head at approximately 48 hours previously.

Now Cortez, sitting tall in his handcuffs and orange jumpsuit, conferred in whispers with his lawyer as Alexa entered the interrogation room.

With her came Stuart and Phoenix Homicide Detective John Rebstock.

"*Hola Jero, cómo estás*?" Rebstock asked in fluent Spanish as he settled his heavy frame into a chair across from the prisoner. The chair squealed in protest at having to take his 300+ pounds. The man stood six-five, with a drinker's nose, a wrinkled summer suit, and gave off an air of cheap aftershave and too many cigarettes.

Jeronimo Cortez looked him over.

"The pigs are sending out the big guns, eh?" the gang leader said. He did not say this with any trace of sarcasm. Everyone in the Phoenix criminal world knew how capable John Rebstock was.

Alexa and Stuart sat down on either side of him, both having to edge their seats away to get room.

"We dug up your friend," Alexa said. "So now that you've gotten our attention, we'd like to know what you have to offer."

The attorney made a small hand motion to Cortez and spoke.

"My client is willing to share information on an individual in his organization who has committed a series of murders in Arizona and plans on continuing his killing spree over the next few weeks. In return, we'd like all murder investigations connected with my client dropped and he'll plead guilty to the drug charges."

Rebstock snorted. "Selling out one of your *compadres* in order to not get the chair? That isn't going to go down well in prison."

Alexa nodded. Like all the major gangs, Los Diablos Auténticos had a lot of people on the inside. Snitches did not prosper behind bars. And if their leader snitched? That would be ugly. Really ugly.

And he hadn't asked to be sent to a different state, something a lot of snitches did in his situation.

"This guy ain't no Diablo," Cortez said.

"Your lawyer just said he was," Stuart said.

Cortez looked him over. Stuart wore the black suit and tie common among FBI agents, a completely inappropriate mode of attire for the Desert Southwest that Alexa still hadn't convinced him to shed.

"Who the hell are you?"

"Agent Stuart Barrett, FBI."

"Am I supposed to be impressed?"

"No. You're supposed to talk."

Cortez leaned back in his chair. "I will if I get a deal. And hurry up. Time is ticking. That *hombre* is going to kill again pretty soon."

"Giving us one body isn't enough to drop charges of this magnitude," Alexa said. "And we have to get the D.A. to sign off on it. You're going to have to give us more."

"I can give you directions to more bodies."

Rebstock frowned. "You know where all the bodies are, and you claim you didn't have anything to do with it? Come on, Jero. I thought you had more brains than that."

"I know because he calls me."

"Calls you?" Alexa asked. This was getting weirder and weirder.

"Or one of my people. He likes to brag."

"You never answered my question," Stuart said. "Your lawyer said he was a Diablo and you say he isn't."

"Un Diablo Auténtico," Cortez corrected. "We got nothing to do with those gringos on bikes."

"Whatever. Answer the question."

Cortez looked at his lawyer, who gave him a slight nod.

"He was an Auténtico, but we burned him on the altar."

Alexa felt a chill go through her.

"Huh?" Stuart said.

Cortez laughed and pointed at him.

"Where did you get this gringo? D.C.?" he asked Alexa.

"As a matter of fact, I did," she admitted.

"Tell him what burning on the altar means. You're Arizona born and bred. I can tell. Also tell him to change his clothes. He looks like he's going to a funeral."

"It will be yours if you don't give us something." Alexa turned to Stuart. "Burning on the altar is something the Latino gangs do to kick someone out. They make an altar and decorate it with a cross and pictures of saints, then burn a photo of the person on it. Then everyone in the gang swears to kill him if they ever see him."

"They haven't done a very good job," Stuart said.

"Some tried," Cortez replied. "That's why the body count is so high."

"And you're saying this guy is going to kill again?" Detective Rebstock asked. "Not many of your people out on the streets after last night."

"You know that ain't true. And he ain't just going after my people. He's going after anybody he feels like."

Alexa traded looks with the detective and the FBI man. Cortez sounded sincere. Sure, he wanted to avoid the death penalty, but he also knew that was all he would get. With his priors, and the several kilos of meth and heroin they had seized, he would spend the rest of his life behind bars.

Rebstock seemed to think the same thing, and representing the city, who had officially made the bust, it was his call.

"Give us details on those bodies and I'll talk to the D.A.," he said.

"Just so I know you play straight with me, let me tell you that I got more information. Information on how to catch the guy. You'll get that if we make a deal."

"All right," Rebstock said. "Spill."

"There's a construction site on the west side of Arizona City. Luxury apartments. 'Enjoy the desert sunset' and all that crap. Except the developer went bust. So it's only half built. Been abandoned for months. He buries them there. I don't know where exactly. You'll have to search the site."

"We'll do it," Alexa told Rebstock. Stuart nodded.

"All right," the homicide detective said. "I'll send you with a K9 unit trained to sniff out bodies."

Cortez snorted. "With the number he killed, you won't need dogs to smell it."

* * *

Arizona City was one of the many new developments dotting the sides of Interstate 10 between Phoenix and Tucson. When Alexa had been a kid, you could drive the 110 miles between the two cities and see only desert, the occasional ranch house, and a couple of small towns. No more. More and more towns had popped up, and outlet centers, and rest stops. Pretty soon, she feared, it would be a continuous stretch of concrete.

Stuart drove with Alexa in the passenger's seat. Behind came the police K9 unit van with two officers and a friendly German Shepherd named Nosey. Not the most original name for a sniffer dog, but Nosey knew her job.

They found the development easily enough, well off the Interstate and at the end of a half a mile of paved road with nothing on it. Desert stretched out on all sides, except for Arizona City to the east.

Beyond a chain link fence stood a series of large townhouses, each one alike. Their roofs had been put on, but their walls hadn't been surfaced and the doorways and windows remained empty rectangles. No construction equipment was in sight. This place looked like it would never be finished. Instead, it would just stand as a useless blight in the desert.

"There," Stuart said, pointing. He parked in front of a large hole cut in the fence.

They got out. The male and female officers from the K9 unit parked and got out behind them. As they opened up the back of the van to get Nosey, Alexa ducked through the hole in the fence and started walking toward the construction site.

The hard-packed earth didn't show any footprints, and she was surprised not to see the beer cans and graffiti one usually found at abandoned sites. The local kids must have preferred someplace a little closer to get drunk and cause trouble.

Alexa walked across a barren stretch of desert, the wind rustling a few dry clumps of grass. Otherwise, there was no sound. A playful bark from the dog sounded alien in this bleak landscape.

She came to the first of the townhouses and peeked through a window. The place wasn't even half finished. No wiring, no plumbing. The stairs were a set of concrete treads.

Alexa moved to the next one. It looked the same.

"Spooky place," Stuart said.

Alexa jerked. She hadn't realized he was behind her. Two tours of duty in Iraq had made him pretty good at walking quietly, even in dress shoes.

"Wouldn't want to be here at night," Alexa agreed.

"Jeronimo's friend would, though."

"You think he's telling the truth?"

"My gut says yes."

"So does mine."

Something beyond the gap between the second and third houses caught her eye. A rough patch in the soil, situated between a heap of dirt left by some backhoe and a concrete platform that would have served as the base for something that would now never get built.

Alexa walked toward it. Yes, the soil was definitely disturbed here, and recently.

She stopped at the edge of it, an area about ten feet to a side. She could see where someone had used the flat part of a shovel to tamp down the earth in an attempt to make it look undisturbed, but her desert-trained eye spotted a slight difference in the soil color. The topsoil layer in Arizona gets so baked by the sun that it's lighter than the soil beneath, even if the lower layer is equally dry. So whoever had dug up the soil had left a large, darker rectangle on the desert floor.

He or she or they must have known this would happen, because they dug in an area blocked from view on three sides. If she hadn't looked at just the right angle as she passed between the houses, she would have missed it.

"What you got?" one of the K9 team called as they came up to them.

Nosey pulled on her leash.

"Find something, girl?" the other cop asked. He let her go, and Nosey rushed over to the darker section, circled, and barked.

"That was quick," the K9 officer said.

The dog kept circling the disturbed area, and it would not stop barking.

Alexa let out a long, slow breath. This was going to be a tough day.

CHAPTER FOUR

Alexa watched as the forensics team carefully scraped the soil away with all the care of an archaeological excavation. They had already stripped off six inches of soil to partially uncover a dozen bodies. They lay in an orderly row, all men, mostly young and mostly Hispanic.

Alexa and Stuart had watched this meticulous, grisly process for the past couple of hours, phoning in regularly to Rebstock to keep him updated. He hadn't been out yet. He was on the scene of another murder, a sixty-year-old man who had stabbed his wife of thirty years to death with a pair of scissors. The evil of the world did not rest just because they had uncovered a major tragedy.

The CSI team brushed away dirt from the faces and worked around the edges of their bodies to reveal more of their appearance. The corpses looked like ghosts materializing out of the earth.

The team's head, Annette Guevara, was everywhere, checking, making notes, giving instructions. A genius at her work, she could tease out clues from even the subtlest crime scene.

With something like this, she could discover volumes.

At the moment she crouched over the head of one of the bodies in the middle of the row, staring at it. Her long brown hair was tied up in a bun, and her pretty features were set in concentration. She looked younger than her age, almost like a teenager, although no teenagers Alex had ever met could concentrate this hard on anything.

At last she stood, wiped the dirt off her knees in an absentminded gesture, and walked over to them. Without preamble or even a hello, she started talking.

"We're dealing with a left-handed male who is fairly strong but not overly so, and with great physical reflexes. His preferred weapon is a 9mm automatic, but he killed several of the victims with blunt force trauma. In every case, he shot them in the back of the head execution style, often a couple of hours after they were dead."

"That's odd," Stuart said, handing his girlfriend a double espresso he had bought at the last gas station they'd passed. Alexa stifled a smile. He was like her puppy dog, if puppy dogs could buy espressos at gas stations.

"Thanks, baby," Annette said. "It was done in what looks like a ritual fashion. For the ones who were already dead, and therefore a bit more cooperative, he would stand in the exact same position. About five or six feet behind and a little to the right."

She took a sip of her coffee and went on. "Time of death ranges from eight to ten days to two days. In each case he remembered where he buried the previous victim and dug a grave right next to him. He made an orderly row with the first victim on one end and his final victim on the other."

Alexa considered this. It would have been a difficult thing to do in the dark.

"Any sign that he got injured in any of these fights?" Alexa asked.

"Nope. None of the knuckles show any scraping or bruising from throwing a punch. I'll have to check the knees when I undress them, but I doubt I'll find anything. There aren't many defensive wounds and any of those are glancing. That's one of the ways I know he was quick."

"What do you mean by glancing defensive wounds?" Alexa asked. Sometimes you had to bring Annette down to earth.

"Meaning that when the victim brought up his arm to stop some blunt force trauma, the bruise or break wasn't directly on the arm. It was on the edge of the arm because they didn't get the arm up quick enough. In at least one case, the guy lying three bodies away from us, tried to block his face, but the weapon barely hit the forearm before continuing on to break the right cheekbone. I'll probably find more examples once I get them cleaned up."

"So what was this blunt weapon?" Stuart asked.

"Different in each case. One looks like the wooden handle of a tool. Another was probably a wrench—the victim had grease stains on his clothes and under his nails, so he probably worked in a garage or body shop—and a couple with what looks like a tire iron. Most victims had only bullet wounds, although I might find more evidence of blunt force trauma when I undress them."

Alexa had the odd thought that because Annette would be so busy tonight with the case, she would be spending time with naked corpses instead of a naked Stuart.

Ugh, why did I even think of that? This job is getting to me.

“Thanks, Annette, keep us posted,” Alexa said, trying to keep her voice level.

“I always do.”

The CSI team leader reached out and brushed Stuart’s chest with her fingertips as she turned and walked back to the mass grave.

“Looks like Cortez told the truth in a bigger way than we ever imagined,” Stuart said, watching her go.

Alexa nodded.

Yes, the gang leader had been right.

Cortez was right about something else too. They did have him on surveillance, and he hadn’t been out of Phoenix in two weeks. It would have been impossible for him to commit the bulk of the murders.

He could have ordered them, though.

Alexa had some tough questions for him at their meeting this afternoon.

* * *

Once again, they sat in the interrogation room with Jeronimo Cortez and his attorney. Homicide Detective Rebstock came with a folder tucked under his arm. The deal with the D.A.?

She and Stuart flanked the detective like before. For a moment, both sides stared at each other in silence.

“So?” Cortez asked at last.

“Twelve bodies,” Rebstock said. “All shot in the back of the head, execution style. Some had other wounds, a few fatal, but your man finished them off with a shot to the back of the head, even if they had already been dead a couple of hours.”

Cortez nodded. “That’s his way.”

“Five were in your gang. A couple more we’re not sure about. A few others had records. Drug dealing. Armed robbery. But at least three seem to be civilians. That includes the two most recent ones.”

“He’s going after my people, but if he can’t find one in time, he takes somebody else out. Now that you busted twenty of my guys and sent a few more to the hospital and the morgue, he’s going to have slim pickings. He’ll be going after civilians even more now.”

“What do you mean, ‘in time?’” Alexa asked.

Cortez made a face. “He likes to kill. I mean, when you do what we do, killing is something that happens. Not that I’ve ever had to pull the trigger." Rebstock snorted. "But he actually *likes* it. He was one cold guy. Then about a month ago he changed. I don't know why. He just started capping people for no reason. Usually guys from other gangs, so we didn't complain too much, but it caused problems. We don't start beefs. It's bad for business. He got the whole city going crazy."

Alexa remembered there had been an uptick in gang shootings in and around Phoenix, as well as a few known gang members going missing. This killer was responsible for all that?

"We need a name," Rebstock said.

Cortez looked at the folder the homicide detective had placed on the table in front of him.

"I need a deal."

Rebstock slid it over to the lawyer, who opened and read it. Cortez leaned in and read it too.

Alexa and Stuart traded glances. Assuming Cortez hadn't made the hits himself, trying to weasel his way out of them in a very unusual fashion, this was big. Really big.

And if Cortez didn't take the deal, a lot more people would die before they tracked the killer down.

Plus, there was no way to threaten Cortez. They had nothing to hold over him. He was already facing life in prison and a very good chance of execution. This was his one lifeline. If he tossed that aside, they had no power over him.

The lawyer frowned.

He gave Rebstock a sharp glance and said, "I need some time alone with my client."

Rebstock lifted his heavy frame out of the chair and motioned for Alexa and Stuart to come with him. Out in the hall, he said,

"He's probably going to hold out for more concessions. The D.A. gave me a fair amount of room to maneuver. I'll keep the pressure up, though. I know Jero. I busted him years ago when he was just a low-level runner and I was a street cop. He cares about his people. Los Diablos Auténticos is like a family to him. While he wants to protect himself, he wants to protect them too. If this ex-member is really on a rampage like he appears to be, Jero will crack before long."

Alexa noticed Rebstock used the familiar short form of Cortez's first name. This was something she had seen in many cops who had been around for a while. They got to know certain criminals so well they were almost like troublesome friends. She'd even known cops who visited the guys they busted in prison. The cons felt the same for some officers.

She even knew of a case where a cop was the victim of a nonfatal shooting and a guy the officer had arrested for stealing cars snitched on the shooter, at great risk to himself.

Cops and criminals were enemies, no doubt about it, but their lives grew so intertwined that with some of them, a level of mutual respect and camaraderie was bound to develop.

They walked down the hall to the main office, heading for the coffee machine. It had been a long day already and it would continue to be so. The office buzzed with activity. Cops and detectives took calls or interviewed witnesses or busied themselves on their computers filling out the endless paperwork that every officer of the law got burdened with on a daily basis.

As they came to the coffee machine, the scanner nearby crackled to life.

"Report of bodies found at 702 Finch Lane. I need a unit to respond."

"Unit 32 here. We're a couple of blocks away. We'll take it."

"Aw, hell," Rebstock said. "That's a drug house. The narcotics division has been gathering evidence on them."

"A drug house?" Stuart said. "This could be our man. Cortez said he's been killing people from other gangs."

"Let's go," Alexa said.

They hurried out of the building. The coffee would have to wait, even though a long day had just gotten a whole lot longer.

CHAPTER FIVE

By the time they got to the house, the responding unit had sealed off the yard and a second unit was just pulling up.

Alexa got out of the car as Stuart parked, a sick feeling in the pit of her stomach. Could this really be the work of the same guy?

She and Stuart ducked under the police tape and walked up to the officer standing guard outside the house.

"So what's the story?" she asked. Rebstock walked up. He had parked right behind them.

The officer nodded toward the inside of the house. "The owner's girlfriend came here an hour ago. Let herself in and found the owner dead, along with three other males and one female. The girlfriend is in that patrol car over there, giving a statement."

Alexa glanced across the street and saw a female officer talking with a pretty young Hispanic woman, who was shaking uncontrollably.

"Let Officer Menendez take care of the interview," Rebstock said. "I want to see what's inside."

The cop made a face. "I wish I could unsee it."

They entered and found a massacre. Three Hispanic men in their twenties lay in a row face down on the floor, each with a bullet wound to the back of the skull. From the blood patterns on the furniture and walls, it was obvious they had been shot and killed where they had been sitting, and then arranged for a postmortem execution in the middle of the floor.

Alexa felt a chill. This was definitely the same guy. Quick and remorseless.

"No one called this in? No one heard any shots?" Stuart asked.

"This isn't the kind of neighborhood where people hear shots," Rebstock replied.

Stuart shook his head in disbelief. "That saturated with gangs, eh? Which gang was this?"

"Los Caballeros run this area. The Knights. Not a very big gang. They flew under the radar of Cortez's outfit by mostly selling weed, ecstasy, and psychedelics. Los Diablos Auténticos only do meth and heroin."

An officer appeared in the doorway at the back side of the room.

"The other two are in here, sir."

They picked their way around the grisly scene and entered a bedroom. The sloppiness and sports posters showed it to be a man's bedroom, perhaps the same man who lay face down with a gunshot to the back of the head. Right next to him lay a young girl.

"Damn," Stuart said. "She's little more than a kid."

"Customer?" Alexa mused aloud. "Probably not one of the victims' girlfriends."

"Yeah," Rebstock agreed. "Too well dressed. She belongs in Scottsdale, not here."

He bent down with a grunt and a cracking of knees and felt inside her pockets, coming out with a wallet and several little bags.

"Heroin," he said, holding them up. "Looks like they were muscling in on Los Diablos Auténticos."

"That might be a motive," Alexa said.

"Except our boy got burned on the altar," Rebstock said, standing up with visible effort.

"Supposedly," Alexa replied.

"Supposedly," Rebstock agreed.

He opened the wallet and pulled out the girl's driver's license.

"Oh, sweet Jesus."

"What?" Alexa asked.

"Brianna Silverman."

"Is she related to the senator?" Stuart asked.

Alexa cocked an eyebrow. Looked like he had been reading up on Arizona.

"His daughter," Rebstock said. "Only nineteen. We busted her three years ago on a marijuana possession charge. The story never made the papers because she was a minor. Oh, hell."

The homicide detective slumped.

Alexa noticed a wooden box on the dresser, elaborately carved with geometric decorations on the sides and lid. She pulled out a ballpoint pen from her pocket and used it to open the box.

It was nearly filled with more packets of heroin.

She looked around the room. A pistol lay on the floor. She looked at the doorway and the wall opposite. No bullet holes.

Quick reactions, that what Annette said.

Stuart looked in the open drawer of the bedside table.

"Big packet of money in here. Also, a box of ammo. Looks like this is where he got the gun from. Our perp didn't take the drugs and didn't take the money. Why not? Is Cortez right? Is this guy really just killing for the thrill?"

"Seems hard to imagine," Alexa said. "This guy sounds like the gang enforcer. They tend to be the most self-controlled of the bunch. Usually a little older, more experienced. Cold."

Stuart gestured at the room. "This is anything but cold and self-controlled."

Alexa nodded. "It does seem strange. And he's not fitting into his pattern. He didn't take the bodies away and bury them."

"Probably noticed us excavating his mass grave," Rebstock said, pulling open the drawers one by one, using a handkerchief so as not to interfere with any fingerprints. "Maybe not him, but he might have a lookout in Arizona City."

"Some sidekick too terrified to sing like Cortez wants to do? Maybe," Alexa said. "But I'm thinking this guy works solo."

"Which means he's watching us," Stuart said.

Alexa suppressed a shudder. "Yeah."

Rebstock's phone rang. As he answered it, Alexa continued her search through the dresser. The homicide detective had already found a bag of weed, too small for distribution so probably personal use. In another drawer she found several bottles of opioid painkillers. Just as dangerous as heroin if abused.

Rebstock put his phone away. "Cortez has accepted the deal if we make a couple of concessions that I'm already authorized to make."

"Let's go find out this guy's name," Alexa said as they hurried out the door.

She was glad to get away from that scene of butchery but feared she might be seeing another one all too soon.

* * *

"We call him *El Carnicero*," Cortez said, then turned to Stuart. "That means 'butcher,' gringo."

"What's his real name?" Alexa asked.

Cortez shifted in his seat, his face twisting.

"It's OK, Jero," Rebstock said, in a voice that sounded like a father encouraging a wayward son to do the right thing. "You burned him on the altar. He's killing your people. With so many of you behind bars, only we can stop him."

Cortez nodded—a quick, tense movement—and Alexa could see his features change from agonized to resigned as he finally made the decision to snitch.

"Vicente Pérez. He lives on 209 E. Alameda."

Rebstock leaned forward. "You did the right thing, Jero."

"Does he have any assistants? A girlfriend, perhaps?" Alexa asked.

Cortez shook his head. "He's a loner. Hardly ever came to the parties. Fine by us. Even when he was in control before ... all this, he gave us the creeps."

"How did he join your gang?" Alexa asked.

Cortez shrugged. "Same as anyone else. He joined early, back in the day when I was just a runner."

"What about family?" Rebstock asked.

"All in Mexico. He never talked about them. Probably to keep them safe. Pérez might not even be his last name, but that's what's on the records here. I've seen his car insurance."

Alexa's brow furrowed. "Why would you have seen that?"

"We were in his car. Snuck a peek when he was getting gas."

Spying on a fellow gang member? One above you in seniority if not in rank? That's kind of odd.

"And no girlfriend at all?" Stuart asked.

"No. He'd go to high-end hookers. Always the best. He had tons of cash and didn't waste it like a lot of my brothers."

"Could he have a wife back in Mexico?" Alexa asked.

"If he does, he never mentioned it."

"You got a photo of him?" Rebstock asked.

"You kidding? If anyone tried to take a photo of him, he would have shoved their phone up their ass."

"Give us a physical description."

"About thirty-five. About my skin color. Lean but quick. Five-ten. Always dressed in black. Good quality clothes. Has a pair of really expensive black cowboy boots, the kind you got to get on a waiting list for from some artist down in Mexico. Speaks English fluently but with a bit of an accent. When he speaks Spanish, he talks like someone from Mexico City."

"Did he ever mention Mexico City or his life in Mexico?" Alexa asked.

"No. He don't talk much."

I guess that's why you checked up on him.

"Besides his house, where does he hang out?" After this rampage, Alexa didn't expect to find Vicente Pérez at home.

"Nowhere in particular."

"No favorite bar? Strip club?"

"He always went to the best, but I don't know of any favorites. The guy didn't keep much of a schedule. Unless you called him and asked him to come over, you had no idea where he was. I never bumped into him when I went out, and he didn't hang around the barrio."

Rebstock cut in. "I presume he ditched the last of his burners when he went rogue?"

"Yeah."

"Then how did he call you when he bragged about his killings."

"With new burners, I guess."

"Anything else you can tell us?" Rebstock asked.

Jeronimo Cortez shook his head. "No, sorry. He kept himself to himself."

"Well, you got your deal, Jero," the homicide detective said. "Immunity from the death penalty and the chance for parole in thirty years. Not bad considering the circumstances."

"I just want to save my people."

And save a glimmer of hope for yourself. Alexa tried to imagine him stepping out of prison in his early sixties. What kind of life would he have then? It didn't seem like much to hope for, but it was better than nothing.

But as Alexa looked into Cortez's eyes, she saw what looked like genuine concern. Maybe her cynicism had been misplaced. Gangs were like family for some people, and Cortez had grown up in Los Diablos Auténticos.

Maybe you really do want to save your people.

Well, we want the same thing, so you better be straight with us.

They rose.

"Time to check on that address," she said.

"I'll get a couple of units mobilized," Rebstock said.

CHAPTER SIX

Special Agent Stuart Barrett drove toward the house that the leader of Los Diablos Auténticos had given them. The police were already getting into place, monitoring the neighborhood, sending plainclothes officers to pass the house, and gearing up.

I thought when I mustered out that I'd be done with all this, and here I am doing it all again.

Well, you volunteered for it.

In the trunk of the FBI vehicle Stuart drove was his and Alexa's Kevlar, as well as a shotgun and assault rifle. They had decided that given the nature of the case, they should keep that gear with them at all times.

Not that Vicente Pérez would be hanging out at home waiting for the Phoenix P.D., the U.S. Marshals Service, and the FBI to come swooping down and arrest him. He would be hiding out somewhere. But maybe, just maybe, they could find some clues at his place.

And even if the house was abandoned, Stuart was going in carrying the assault rifle and wearing full Kevlar.

On the Drake Logan case he had nearly been hit with a bomb wired to blow when they went into one of the killer's safehouses.

That still gave him nightmares. He'd dealt with a lot of IEDs in Iraq, some way bigger than the crude bomb left by Drake Logan's henchmen, but it was this last one that bothered him most.

Because it went off in America.

He had done a pretty good job putting Iraq behind him, certainly better than a lot of his old Army buddies who still struggled with PTSD, depression, and substance abuse. But dealing with a bomb in a peaceful cabin in the desert in Arizona? That had hit him hard.

"You're awful quiet," Alexa said.

"Getting ready," Stuart replied.

"He won't be there."

"He knows we're coming. He might have left a surprise."

"They're bringing a bomb sniffing dog."

Stuart's jaw tensed. Was he really that obvious?

He dismissed it with a laugh. "We getting Nosey again?"

"No, she's only trained for bodies and articles of clothing. We're getting Sniffer. He does the bombs."

"Nosey? Sniffer?"

"These are cops, not poets. What do you want them to be called? Jane Austen and Nebuchadnezzar?"

They both laughed. For a moment there was silence, and then Alexa said in a quiet tone,

"Don't be mad, but I looked into Stacy's disappearance."

"What?"

Stacy Fielding was his high school sweetheart, who vanished from an abandoned cabin in the woods where they used to make out. She had disappeared moments before he came to meet her one night.

Why the hell was she looking into that?

"Stuart, I know it's sensitive, but—"

"Jesus Christ, it's none of your business!" he said overcome with outrage.

"I know, but I think I can—"

"Just drop it, all right?"

Who the hell did she think she was? Didn't she have enough on her plate without digging up a nearly twenty-year-old cold case on the other side of the country?

And it was *his* case. Did she think he hadn't gone over every bit of evidence a million times?

Oh, he knew why. Because his Stacy had the same name as her Stacy, a thirteen-year-old neighbor girl with drunken parents Alexa had taken under her wing. He remembered Alexa's face when he had told her about his Stacy.

So she had taken it personally, and charged into the case like a bull, the same as with every other case.

Damn, how much had she dug up? Wasn't it bad enough that she had snooped around his military and FBI record? Now she was doing this?

She was investigating him like some criminal.

They made it a couple of blocks away from the house and parked next to one of the police's unmarked vehicles.

"Let's get this done," he growled. "And try to focus on the case you're actually assigned, all right?"

Alexa didn't reply. He had no idea what kind of expression she had on her face because he didn't bother looking at her.

He opened the trunk, and they donned their Kevlar as a member of the Phoenix police department came up.

"We're all in position. Kicking off in five minutes," he said.

"Good," Stuart grumbled. A bit of action would make him feel better.

He grabbed the assault rifle.

The neighborhood had grown quiet. No one was out on the street. While this was a middle-class neighborhood with nice houses and lawns, even these civilians could sense trouble was brewing. The last neighborhood they had been in saw stuff like this all the time. For those who lived here, this must look like Armageddon.

Once geared up, the three of them jogged a block over to where several police officers hid behind a large house. Several carried shotguns and all wore Kevlar. Stuart could see the terrified face of the homeowner peeking out the window.

"We're all ready," the sergeant said. "Target is the gray building with the saguaro in the front yard. When we get around this house it's across the street at eleven o'clock."

"Let's do it," Stuart replied.

The sergeant sent out a command on his walkie-talkie.

"Go!"

They rushed around the corner of the building and Stuart immediately saw the target. He also saw teams advancing down the street from both directions, using the houses as cover. A fourth detachment would be coming up on the house from behind.

He saw no car in the driveway, no lights in the windows.

This is going to be a bust. Where the hell is that bomb-sniffing dog?

There he was, being led by a cop in the detachment coming in from the right. Now that he had that reassurance, Stuart had eyes only for the house, watching it through the sights of his assault rifle as he jogged across the street.

While he kept an eye on the windows, he spared a glance all around the house—the roof, the lawn, the garage door. You had to take in everything in a situation like this.

When his gaze flicked to the garage door, he noted an oil stain on the driveway in front. It looked dry. Hardly surprising in the searing heat of Phoenix, but it looked dry and a bit faded.

He had no more time to think about that as they rushed up the stairs and the lead man kicked the door in.

"POLICE! GET FACE DOWN ON THE FLOOR WITH YOUR HANDS BEHIND YOUR HEAD!"

They poured into the house by the numbers, spreading out, taking every corner, checking every room. The bomb sniffing dog ran through the house without a bark. Stuart was impressed. The Phoenix police were almost as good as an Army squad. Given the amount of drugs and gang violence in their city, he wasn't surprised. They did this a lot.

It took less than a minute to clear the house. Vicente Pérez was gone. Even worse, there weren't too many possessions lying around. Nothing of value on any table or counter. A half-empty closet. It looked like he had moved out.

Damn. Got the jump on us.

Stuart moved back into the living room as the police began a more extensive search, hoping to find clues. He found one on the coffee table.

He ran a finger along it, leaving a darker trail on the dusty surface and then held his dirty finger up for Alexa to see.

"He's been gone a while," Stuart said.

"Damn it! Cortez played us. They've been hunting him for two weeks. This would have been the first place they checked. Cortez must have known he wouldn't be here!"

"Great," Stuart grumbled, his already bad mood growing worse. "Now where the hell are we going to look for him?"

Alexa's phone rang. She pulled it out and looked at the screen.

"It's Marshal Hernandez," she said.

The head of the Arizona office and her direct superior.

Great. Perfect timing.

"Put it on speaker so I can hear," Stuart said.

She did, then answered it.

"Yes, sir?" Alexa said.

The Marshal's gruff voice, with a hint of a Hispanic accent, came over the line. "Detective Rebstock says you and Agent Barrett have been tagging along on his investigation instead of performing your usual duties."

Alexa gulped. "Yes, sir."

While they had been invited to be part of the raid against Los Diablos Auténticos, they hadn't actually been assigned the follow up case against the killer.

Her boss chuckled. "You just go right for what you think is most important no matter what you're really supposed to be doing, don't you?" Alexa cast a nervous glance at Stuart, who frowned.

You got that right, Marshal. She thinks every case is her case.

"Um, sorry, sir," Alexa said.

How about saying sorry to me?

"Well, you guessed right as usual," Marshal Hernandez said. "I just got off the phone with the Senator Silverman. He's shattered, as you might expect. He wants the best people on this case, and that means you and Special Agent Barrett. So keep doing what you're doing. And take care. The media has already been talking about the uptick in murders and disappearances. When they hear about the mass grave and Brianna Silverman, there's going to be hell to pay."

"I understand, sir."

"Under no circumstances talk to reporters."

"I won't, sir."

Stuart saw Alexa cringe. That had been a reference to her sister-in-law Melanie, who worked for Action News in Phoenix. An ambulance chaser if there ever was one.

"We'll get right on it, sir," Alexa said, and hung up. She looked around for a moment, unsure what to do next. Neither was Stuart.

Then he got an idea. He pulled out his phone.

"Who are you calling?" Alexa asked.

"That scuzzy lawyer Cortez hired. He knows more than he's telling, and this time, we're going to find out what."

"He'll play dumb."

"He can play dumb all he wants, but he didn't give us any real information. We can make a case that that invalidates the deal. If he wants to protect his people and save himself from a lethal injection, he's going to spill."

CHAPTER SEVEN

Alexa studied Jeronimo Cortez and his lawyer from across the table in the jailhouse. Stuart and Rebstock sat by her side. This was getting repetitive.

"You lied to us," she growled.

The lawyer leaned forward, raising a protesting hand. "My client promised you information on the alleged killer and provided it. He gave you a name, all the biographical details he knew, and his home address."

"He gave us a name that could be false, a bunch of vague stuff we can't check, and an address that's been abandoned for at least a week. And he knew that Pérez or whatever his name had already left. That house would have been the first place Los Diablos Auténticos would have looked for him."

"We never went there," Jeronimo Cortez said.

"Oh, come on! Cut the bull!" Stuart said. He was still in a pissy mood thanks to her slipup on the ride over to the suspect's house. She had been stupid to tell him she was looking into the case. She should have just worked quietly until she had found something more solid.

But in a cold case like that? A tall order.

One case at a time.

"We need more if we're going to catch this guy," Alexa said. "And you can provide it. So do it, or the deal's off."

Cortez gave her a smug smile. "The deal is signed."

The lawyer looked less confident. "If you renege on the agreement, we'll sue."

"Sue all you want. Your client is a felon half a dozen times over. He's going inside until he dies of old age, assuming he doesn't get the needle first."

Cortez crossed his arms over his chest. The lawyer leaned in and whispered to him. The whispering went back and forth for a minute, then the lawyer turned back to them.

Here we go.

"My client wants an assurance that he will be placed in the prison in Tucson."

Alexa and Rebstock looked at each other. She saw he realized the same thing she did. Los Diablos Auténticos dominated every maximum-security prison in central Arizona. Down in Tucson, however, they were only one of several gangs. Cortez wanted to lead his compadres in expanding their prison empire.

Rebstock looked uncomfortable.

"What do you have in exchange?" the homicide detective asked.

"I got another address for you," Cortez asked.

"You could have mentioned that before," Stuart snapped.

Cortez shot him a contemptuous look. "Sorry, gringo. Slipped my mind."

Stuart grunted. "Like hell it did."

"I can authorize his placement in the Arizona State Prison Complex in Tucson, but the men arrested in the raid will all go to other facilities," Rebstock said.

Cortez looked like he had just bit down on something sour. Rebstock went on.

"And the placement in Tucson is conditional on us finding solid evidence at this new location."

The lawyer leaned in, and he and his client had another whispered conversation.

"We can do that," the lawyer said after a moment.

"So where is this place?"

Cortez hesitated.

"Come on, Cortez," Alexa snapped. "You said you wanted to protect your people."

"Hardly any of my people left on the outside."

"You want revenge, though, right?"

Still Cortez hesitated.

The lawyer gave him an encouraging gesture, looking exasperated. Alexa almost pitied him. Being stuck with a stubborn and obviously guilty client like that must have been a rough road. But he was no public defender. He was being paid top dollar to defend Jeronimo Cortez and several other members of the gang. Alexa wondered how he slept at night.

Just fine, probably. On silk sheets.

At last Cortez spoke. "387 West Palm Street. It's a safehouse we use. We paid an old man in another state to buy it in his name so it couldn't be traced to us. Only a few people know about it. All those people either got killed by Pérez or arrested the other night."

"But Pérez knows about it."

Cortez nodded. "Go quick, though. He's always moving around. I don't know if he'll be there for long."

Rebstock turned to Alexa and Stuart. "I'll bring along a couple of units. My best people. We'll get this guy."

Alexa stood. "We're coming along too. Marshal Hernandez has approved us being part of the investigation, and we both want to be there when this guy goes down."

Assuming Cortez has finally decided to tell the truth.

* * *

Vicente Pérez sat at 387 West Palm Street and considered his next move. It was already getting dark. Almost time to strike again.

Strike against the people who had corrupted him.

And there were so, so many.

He looked around the dumpy old house, one built in the Sixties when they still used adobe. Cool in the summer and warm on the cool winter nights. Why the gringos switched to concrete or particle board he'd never know. Sure, it was cheaper, but it was no kind of house for the desert. The gringos had been in Arizona for two hundred years and had never really adapted.

But while the design of the house was perfect for the climate, Los Diablos Auténticos hadn't kept it up. The carpet was disgusting, the walls stained, and he had given up trying to clear out all the cigarette butts and empty beer bottles. Still, it was a place to hide, and the old adobe walls were bulletproof.

That's why Jeronimo Cortez had chosen it as a safehouse.

And put in a few little … additions.

Smart guy, Jero. Tricky. He'd do well in prison. Probably end up running the place within a year if someone didn't shiv him first.

Pérez wouldn't mind the chance to do it himself, but even he couldn't reach someone in police custody.

Yes, they should all die. Especially someone like Jero.

Jero reminded Vicente of himself. He'd watched Jero rise in the ranks from a runner everyone picked on for his small size to a deadly leader of the gang he had once been a tagalong for. Now everyone feared him and deferred to him.

Vicente had been much like that. He'd grown up in the slums of Mexico City in the late Nineties, where the poverty was grinding and the narco money never made it to where he lived. Neither did running water or reliable electricity. Vicente's first memories were of a one-room shack shared with his hardworking mother, his father paralyzed in a work accident that he had never been compensated for, and three younger siblings.

With nothing at home except stifling air and his father's groans, Vicente spent his time on the streets and alleys. He stole what he could, which wasn't much since no one had anything, and fought with the other boys. While he wasn't big, he was quick, accurate, and aggressive. He could poke a bigger boy in the eye and knee him in the crotch while the kid was still winding up for his first punch.

That earned him respect, and also made him a target. He got in more fights, and he didn't always win.

By age eleven he started carrying a knife. It was a little thing, just a three-inch blade with a cheap pink plastic handle that he had swiped from a stand selling fish tacos. A local tough, fifteen years old and way bigger than him, called him a *maricón* for carrying a pink knife. A slash across the face stopped that joke.

After slashing the kid, Vicente had run off behind a shed and puked his guts out. The sight of the blood spurting from that hairless cheek had disgusted and horrified him. But he couldn't let someone call him a *maricón* and get away with it. If people thought you were like that, especially if you were a boy and small for your age, terrible things would happen to you.

He had to do it, and he had to pretend it was nothing more to him than pissing against a wall.

The next day he sauntered down the street where the older boy and his friends hung out. The older boy wasn't there. His friends were. None of them approached him and none called him a *maricón*.

Vicente began to get respect, began to get a name.

And that's when the real trouble started.

"Why don't you run with Los Verdugos?" a local weed dealer asked. This was no street kid, but a man. Twenty years old who had already spent a year in prison.

Los Verdugos, "the executioners," ran all the drugs in his part of the shantytown. They also strong-armed street vendors into freebies or bribes. When they weren't doing that, they fought rival gangs in a war of constantly changing boundaries and constantly rising casualties.

Vicente got a job as a runner, the same way Jero had started out. He got a reputation as the best because he could run fast to avoid trouble, and if trouble cornered him, he had his knife.

Vicente hated to use it, but what could he do? The local bullies had forced him to be tough. Poverty and no opportunities sealed the deal.

And it was seductive. A small kid with smarts could get respect. Money. Food.

Of course, his parents noticed. Mother screaming. Father lecturing from where he lay in bed. He tried to explain. Tried to give them money they threw out the window. They were proud, the Pérez family. Mother ironed and cleaned for middle-class homes in town, working twelve, fourteen hours a day. Father agonized in his bed that he couldn't be a man and support his family.

"That's what I'm trying to do, Papa," Vicente explained. "Be a man."

His father glared at him. That look still had the power to make Vicente's knees shake even though he knew his father didn't have the strength to hit him like he used to.

"You're not a man," his father growled. "You're an animal."

At least he could feed his little brother and two little sisters on the sly. Buy them food from the street vendors when their mother was at work.

Then one night his little brother Luis, only nine, bragged that the leader of Los Cabelleros had given him a job as a runner. That had earned Luis a slap from his mother and a fit of rage from his father.

"Vicente, it's bad enough what you do, but don't take my other son. What's next, you'll turn Concepción and Inez into streetwalkers?"

"What's a streetwalker?" Inez, only three, asked. Concepción blushed. She was seven, but she already knew.

"Out of my house!" his father bellowed.

Vicente fled, trying not to cry. Crying was weakness, and weakness could get you killed.

"Hired Luis? Your little brother?" his gang leader said when Vicente confronted him. "Hell, no. The kid was just bragging. Don't worry about your folks kicking you out. You can stay here."

Vicente looked around the adobe house Los Verdugos had hired some local men to make. Three bedrooms and a big living room. He'd have to share a room with two older guys, but he was used to sleeping crowded in with other people. He'd done it all his life. What he wasn't used to was the mirror on the table with lines of cheap street coke, called "nose bleeds" by the locals because it was cut with laundry detergent. And he wasn't used to the half-dressed girls lounging on the sofa. And he wasn't used to spending the night here, instead of just passing in and out on errands.

At that moment Vicente Pérez realized he had only been in the gang part way. Now he was inner circle.

One of Los Verdugos, his arm around a girl and the other holding a joint, smiled.

"Don't worry, Vicente. We're your family now."

From there he had climbed up the ladder. It wasn't long before he learned the gang leader had lied. He had talked to Luis, knowing the boastful little boy would mention it to his parents. The gang leader had wanted Vicente kicked out of the house so he could work for Los Verdugos full-time.

Vicente swore revenge.

At sixteen he got it, setting up a situation where it looked like the gang leader had ripped off some other Verdugos. That gave Vicente the excuse to kill him.

He ended up running the show, but not for long. The narcos had noticed him. His reputation had spread enough that they offered him a job as an enforcer. It involved a move to Sonora, a move away from his siblings and his mother's early grave, but he took it. He could send money home.

But that money always came back. And the letters he sent never got answered. The Pérez family, struggling, half-starving, were too proud to take money from a narco. Vicente Pérez would have cried had he remembered how.

Step by step, the wolves that preyed on poverty and desperation had pulled him away from his family. They had acted like his friends and made him the loneliest man he knew.

They had to pay for that. They all had to pay.

The image of that teenaged white girl who he killed at the drug house passed through his mind. She had never done anything to him. Did he feel a flicker of guilt?

No, she was part of it too. These gangs wouldn't exist without customers. Stupid rich kids like her were the ones who spent the most money. That gave the gangs power.

And that seduced desperate kids like him into a life of crime.

Vicente Pérez pulled out a faded photograph from his wallet. It showed the whole family together, back when his father had a job and could afford the luxury of having his photo taken with his family. At a little studio the size of a walk-in closet. His father had never been rich enough to own a camera.

There they all were in their Sunday best, Father with his arm around Mother, who held the infant Inez. In front of them the three other children all in a row, looking serious and a bit in awe of the giant antiquated camera on a tripod the photographer used.

A soft sound outside snapped him out of his thoughts. He cocked an ear. Nothing. But it wasn't the quiet of a street already settling into night, it was the silence of a street gone to ground, knowing something was about to kick off. The silence you hear in the forest when a predator is on the prowl.

There was only one predator left who would come after him.

The cops.

How could they know about this place? Jero must have sold him out!

In a fluid motion he returned the photo to his wallet, his wallet to his pocket, and checked that his gun and knives were loose in their holster and scabbards. Knives would be best for what he had planned.

All that took less than two seconds, and by that time he had made it to the wall between the living room and kitchen.

Another sound. The cops were in a hurry and not sneaking well tonight.

He pushed on the wall.

Just then he heard the front door get kicked in.

CHAPTER EIGHT

Alexa was third inside the safehouse. First was a Kevlar-clad man-mountain from the Phoenix P.D. Next came Stuart, toting an assault rifle he had managed not to give back to the SWAT team. Alexa was next, followed by another officer and Rebstock. A trio of officers covered the other sides of the house. The place was pretty big. Alexa worried Pérez would hole up in one of the back rooms and shoot it out.

They passed through a short front hall. To the left was a tiny bathroom that the lead man had already cleared with a simple glance. The hall led to a dingy living room. Beyond that was another short hallway leading to the kitchen and more rooms.

Rebstock, the only man not wearing Kevlar, because no suit would fit him, guarded the front door. He stood on the front lawn, out of sight of the interior, with his gun covering the entrance. The rest of the officers fanned out. Two veered right to check out the kitchen. The man-mountain, Stuart, and Alexa continued down the hall.

A bedroom. Laundry room. Another bedroom. Master bathroom. Where was this guy?

They got all the way to the back, where a door led to the backyard. It was locked from the inside. Alexa opened it and peeked out, leading with her gun.

No one except for a cop hiding behind a palm tree on the other side of the fence. Aiming at her. He gave her a thumb's up.

A little early to say mission accomplished, buddy.

Standing in the doorway, she looked around the yard. Empty other than for a few lawn chairs, a firepit, and a barbeque. Nowhere to hide.

No shouts from inside. Had Pérez already fled?

Damn, he's still one step ahead of us.

Unlike at Pérez's home address, Alexa had seen plenty of clothing and personal items in the various rooms. But how to tell if any of it was his?

Just as she turned to go back into the house, she heard a thump, a cry, and the sound of running feet.

Then she heard Rebstock shout, "Drop the weapon!"

She found herself running down the hallway with Stuart, glancing into every room they had passed, finding no one except a cop on his hands and knees looking under one of the beds. They came into the living room, to find Rebstock blocking the short front hall leading outside.

"He tried to come out. Didn't get a shot before he ducked back in."

Rebstock stayed where he was, blocking the one entrance. The cop in the backyard could cover the other entrance. The windows were barred. They had him trapped.

"In here!" someone shouted from the kitchen.

Alexa and Stuart were across the living room in a heartbeat. They found an officer kneeling beside another officer, who sat with his back against the dishwasher, gripping a hand to a bloody throat. The uninjured cop was pulling out a small First Aid kit from his vest.

The injured officer croaked out, "Got me from behind. Didn't even see him. How could he—"

A cry of pain from somewhere else in the house got Alexa and Stuart running for the source of the sound.

Across the living room, they passed Rebstock still blocking the front exit.

"Didn't see anything!" he shouted as they passed.

But to pass from the kitchen to the other part of the house, he'd have to run right past you.

They paused at the entrance to the back hallway. The house had gone silent again.

Looking down the sights of her Glock, Alexa faced an empty hallway. Stuart stood just behind her, the front of his assault rifle sticking out just over her shoulder.

They began to advance.

The first two open doorways stood right across from one another. With an unspoken agreement born of training and trust, Alexa ducked right while at the same instant her partner ducked left. The argument in the car was forgotten for the moment. This was duty. This was survival.

Nothing in her room. She turned and found Stuart coming back into the hallway. His expression told her they needed to continue the search.

They paced down the hallway, the only sound they heard being the soft voice of the police officer in the kitchen reassuring his injured partner, then getting on the radio to call for backup and an ambulance.

Neither will get to us in time. We're alone with Pérez.

And why do I get the feeling that the odds are still in his favor?

A doorway to the left. Alexa went low and Stuart high. In the middle of the bedroom lay the officer who had been checking under the beds.

Alexa rushed over to him. He had a big bump at the base of his skull, just below his helmet. He was breathing but knocked out cold.

What the hell?

When she turned to Stuart, she got another surprise. He was staring at the walls, first in this room, then out in the hall, before passing to the laundry room.

"Look," he whispered. "The walls are too thick."

"The walls are too thick?"

He ran his hand along the wall between the hallway and the bedroom where the officer lay knocked out.

"I saw this in Ramadi."

He tapped lightly on the wall with his fingertips. It sounded hollow. He moved around to inside the bedroom and stared for a moment, then pressed on a spot in the wall.

A doorway popped open. Alexa's breath caught. Inside was a narrow space just wide enough to edge along. It was dimly lit from above, where some unseen lightbulb shone from between the ceiling and the roof. The hidden passageway led all the way to the next room, turning right.

"I bet it goes around to the living room," Alexa whispered, not believing her eyes.

"This hallway and the front door cut the house in half. There must be another passageway leading to the kitchen."

He stepped across the hall to one of the unoccupied rooms and felt along the wall.

"It's got to be here somewhere," he whispered. "I bet there's openings in every room. When I was in Ramadi—"

Just then the wall opened right in front of Alexa and Pérez leaped out, knife flashing.

The keen blade swept sideways, aiming for Alexa's throat. She backpedaled, knowing she wouldn't make it in time.

A clang of metal. Stuart had brought the barrel of his assault rifle down on the knife, it screeched across the front of her Kevlar vest.

Pérez didn't miss a beat. With a vicious backhand he smacked the pommel of his knife across Stuart's jaw, slamming him into the wall, then kicked at Alexa just as she brought up her gun. Her bullet punctured the wall, but Pérez was unharmed.

Then she was stumbling back. The combination of her trying to jump out of the way of that knife and his foot hitting her hard in the Kevlar vest made her lose what remained of her balance.

She ended up on the floor, retaining the grip on her weapon, feeling sure he would pounce on her the next minute.

He didn't. He ducked out the door.

Alexa scrambled to her feet, saw Stuart on his knees trying to maintain a hold on consciousness, and followed Pérez out the door.

The clatter of metal from the next room over told her where he had gone.

She rushed into the room just in time to see the metal bars on the open window shaking. Shots rang out from the side of the house. Crossing the room in three quick steps, she saw the bars were actually a grate that could be lifted up. An escape hatch.

Another shot. She peered out the window, keeping low, only her eyes visible between her helmet and the window frame.

The cop guarding the side of the house was shooting at something to her right, toward the back of the house. Return fire made him duck out of sight. Then the fire shifted to the back of the house.

Pérez was getting away.

Alexa lifted up the grate and shoved her legs through the window, landing on her feet outside, the closing grate smacking down on her helmet with a sharp *clank*.

She found herself in a space a couple of yards wide enclosed by the house on one side and a low wooden fence on the other. Another shot rang out. She rushed to the backyard in time to see Pérez leap across the back fence. Alexa fired. He didn't flinch as he ducked out of view behind the fence.

He could be running, hunched low and out of sight, or he could be waiting for her to cut across the backyard in pursuit. She had to take that chance. Alexa pelted across the open yard, completely bare of cover, and got to the fence. The officer covering the back lay on his back behind the palm tree he had been using as cover. He didn't move.

Alexa scanned the adjoining backyards of the neighboring houses, her view partially blocked by a tool shed, a kid's brightly colored jungle gym, and a couple of palm trees. At least the fences over there were of chain link, not wood. Otherwise, she wouldn't be able to see a damn thing.

But she still couldn't see Vicente Pérez.

Hopping the fence, she raced across the backyard, keeping her eye on the tool shed as the most likely ambush point.

She got to it, eased around one side, and jumped the last corner.

He wasn't there.

A movement from the next yard over caught her eye. Pérez darted from behind a house and leapt over a wooden fence into the next yard. Alexa sprinted for the spot where he had disappeared. Out of the corner of her eyes she saw a couple of people peeking out of windows, dangerously exposing themselves. Civilians often did stupid things like that where there was a gun battle. At least everyone had remained inside.

She got to the fence, looked over. He wasn't there.

He stood behind the corner of the next house, just popping out to take a shot at her.

The prey had turned on the hunter.

CHAPTER NINE

Alexa and the killer fired at each other at the same time.

Both hit.

Just as she saw Pérez flinch from her bullet, Alexa felt something slam against her chest. For the second time in the past couple of minutes, she found herself flat on her back.

She lay there for a second, stunned and disoriented. A tight ache in the center of her body felt like a fist had reached into her body cavity and squeezed.

Looking down at her chest, she realized why she wasn't dead.

The bullet was embedded in her Kevlar vest, its back end looking like a button just below the neckline. At worst, she had a broken chest bone, more likely just the world's ugliest bruise.

Another shot. Alexa rolled over to get on her stomach. A return shot from a different caliber weapon told her Pérez had gotten into it with someone else, hopefully not some overeager civilian who would only end up getting himself killed. She shifted her position a yard to the left and cautiously rose, keeping her head low while agonizingly aware that this wooden fence was not bulletproof.

She ducked back down as she heard a sound behind her. Stuart, a bruise the size of a golf ball blossoming on his jaw, paced forward, assault rifle leveled.

More shots. Alexa got back up in time to see Pérez heading for another house. Alexa and Stuart fired. Neither hit.

Alexa and Stuart ran after him, sweat already pouring down their bodies under the stifling Kevlar. Alexa's chest felt sore from the impact of the bullet and every breath ached. She ignored the pain and kept on running.

Rebstock huffed around the corner, his service pistol in his hand, his face looking red as a tomato and ready for a heart attack. Nevertheless, he kept pace with them as they hunted through the backyards and the street beyond.

It was no good. That man was the fastest runner Alexa had ever seen outside of professional sports, and he obviously knew the neighborhood like the back of his hand.

Sirens wailed in the distance. Alexa got on the radio and requested helicopter backup.

She knew it wouldn't matter, though. Vicente Pérez was long gone, free to kill again.

* * *

Alexa was right. Despite a hurriedly constructed police cordon and a helicopter swooping low over the neighborhood, they didn't find a trace of Vicente Pérez.

At least none of the officers got killed. One had been slashed, another knocked out cold, and the cop behind the palm tree had been stunned by a bullet ricocheting off his helmet. Like with Alexa, his Kevlar saved him.

He must have a hell of a headache, Alexa thought as she rubbed the bruise on her chest.

Now the search was winding down. A physical description had been sent to the media so they could warn citizens to be on the lookout. They didn't have a photo to go along with it, though. No one named Vicente Pérez came up in the arrest records for the entire state.

It was like they were hunting a ghost.

At least they got a bunch of his clothing. Nice black shirts and slacks like Jeronimo Cortez had said he wore. Those would give DNA matches that they might be able to connect to the murders. Annette Cruz was an expert at finding DNA at crime scenes. They could use that to convict, assuming they caught him. Assuming they ever saw him again.

They stood by the ambulance as the last police officer was taken away, trying to think out their next move. The officers who hadn't been injured stood around, stunned.

One man. One man had bested an entire squad of experienced officers who had him surrounded.

It seemed unreal.

Detective Rebstock watched the ambulance go and hung his head. "Damn. I wish I had shot him when he appeared at the door. It was all so quick."

Alexa put a hand on the older man's shoulder. "You didn't because you weren't sure if one of us was right behind him. You were thinking of your fellow officers, as you always do."

Rebstock nodded, still looking at the pavement. "If I only had another moment."

"Don't blame yourself. We can't always protect our team."

Rebstock looked her in the eye, no doubt knowing she was referring to the loss of her partner, Robert Powers. He had been killed right in front of her when followers of the serial killer Drake Logan had ambushed his prisoner transport vehicle and broke him out.

Vicente Pérez is just as deadly as Drake Logan.

And if we don't hurry up and catch him, he'll kill just as many people as Drake ever did.

Her phone rang. Marshal Hernandez. She put it on speaker and answered.

"I heard what happened," he said. "The two of you all right?"

"Agent Barrett got a slight bruise," *actually a terrible bruise,* "but he's all right. I didn't get hurt at all." *Unless you count nearly taking a bullet and having an ache in the chest that will probably last all week.*

"Thank God." Pause. "I want you to know this is being done over my protest."

Alexa blinked. "Sir?"

"The senator is livid. He called the governor and thinks you screwed up. I know that's not the case. I told him I'd put my best people on it, and I did. But he's insisting we reassign the case to someone else."

Alexa and Stuart glanced at each other, shocked. Detective Rebstock frowned and muttered something.

Alexa struggled to find the words. "But sir, this is an extremely dangerous suspect. We had him surrounded and he injured four officers. One had to go to the hospital and will need a bunch of stiches. We need to—"

"I know, I know. You and Agent Barrett should stay on the case. But it's out of my hands. The governor is going with the senator on this. Senator Silverman is working on next year's budget and trying to get extra development money for the western states. If that goes through, it will help the governor's reelection campaign. So the governor is going to give the senator everything he wants. And I can't really blame the senator for being irrational. He's beside himself with grief. He's lashing out at everyone. He was literally screeching at me on the phone because we hadn't caught Pérez yet. I tried to make him see reason, but he just lost his daughter. He's insisting, and with the governor going along with him there's nothing I can do."

Stuart leaned forward so Marshal Hernandez could hear. "Sir, with all due respect, this is a huge mistake."

"I agree, Special Agent Barrett," Alexa's boss replied in a grim tone. "But it's a mistake the senator and governor are making, not us. Let's pray the new team will be almost as good as the last. Is Detective Rebstock there?"

"I'm here, Marshal," Rebstock replied.

"Since you are directly responsible for the homicide division in Phoenix, you will remain on the job. A member of the governor's taskforce on crime will be assisting you. Yes, he's a civilian, and no, he doesn't have any background in law enforcement. Try to be patient. And be careful. The governor is looking for sacrifices."

Rebstock did not seem impressed. "Marshal, I've been through so many administrations I've lost count."

"Good man. Deputy Marshal, Special Agent, I'm giving you the next two days off. After that, come into the office and we'll assign you a new case."

Alexa couldn't believe her ears. "Marshal, this is—"

"And when I saw take two days off, I mean *off*, Deputy Marshal."

"Yes, sir," Alexa mumbled, rubbing the tender bruise on her chest.

We'll see about that.

He nearly killed me. He nearly killed all of us. And you think I'm just going to kick up my feet and sip a beer in front of the TV?

* * *

Back home on her little ranch just outside Phoenix, Alexa enjoyed a rich sunset from her back porch, the western sky turning a brilliant orange before deepening into red, a few striated clouds absorbing the color to highlight the beauty. She stood staring, a cup of coffee in her hand, as the sky's color slowly mellowed and turned blue.

Not many things could soothe her mind and make her forget the cares of her day. This was one of them.

Smith and Wesson, her two horses, snorted and trotted around the corral, enjoying the cooling air. Alexa smiled. Horses were another thing that could take her mind off her troubles.

The evening dimmed further, the saguaros becoming silhouettes, the distant hills blending with the darkening sky. A coyote howled, signaling the start of the night and the creatures that lived in it. Alexa took a deep breath.

A loud, braying laugh from the neighboring trailer told her Mr. and Mrs. Carpenter had started boozing it up again. Even though their trailer was half a mile away, the sound carried clearly over the still air. The way they partied, they could have been living in the middle of the city and Alexa would probably hear it. And it would only get louder as the night wore on.

Alexa moved back inside and started cooking some macaroni and cheese for two. Now that she was out of sight of Arizona's natural beauty, her mind began to hum. She could not leave this case alone. Not after what she had seen.

Now that Vicente Pérez was on the run, he'd be twice as dangerous. She'd seen it before. A guy (and occasionally a woman) would decide to go on a killing spree. As the spree continued, all but the most deranged mind would become aware that the police were onto them and closing in. The killer would get more desperate, more daring, knowing their time was running out. The killing would increase in pace.

And unlike most of the people she had hunted down, Vicente Pérez was a professional killer. That had been his job for several years.

Cortez had told them that Pérez had come up from Mexico. No doubt he had gotten his start there, probably with one of the many narco organizations. Then he had come to the United States. Why? Had he been sent by the narcos to be the enforcer for Los Diablos Auténticos? That would make sense. The gang controlled so much of the lucrative drug trade in central Arizona their annual turnover must have been in the tens of millions. Their raid on the warehouse had bagged heroin and meth with a street value of $1.2 million, and that was just one month's supply.

So Pérez didn't just work for Los Diablos Auténticos. He worked for one of the powerful families that supplied them.

The big narco families had all but taken over some regions of Mexico. Through a mixture of violence and bribery, they kept the police sidelined. Any rival organizations were likely to be killed and suspended from bridges as an example to morning commuters. The central government tried to fight the good fight but got hampered by local officials who were either in the narcos' pocket or too terrified to enforce the law.

This meant the narcos had a reasonably stable business, considering the nature of that business. Other than wars with rival organizations and trouble from a few courageous officials who put law and order over their personal safety, they didn't have much to worry about.

So how would they react to Pérez going rogue? Surely Cortez must have told them. The answer had probably come back to take him out. Pérez was disobeying orders and rocking the boat. The narcos had only one solution to that. When Cortez sent men to kill Pérez and they ended up dead themselves, what did the gang leader do?

Called for backup, probably.

That meant someone worse than Pérez was coming up from Mexico.

A chill went through her.

Then she heard the back door open.

CHAPTER TEN

Alexa took in a sharp breath and grabbed a butcher knife lying on the counter nearby.

Stacy, the Carpenters' thirteen-year-old daughter, huffed her way across the kitchen without so much as a hello and disappeared down the hall. The kid was so angry she didn't even notice Alexa wielding a giant knife.

Alexa let out a sigh of relief. Until now she hadn't realized how much this case had gotten to her. Being taken off it made her feel helpless. Vulnerable.

The real vulnerable one just walked through the door, Alexa reminded herself.

This happened every night Stacy's parents got hammered, which was most nights. The guest bedroom had half of Stacy's clothing (most of which Alexa had bought her) and her posters on the walls. The kid took care of Smith and Wesson when Alexa was gone and even did her own cooking when Alexa was away. Her visits had become so predictable that when Alexa heard the Carpenters begin to party it up, she had automatically begun cooking for two.

"Dinner will be ready in five minutes!" she called out.

The only response was the TV turning on.

Alexa shrugged and set the table. That was Stacy's chore—the kid needed chores to add some much-needed structure to her life—but Alexa would let it slide tonight.

Once she set the table, she gave Stacy a heaping portion plus a glass of milk, nonalcoholic beverages being a rare commodity in the Carpenter home, and went to the living room, absentmindedly rubbing the sore patch on her chest.

Stacy lay curled up on the sofa texting. Another advantage of Alexa's place besides the lack of drama, the full refrigerator, and the general cleanliness, was access to WiFi. A documentary about the Amazon rainforest played on the television.

"Hey," Alexa said.

"Hey." Stacy did not look up.

"How was school?"

"Meh. Rachel got caught smoking weed in the bathroom."

"Shall I go arrest her?"

That got a smile. "She got suspended for a week. That's not a punishment, that's a vacation."

"Weed makes you stupid. Don't try it."

"There's a reason they call it dope," Stacy said, repeating Alexa's old line.

"Mac and cheese is ready."

"One sec," Stacy said, still texting. "Did you hear about the senator's daughter?"

"Yeah," Alexa sighed.

"They said she was found in a drug house with heroin on her."

Alexa gaped. "That part made it to the news already?"

"Melanie reported on it."

"Ugh." Her sister-in-law was a serious pain. The fact that she had a talent for digging up information made her doubly so.

Even worse, she smelled a story about Alexa's relationship with Stacy. "Hero Cop Takes In Child Of Drunk Parents," or some such headline. Good clickbait that would guarantee Stacy's parents would never let her see her again.

That's not what Mr. and Mrs. Carpenter thought they would get. Melanie had pumped them up with the idea that Stacy would be made into some sort of country-girl starlet.

Perhaps wondering why Alexa had gone silent, Stacy looked up from her phone, big blue eyes fixing on her. "Are you on that case?"

"I was but then got … reassigned."

"Reassigned? But you're like the best cop in the world."

Alexa smiled. "Hardly. We tried to catch him, but he got away. That made the senator mad, and he got us reassigned."

"Politicians are stupid."

"He just lost his daughter."

"Yeah. I guess that would screw him up."

"Did Melanie try to contact you about this?"

"I ghosted her ages ago."

"Good girl. Let's eat."

Stacy grinned, cheerful again. It took so little. Just a compliment and a hot meal.

But that little bit had to be constant, a daily shoring up of her self-esteem and a glimpse of normality to offset the indifferent chaos at home.

The problem was, Alexa couldn't provide that every day.

Her brother Wayne's words came back to her, as they came back to her often.

"Maybe it would be better if you didn't get so involved ... you don't have the time to raise her. That's what you're after, isn't it? Having a kid? But you spend most of your time running around the entire Southwest chasing killers, drug dealers, and escaped convicts. How can you raise a kid, especially a needy one like her, when you're doing all that?"

Alexa didn't have an answer for that. She knew she wasn't providing Stacy enough, but too little was better than nothing. Over dinner she tried to think of a solution to that problem. Child protective services would be no help. Cold cuts and a dirty trailer made for better food and housing than some kids got in Arizona, and her parents didn't take illegal drugs. They also didn't hit or molest her. No way Alexa could get her out of there through official channels.

After Stacy washed the dishes, she did her homework at the kitchen table, much more peaceful than trying to work at home. The loud laughter and thudding rock music were distracting enough here. In that tiny trailer, any sort of concentration would have been impossible. Alexa confiscated Stacy's phone, that other distraction, until she was done.

"I got a bit of work to do," Alexa said, squeezing her shoulder.

"I thought they told you to take two days off."

Alexa smiled. "They should know me better than that."

Stacy gave her a high five and Alexa walked down the hall to her home office. There she had a desktop computer and a police scanner attached to a rooftop antenna high up and sensitive enough to pick up signals from downtown Phoenix.

The scanner she kept off so as not to disturb Stacy. Instead, she fired up the computer and checked her email.

A pile of routine stuff, plus a message from Annette dated two hours before. She opened it.

"Some more results from the drug house and the mass grave. Definitely the same shooter. I won't list all the details, but we can prove in court that the same shooter committed both mass murders.

Ballistics, angle, height of shooter, you name it. We got him if you can get him."

"Also a heap of DNA. Already matched the DNA from Pérez's home to traces at the drug house and on one body from the mass grave. Our boy isn't too careful with that. Any idea why?"

"Heard about you getting kicked off the case. Idiots. Don't worry, I'll keep you in the loop. I'll keep Stuart in the loop too. He's sure keeping me in a loop, wink wink."

"Have you ever gotten him to give you a BACKRUB???"

"Oh. My. God."

Alexa rolled her eyes. She knew that Annette and Stuart had enjoyed a torrid relationship ever since they had met on a previous case, but did they have to stick her nose in it?

Alexa had been single for a long time. Between her responsibilities to Stacy, her immense workload, and the emotional damage that came with the job, she hadn't had any spare time or energy. That didn't stop her from wanting a boyfriend, though. She had felt that desire growing within her for a while now.

Not that she had a lot of choice in men. Once you got to your middle thirties like she had, the number of candidates grew slim. Most decent guys were married with small children. Others were already divorced. Those that remained weren't all that interesting. The barflies. The underachievers. The perpetually unemployed.

While she didn't have unreasonably high standards, she'd rather be single than settle for second best.

Alexa wanted a real man. Someone who could take care of themselves and wasn't looking for a mother figure to do everything for them. Someone with a strong sense of self. A strong sense of right and wrong too. Someone with a good career. Maybe in law enforcement. Her previous boyfriends had never understood her drive and constantly worried about the dangers of her career. A man in law enforcement would understand.

Someone like …

Stop. He's entirely inappropriate. He's taken and he's your partner. Plus, he's pissed at you right now.

OK, not him, but someone like *him.*

Is there anyone like him?

STOP.

A noise outside made her perk up.

It had been a soft sound, the sound of someone trying to walk quietly. A person sounds very different when they are sneaking than when they are walking normally, not just softer but stealthier. Slower. More deliberate.

Someone was sneaking around her property.

Then she noticed something else. While the rock music still blared from the Carpenters' trailer, Alexa didn't hear them shouting anymore.

Alexa grabbed her pistol from where it lay on her desk. Even at home, she was in the habit of keeping it in the same room with her. She had dealt with far too many killers not to have protection at hand at all times.

That wasn't paranoia, that was self-preservation.

Burglars weren't unknown in these parts, but more likely it was Stacy's mom or dad snooping around. They had grown increasingly belligerent about her relationship with Stacy.

Alexa took her gun, just in case.

Returning to the kitchen, she found Stacy bent over a notepad and a math textbook. Alexa kept her gun on the far side of her body so the kid wouldn't see. No point scaring her. If it was one of her parents, hopefully Alexa could get them off her property without Stacy knowing. She'd be terribly upset if her parents were spying on them.

And if it was a burglar? She didn't want the guy to hear her say anything to the kid. Better to get him by surprise.

Stacy didn't even look up as Alexa passed to the back door, no doubt assuming she was going out to check on the horses as she did every night. Alexa grabbed the mini Maglite that stood on the counter next to the back door and eased the screen door open.

She stepped out into the warm evening. A few moths circled around the backdoor light and one of the horses dipped its head to drink from the trough. Otherwise, she saw no movement.

Her office window was on the side facing the Carpenters' trailer, all lit up and clearly visible in the distance. She didn't see anyone moving over there.

The light on the back door was the only one that shone on the outside of Alexa's house. There was some light filtering through the Venetian blinds on the windows, but not much.

She got to the corner of the house and steadied herself, gun in one hand and the mini Maglite in the other.

Most likely it's the Carpenters, she told herself. *Go easy and don't scare them.*

She whipped around the corner, turning on her flashlight in the same instant. If she shone it in their faces, they wouldn't see the gun and maybe they wouldn't let out a loud, drunken squawk.

They didn't, because they weren't there. Nobody was.

She paced forward, swinging the beam of her light around. There was nowhere to hide anywhere close. The few scraggly bushes and cacti couldn't hide so much as a coyote.

Alexa stopped short. A section of the soil near her office window was disturbed. She had dug it up herself a few days ago to fix a pipe, and unlike Pérez she hadn't tamped it down to hide the fact that she had been working there.

That had left a good surface to show several fresh boot prints.

She crouched down to examine them. Work boots, about the same size as Stacy's father wore. She cursed softly under her breath.

But where was he?

Slowly she moved around the house, swinging around each corner, ready for anything, but she saw no trace of anyone.

In the time she had taken to get out of the house and look all around it, Mr. Carpenter had managed to sneak off. In two directions there was plenty of cover. In front of her house stood several large outcroppings of rock, and in the other direction a cluster of mesquite trees and a slope down. It wouldn't have taken much time for him to sneak away.

And on the off chance it was a burglar, she had succeeded in scaring him off.

No, more likely it was Stacy's dad. There hadn't been a break-in around these parts for more than a year and all the locals knew she was in law enforcement.

She tucked her gun in the waistband in the small of her back and covered it with her shirt. Then she went back inside and locked the back door.

"Getting time for bed, kiddo," she told Stacy, who was just packing up her homework.

"You were out there for a while."

"Thought I heard a coyote. Wanted to make sure it wasn't going to spook the horses."

Alexa felt bad about lying to the girl but sparing her the truth was the better option.

"You going to bed too?" Stacy asked.

"No, I'm going to do a bit of work."

I'm going to look into all of Pérez's victims. Maybe I can find a pattern to who he's targeting, something Cortez didn't share or doesn't know.

No way I'm going to stop hunting this guy, not after he tried to kill me and Stuart.

CHAPTER ELEVEN

Vicente Pérez was getting desperate. He had barely made it out of his neighborhood alive. A patrol car had driven not ten yards away from him while he hid behind a parked van, and then the police helicopter had shone its light so close he felt sure they had seen him.

They hadn't. He had gotten away. But for how long?

Now there would be a city-wide manhunt for him. His description would be on every news source. Police sketches would soon follow. Thank God he had never let anyone take his picture, and he had never been arrested. They'd have a hard time tracing him.

They'd try, though. Unlike a lot of the young hotheads in the gangs, he didn't underestimate the police. He'd read up on Homicide Detective Rebstock. He'd cracked a lot of tough cases, and he seemed to have the cooperation of the U.S. Marshals office and the FBI too. That could cause serious problems.

A more immediate problem was the graze along his side, given to him by that Deputy Marshal. It had dug a furrow along his ribs, tearing his shirt and leaving a long wound that had soaked his shirt and pants in blood. Holding a bandanna to it, he had managed to stop the bleeding, but it hurt like hell and threatened to open up with any sudden movement.

He needed shelter. Now.

Vicente had walked at least a couple of miles, cutting across yards and setting a dozen dogs to barking. He'd ended up in a richer neighborhood. Bigger houses set further apart. Good. That offered some opportunities. Problem was, rich folks in Phoenix fortified their houses. The high crime rate meant barred windows, double locks on doors, and suspicious owners. They weren't going to open up to some Mexican with a torn shirt.

Then a pizza delivery car drove past on the street ahead, going slow, obviously looking for a particular address. Perfect. Vicente increased his pace, following the car down the road. No other pedestrians about. That made him conspicuous but also reduced the number of witnesses.

The brake lights went on. Vicente slowed.

The car pulled to a stop in front of a house. Vicente walked on the other side of the street, trying to time it just right.

A kid got out in a bright uniform and baseball cap, carrying a pizza box. He didn't look more than nineteen. Probably a university student trying to make a bit of extra money. The car looked pretty nice. Probably a graduation gift from his parents or grandparents. Vicente could never dream about having a car when he grew up, not that he resented this kid. What Vicente had to do was necessary, not personal.

And with the drug dealers? That was another story.

He strolled across the street, trying to look casual and hoping the tear in the side of his shirt wasn't too visible under the streetlights. He kept his arm close to his side just in case.

The kid didn't notice him. He was at the door now, ringing the doorbell. Vicente didn't break his pace.

The door opened, and a middle-aged man with a gut greeted the pizza guy. Vicente strolled up the walkway. The homeowner didn't notice him at first.

Civilians. A bunch of sleepwalkers.

Vicente got halfway up to walkway before the homeowner, cash in hand, looked past the delivery boy and fixed his eyes on him. His eyes didn't register much surprise, only curiosity. Being well dressed always helped. That was something he could never get Jeronimo and the others to understand.

"Excuse me," Vicente said, trying not to let his accent show. "Could you tell me how to get to Birch Street?"

"Birch Street?" the homeowner said.

The pizza guy turned around. "I've never heard of Birch Street."

"Yeah," Vicente said with a nod. "Yeah, I made it up."

Vicente pulled his gun just as he stepped up next to the pair. The teen and the middle-aged man gaped.

Just then there was a cheer inside.

"Yay! Pizza!"

A trio of children ran up to the front hall. A boy and two younger girls. Vicente froze.

"Kids," the homeowner warbled. "Go set the table."

The kids stood staring at the gun.

"GO!" the man shouted.

The kids ran off.

The man turned back to Vicente, holding out the cash in one hand and his wallet in the other. “P-please. Take it and go.”

“I got money too,” the delivery boy said.

“I don’t need money; I need shelter. Get inside.”

The delivery boy hurried to obey. The homeowner took a stand.

“You’re not going to hurt my children.”

“I will if you don’t do exactly as I say.”

The man hesitated.

“They’re safe if you obey.”

The man stared at the gun. Vicente tensed. He had been visible with it in the light of the doorway for too long already. He didn’t want to fire while he was outside.

Still the man hesitated. Vicente gave a little jerk forward. The guy yelped and retreated inside.

Vicente entered a front hall of tile and Mexican decorations, the kind white people who love the Southwest buy at boutique stores rather than venture south of the border. He closed the door behind him and turned to face the homeowner.

Only to realize the pizza guy had disappeared.

Vicente pistol whipped the homeowner, who fell to the floor with a thud, and ran into the interior of the house. The three children stood in a little cluster in the center of the living room, the overturned pizza box nearby staining the carpet, while the teenaged delivery driver fumbled with the lock on the sliding glass door leading to the backyard.

“Stop,” Vicente said in a casual voice. The pizza boy froze. One of the kids started sniffling. He turned to them.

“Where’s your mother?”

One of the girls answered. “A-away on a business trip.”

“Stay here.” He turned to the pizza boy. “You. Come with me.”

“P-please.”

“Move.”

He prodded the teen with the muzzle of his gun. The pizza boy hung his head and allowed himself to be herded back into the front hall.

“Oh my God,” he whispered when he saw the homeowner lying unconscious on the floor.

“He’s not dead.”

The pizza boy let out a breath of relief, only to have it caught short as Vicente whipped out one of his knives and buried it deep in the small of his back, going straight through one of the kidneys.

The boy's body arched, he let out a small gasp, and this too was cut off as Vicente yanked out the knife and slit his throat.

As the pizza boy slumped to the floor, Vicente stepped over him and dispatched the homeowner.

He cleaned the knife on the man's pants, locked the door, and put away both weapons. Then he returned to the living room. The kids hadn't budged. Good. They were spared the sight.

The boy, about eleven, stood up a little straighter, although he could not meet Vicente's eye.

"You do anything bad with my sisters and I'll tell my teacher."

Vicente smiled. "You're a tough kid. This will make you tougher."

"Are you going to kill us?" one of the girls said in a small voice.

Vicente thought for a moment. Killing the adults had been necessary. Killing the kids was also necessary if he planned to hide out here. He had managed to find a house where he could be safe for the moment. Trying to find a second one would be too much risk, especially since these kids would call the cops the moment he left.

He had to stay.

But I can't kill the kids. No, that's going too far.

And slicing the throats of those two civilians isn't? That pizza dude was still young enough to have zits!

Quiet. You did what you had to do so you can keep on going. Your work isn't finished yet, and it's more important than a couple of little ordinary lives.

But what to do about these kids ...

A wet feeling on his side made him look down. The effort to kill those two had opened up his wound again. He needed to patch that up before it started to weaken him.

He couldn't afford to be weak.

He went to the kitchen and rummaged around the drawers, pulling out several cloth napkins. He pulled on one, feeling the pain in his side as he did so. They seemed strong. Good quality.

"What are you going to do?" the boy asked. They still stood in a little cluster, hugging each other for reassurance.

Kill you. I should kill you.

You're being weak, Vicente.

"I'm going to tie you up. I won't hurt you."

"I want Daddy!" the smallest one bawled.

The boy hung his head, tears dropping onto the carpet with a soft patter. He had already figured out what had happened to Daddy.

Vicente approached them, napkins in hand. Their wrists and ankles were small. The napkins would make a tight binding.

"I won't hurt you, but I got to keep you out of the way."

Because I got a lot more killing to do.

CHAPTER TWELVE

Alexa's alarm tore her from too-little sleep. Blearily she looked at the clock. Seven in the morning. About three hours after she finally went to bed. While her chest still felt sore, and her entire body yearned to slap the damn machine to silence and go back to sleep, she had to make sure Stacy made it to the school bus on time, and she had to call Stuart.

She had hit on something.

Alexa stumbled into the kitchen to find Stacy already eating cereal and texting. The girl looked up.

"Morning. Whoa, you need some coffee. Or maybe you should go back to bed?"

"Too much to do," she mumbled, heading for the coffeemaker.

"On your day off? You should rest."

Who's taking care of who here?

"I think I found something important in the case. I need to see Stuart."

"Stuart says you work too much."

"Stuart is probably right. I'm still going to see him. You all ready for school?"

"Yeah."

"Homework done?"

"Yup."

"Bookbag packed?"

"Yup."

"Teeth brushed?"

Stacy rolled her eyes. "I'm not done with breakfast yet. Have some coffee."

They both laughed.

* * *

Two hours later, she and Stuart sat at a bagel shop having breakfast. Since he wasn't on duty, Stuart for once didn't wear his black suit.

Instead, he had on simple jeans, a finely tooled leather belt that must have cost him a pretty penny, loafers, and a polo shirt. The bruise on his jaw had shrunk from the size of a golf ball to the size of a walnut. He had covered it with a bandage. It had probably been oozing blood.

He seemed relaxed until Alexa started talking about the case. Then he rolled his eyes and said, “I knew you couldn’t take a day off.”

Alexa ignored that comment and went on. “Last night I went through the list of murdered people. Minus the innocent bystanders, most had priors and the others were suspected of criminal activity. It was pretty easy to find a method to Pérez’s madness.”

“Which is?”

“He’s taking down the drug networks in town.”

“Well, he is going after the Latino gangs, but that doesn’t mean he’s specifically trying to take down drug trafficking in Phoenix.”

“Hear me out. He hasn’t just been going after any random gang member; he’s been going after the mid-level dealers, the kind of guys we busted in that raid who had come for their monthly pickup. He’s hit three gangs so far, plus the Diablos who came after him.”

“And some innocents.”

Alexa nodded. “Like Brianna Silverman. But all of the civilians seem to have been customers in the wrong place at the wrong time.”

Stuart took a bite of his sesame seed bagel with cream cheese and mulled over that for a moment.

“Then why not go after the bigwigs?” he asked. “People like Jeronimo Cortez who run the local scene?”

“I’m not sure yet,” Alexa conceded. “Maybe he can’t get to them. All the gangs are lying low because of the raid.”

“But he started killing before the raid.”

“True. Maybe he’s working his way up. Or maybe he wants to break the network first, then go after the big guys.”

“Or maybe he’s scared of the big guys. Wait, no. He’s not scared. I don’t think he’s scared of anything. Hmmm … The ritual aspect of shooting people who are already dead is interesting.”

“I’ve been thinking about that. It’s important somehow. We should ask Cortez if Pérez did that sort of thing before going on his rampage.”

Stuart’s eyes twinkled over his bagel and a slow smile crept across his lips.

“I thought we were off the case,” he said.

“Well … ”

“So what else?” Stuart asked.

“What else?”

“That question you could pass on to Rebstock, assuming he hasn’t already thought of it himself. You got something bigger than that. You think you have a lead.”

Now it was Alexa’s turn to smile. This man knew her well.

“I think I know who he’s going after next.”

“Who? How?”

Alexa pulled out a tablet and showed him a mug shot of a light-skinned man with black hair slicked back into a short ponytail.

“This is Pablo Mason, half Latino and half Anglo. Unusual for him to have a Hispanic last name and an Anglo family name. Usually mixed couples go one way or the other. His parents live in the barrio so maybe they wanted to give him deeper roots. His dad ran a McDonald’s there. His mother was a shift manager and they ended up married. Now they run the McDonald’s together.”

“I take it Junior didn’t earn his parents’ work ethic?”

“He did, just not in a legal way. He’s a dealer in the same barrio for a gang called the Mestizo Boys, mixed blood like him who specialize in weed and ecstasy.”

“There are better ways to celebrate multiculturalism. Why do you think he’s the next target?”

“He’s been busted twice for possession of small amounts, and we know for a fact that he’s got several corner dealers working under him. We’ve never been able to pin enough on him to get him to court for a major crime. But the Mestizo Boys are the only gang in Phoenix that Pérez hasn’t hit yet. They’re a smaller gang and Mason is the only mid-level dealer, the go-between getting the drugs from the narcos’ regional supplier and handing them down to the street dealers.”

“Sounds like a good bet. So you’re going to give this info to Rebstock and go back to enjoying your day off, right?”

Alexa and Stuart laughed.

“You’re unbelievable,” Stuart said, shaking his head. “Can I at least finish my bagel first?”

“Sure.”

“Very generous of you.” He grew serious. “You do realize there could be repercussions.”

Alexa grimaced. “I know, I know. It’s just that I never gave up on a case before, and I can’t leave this guy free. He nearly killed the both of us. Two officers are in the hospital.”

Stuart frowned, looking down at the table. For a moment he looked distant, as if he wasn’t sitting at the table at all, not even in Arizona but far, far away.

“Yeah,” he said quietly. “You can’t just see a couple of your men go down and not counterattack. So how do you want to approach this?”

Alexa leaned forward and began to go through the plan. Stuart nodded, eating his bagel as his eyes grew wider and wider. Alexa sensed he had become uncomfortable, but he did not object as she went through everything step by step.

* * *

The territory of the Mestizo Boys was a few blocks along a busy commercial road and the neighborhoods just behind. Alexa drove her Jeep in the slow lane, taking in the strip malls with their liquor stores, cheap outlets, and garish signs offering “cash for gold.” The crowd was a mix of Hispanic and Anglo, all working class. Being the middle of the day, the crowd was a bit thin. Most people were at their jobs. Unlike the neighborhood where the Diablos had their safehouse, most people here had jobs to go to.

Even so, the parasites who peddled drugs made good business and had no problem finding recruits. She spotted three young men, one barely into his teens, hanging out in various parking lots and street corners. The kid stood in front of a boarded-up shop with a can of Coke in his hand, wearing a muscle shirt that he hoped would make him look tough and yet only emphasized his skinny adolescent frame. An older, thickset guy leaned against a telephone pole at the corner of a parking lot two blocks down and across the street. Another block along and across the street from him was a fit man of about twenty who really could fill out a muscle t-shirt.

Dealers stood in a certain way that made it obvious they weren’t simply waiting for a friend or an Uber. They puffed themselves up a bit and looked around them, and they did not move to another location or pace as if impatiently waiting for someone. And unlike everyone else their age, they did not stare at their phone.

It was, of course, obvious to everyone and they knew it. The dealers didn't fear the cops, because they never carried drugs on their person or gave any reason to be stopped and searched. If someone came up to them wanting to buy, and the dealer recognized them as a previous customer or decided they looked safe, they'd give a signal to someone nearby, often in a parked car or nursing a coffee in a restaurant, to come with the drugs. That person would look and act far more nondescript, and Alexa couldn't spot them from a simple dive through the neighborhood.

It didn't matter. She and Stuart weren't after some small-time dealers who would get a year in prison at most. They were after bigger fish.

After getting to the end of the Mestizo Boys' turf, Alexa circled through the neighborhood on the north side of the main thoroughfare, studying each pedestrian and trying to see in each parked car. No luck. She cut south, got onto the other side of the main road, and repeated her search there.

"Maybe he decided to go to a university and he's in his poetry class right now," Stuart suggested.

"That must be it," Alexa said, getting back on the main road to go the other direction.

The Mestizo Boys were sharp. The muscular guy studied them as they passed, obviously recognizing the vehicle as having passed by just a few minutes before. The thickset guy was busy talking to someone and so didn't scope them out, and as they continued down the road even the skinny kid noticed them.

"Pablo Mason runs a tight ship," Stuart said.

Alexa nodded, feeling relieved they were hidden behind tinted windows. Stuart saw what she saw. While he was in the FBI's Behavioral Affairs Unit, specializing in tracking down serial killers, he knew how to scan the streets.

That hadn't helped them find Mason, though.

"We can't do another pass," Alexa said.

"No."

Looping through the neighborhood once could be dismissed as someone having lost their way, but if they came through a second time, all those dealers and their backup would be on the alert for either a nervous new customer—always a liability—or plainclothes cops on the prowl.

Alexa drove out of the Mestizo Boys' turf and parked in front of a strip mall parking lot a block away. The Mason family's McDonald's franchise was visible just down the street. As she got out, Alexa felt a stab of pity for those hardworking parents of a no-good son who was about to have yet another run-in with the law.

"Want to try at the restaurant?" Stuart asked.

"No. I doubt he'll be there, and if he is I'd like to spare the parents. Let's check out the area on foot."

"OK."

They walked through the neighborhood, north of the main thoroughfare. Being a mixed area, they did not stand out other than Stuart being slightly too well dressed. That wouldn't draw much attention. The bandage on his jaw made him a bit conspicuous, though. Alexa felt glad they were in civilian clothes. They could have never done this in uniform.

Stuart must have been thinking along the same lines because he said, "You know you're not authorized to be performing a plainclothes operation."

"Neither of us is authorized to do this at all."

"Nope. Days off with you are kind of interesting."

Alexa felt herself blush. While he meant it as a snarky comment on her obsession with work, she could see it as a compliment, one probably not meant but certainly welcome.

Focus.

At least the tension from the previous day had dissipated. The gunfight had swept away any of Stuart's lingering resentment. It's hard to stay mad at someone who you have to face death with.

Few people were on the streets. In Phoenix, everyone drove everywhere, and it was a school day, so no kids were around. The only people they saw was an old couple walking hand in hand and a young woman in a miniskirt and halter top walking quickly. Late for work or needing a fix? Work seemed unlikely considering how she was dressed.

By unspoken consent, they followed her at a distance.

She cut down a residential road, looking all around her. Not the behavior of someone in a hurry to catch the bus, and she was walking away from the bus line anyway.

The woman came to an intersection, looked left, and darted in that direction. Whatever she saw was hidden from their view by the houses, but Alexa had a feeling she knew.

They got to the intersection and continued straight. From the corner of her eye Alexa could see the woman on the sidewalk half a block away talking urgently with Pablo Mason.

Bingo.

That's the good thing about gang members. You always know where to find them.

"Loop around and come at them from the other direction?" Stuart asked in a low voice.

"Sounds like a plan. He'll have spotted us, so we need to surprise him."

Once Alexa and Stuart got out of sight behind the house at the corner of the intersection, they sped up. It didn't take long for them to get around the next residential block and behind Mason's previous location.

The young woman had disappeared, no doubt rushing home to take whatever it was she had bought. Mason was strolling in the other direction almost a block away. Alexa and Stuart got behind him and started to increase their pace to catch up with him.

Then, bad luck.

Pablo Mason looked over his shoulder. Even from that distance Alexa could see the spark of recognition in his eyes. These two strangers had crossed the intersection ahead of him just two minutes before and now they were coming at him from an entirely different direction?

He began to run.

CHAPTER THIRTEEN

Alexa cursed and sprinted after him, Stuart by her side.

"U.S. Marshal! FBI! Stop and get on the ground!" she shouted.

That only made him speed up.

Trying to catch a man ten years younger who had every reason to not get caught would leave most people in the dust. Not Alexa and Stuart. Law enforcement training involved a lot of things, and one of the most important was physical fitness, especially running. Alexa couldn't count the number of times she'd run down a suspect like a coyote runs down a jackrabbit.

Stuart probably couldn't either. Plus, his years in college football certainly helped his speed. Alexa struggled to stay at his side as he sprinted down the street.

He began to pull ahead, and while that poked at Alexa's ego, she forgave him when he performed a spectacular flying tackle that put Mason down on the ground in a painful looking faceplant.

Too bad. Anyone who pedals drugs deserves a hundred faceplants.

Alexa cuffed him while Stuart held him. The only thing Mason could do was assault their ears with a torrent of swear words in two different languages.

"I'm not too good at Spanish yet, could you translate for me?" Stuart asked.

"Bite me!" Mason shouted.

"No, no, the Spanish ones. I understand English just fine."

Alexa patted him down and came out with a bag of weed, a bag of blue pills with happy faces stamped on them she guessed was ecstasy, and a small bag of heroin.

"The Mestizo Boys are getting into the black tar, eh?" Alexa said. "Los Diablos Auténticos won't be too happy about that. What's left of them."

"I ain't saying nothing without a lawyer."

Alexa and Stuart stood him up.

"We're the ones who are going to do most of the talking," Alexa told him. "You have two priors, so a third conviction for possession is going to see you go away for a long time. A *very* long time. But there's another option."

Mason looked at her curiously but didn't reply. Alexa went on.

"You heard of Vicente Pérez?"

"Yes."

"He's gone rogue. Los Diablos Auténticos burnt him at the altar. He's not taking orders from anyone anymore and is killing all the midlevel dealers. People like you."

"Santa Maria! So it's true." Mason glanced around, as if Pérez might jump out from behind a cactus.

All that tough guy swagger sure disappeared quick. He's terrified of him. Probably everyone is terrified of him. That could come in handy.

Or could be a liability.

"Mason, I can arrest you and you'll go to jail for a while. Years." Alexa dangled the drugs in front of him. "Or I can throw these down the nearest drainage grate and let you go."

Mason blinked. "Let me go? Wait. You want me on the streets so you can flush out Pérez?"

Stuart cocked his head. "You're smarter than you look, Mason. Smart enough to know you shouldn't be doing what you're doing. So why do it?"

Mason frowned at him. "What else should I do? Shift manager at McDonald's, wearing a paper hat and having to smile at every son of a bitch customer who complains he didn't get enough French fries?"

"It was good enough for your parents. Why not you?"

"My parents are slaves to the system. I live free."

"You won't be free if we bust you for these drugs," Alexa said. "We'll search your home too."

A flicker of worry appeared behind the tough façade.

"Ah! Now we're getting somewhere," Alexa said. "You have something to hide at home? This month's shipment? An illegal firearm? I bet that's it. With your priors, you're not allowed to own a firearm, but your job requires it. A convicted drug dealer with a firearm. Damn, you're looking at ten years minimum."

"I don't have nothing, and you need a search warrant."

"The drugs are probable cause for us to reasonably assume there may be a crime in progress at your residence, and that means we don't need a warrant."

Mason didn't have anything to say to that. Criminals at his level always knew the law just as thoroughly as the police themselves.

Still he hesitated. Asking him to be bait for someone like Vicente Pérez was no small thing.

Alexa decided to add a carrot, and a stick.

"Here's the deal. We'll stake you out, the two of us, and jump in as soon as we see Pérez."

"You can't beat him."

"If we get the drop on him, we can. And if you comply, you won't see us in this neighborhood for another year. Think of it, Mason, a whole year."

"You can't make that promise."

"Not for the Phoenix P.D. we can't, but we can for the U.S. Marshals Service and the FBI."

Alexa didn't look at her partner as she said this. She was making a hell of a promise, one that she wasn't authorized to make and would be really hard to keep.

If she knew her partner at all, he would be seriously reconsidering his place in this right now.

But what choice did they have? They had to catch Vicente.

Mason began to waver. She could see it in his eyes.

Now for the stick.

"If we arrest you, we have to put this black tar in the report. You know how word gets around in prison. Everyone knows everything about what people are in for. You're stepping on Diablos' business selling that stuff, and there are a lot of Diablos on the inside."

"Even more now," Stuart added.

Glad to see you're still with me; I worried about that.

Mason looked at Stuart, then her, then at the ground. After a moment he looked up.

"No harassment for a year?"

"None. The police will keep doing its thing, but the federal agencies will stay off your back."

She could practically see the wheels turning in his head. With Los Diablos Auténticos all but destroyed, and members of the other gangs killed or in hiding, this was a prime opportunity for the Mestizo Boys to expand their operations.

If he lived.

That still bothered him.

She couldn't blame him.

Then he lifted his head and put on a haughty look Alexa didn't believe for a second.

"Fuck it. I ain't afraid of Pérez. Let's do it."

Alexa's breath caught. Suddenly she felt cold.

Oh, you should be afraid, Mason. You should be afraid.

* * *

Stuart sat in Alexa's truck, bored and irritated. Stakeouts were always dull, but they seemed to drag ten times as much if you were in a bad mood. They'd only been sitting there for two hours, and yet it felt like some of those twenty-four-hour sentry duties he'd had to pull in Anbar province.

He still resented Alexa poking into his affairs. Snooping around his service history had been bad enough, but didn't she understand how he felt about his old girlfriend? She got so obsessed with tracking down the bad guys that she disregarded everything else.

He didn't say anything to his partner as she sat beside him, scanning the main thoroughfare for any sign of Vicente Pérez. There was no point bringing it up. When it came to a case, she never listened.

Mason had positioned himself in a parking lot near the hefty guy, who looked most capable of handling a fight. The gang leader stood close to several parked cars, obviously intending to use them as cover in case any shooting started.

The skinny kid they had noted dealing in front of a boarded-up shop further down the road had left, only to return twenty minutes later with a large McDonald's bag. Seeing how crinkled it was, Stuart could tell he hadn't just popped down to Mason's parents to get lunch. He went to Mason, then each of the other two dealers, and passed something off to them, each time positioning his body between his friend and Stuart and Alexa's vantage point to keep them from seeing what he was handing them.

Not that they needed to. He was handing out guns.

Fair enough. If Mason was going to be bait, it was too much to ask for him to be a sitting duck.

Stuart felt bad about the whole thing. Mason might have been the black sheep of a good family, peddling drugs to the public, but he didn't deserve to be in this situation. No one did.

Alexa didn't think that way. She figured that using Mason as bait was justifiable because it might prevent more deaths. Even if Mason got killed and they killed Pérez, in the end it would be a win because if Pérez was let to roam free, he would kill far more than some two-bit drug dealer dreaming of the big time.

It was the same calculus generals used in wartime. Yes, you'll lose men in any operation, but it's worth it if it saves the army from destruction.

But this wasn't war, this was a working-class neighborhood in the United States; and they weren't facing a terror cell or an enemy battalion, they were facing one trigger-happy narco enforcer.

And Alexa was no general. Any general worth the stars knew he'd lose men. Alexa thought they could get through without any collateral damage. Her overconfidence could get her killed someday.

Or get somebody else killed.

Not to mention they were going behind their boss's back. Even if they caught Pérez and no one got hurt, they'd get the mother of all chewings out, perhaps even a suspension.

And if things did go wrong? They'd be blamed for whatever happened. It could mean their badges.

This is wrong.

So why had he gone along with it?

He couldn't really answer that. Alexa could be very persuasive, and he found himself trying to please her, even when he was angry at her. There was something compelling about his new partner. Her dedication, her heart, her strong morality, blinded as it was by her deep need for justice. He just wished all those good traits weren't mixed with a supreme level of bullheadedness.

Something on the street caught his eye. A tall, lean man with a cowboy hat pulled low over his face walked quickly toward Mason, who turned to him.

"Could that be him?" Stuart asked.

"Could be. We never did get a good look at Pérez."

Stuart studied him. Blue jeans, white shirt. Cowboy boots of brown leather. Not the all-black attire Vicente Pérez had made his trademark, but it made sense that he'd change up his appearance while on the run.

Mason turned and saw the guy. He frowned and flicked his hand in a dismissive way. Mr. Cowboy Hat stopped, raising his hands as if to say, "What gives?"

The drug dealer shouted at him, pointing down the street. Mr. Cowboy Hat shrugged and walked away. As he turned, Stuart could see he was Anglo.

"Must be killing him to turn away customers," Alexa snickered. This was the third time this had happened.

"Let's just make sure he doesn't get killed for real," Stuart grumbled.

"He won't be."

No general would ever say that.

Another man approached Mason. The drug dealer's back was turned, still shooing away Mr. Cowboy Hat, who kept looking over his shoulder and calling back to him, obviously desperate for a fix and not understanding why the local dealer kept telling him to get lost.

Stuart didn't care about that. He cared about the Hispanic man wearing a baseball cap low over his face and a black t-shirt showing off lean muscles over black jeans. He kept a determined, steady pace as he approached Mason.

"Yo. Eleven o'clock," Stuart said.

Alexa looked. "Might be him. Damn it. Turn around, Mason."

The dealer was now arguing with Mr. Cowboy Hat, who had stopped a good half a block down the street, still pleading his case.

Stuart loosened his gun in its concealed holster. "Should we go?"

"Might just be another customer. If the street sees us, word will get around and we'll never catch Pérez."

The man in black continued to approach while Mason's back was turned, still arguing with the drug addict.

"We should go," Stuart said.

"Let's just wait a second."

The newcomer was only a few paces away now, Mason still oblivious. Stuart pulled his gun, keeping it out of sight under the dashboard.

The man with the baseball cap reached into his shirt and pulled something out.

All Stuart could see was sunlight glinting off steel.

CHAPTER FOURTEEN

Alexa saw the man in the baseball cap pull out a knife. Stuart cursed and leaned on the horn.

Mason turned to face them, caught movement in the corner of his eye, and turned to spot the newcomer just as he charged the drug dealer.

Mason bolted, running around the parked car he stood next to, trying to pull his gun from where it was concealed beneath his shirt.

He had trouble getting it out because he had to sprint to keep away from his attacker, who chased him, brandishing the knife.

The two of them circled the car once, then the man in the baseball cap suddenly switched directions and came around the other side. Mason switched directions too, struggling to get his gun out. It seemed to have gotten tangled in his clothing.

Alexa leaped out of her Jeep, Stuart jumping out the other side. They sprinted across the street, blaring horns and screeching tires warning them that they nearly got run over. They didn't even bother looking at the car that had nearly killed them.

"U.S. Marshals!" Alexa shouted.

The man with the knife stopped the chase and glanced in their direction.

And Alexa could see quite clearly that this was not the man they had fought in the Los Diablos Auténticos safehouse.

So who the hell was he?

Alexa leveled her gun at him. "Freeze!"

The man bolted.

Stuart cursed and got into gear, pelting across the concrete, arms pumping, bypassing Mason and angling across the parking lot for the knifeman.

Alexa slowed long enough to ask Mason, "Who was that?"

"Independent dealer. He's angry because we pushed him out of most of his business."

Alexa turned her attention back to the chase.

Only to find it was already over.

A car screeched to a stop in front of the attacker, the passenger's side door popping open, and he jumped inside headfirst. The car made a tight u turn, scraping against a parked van, and sped off, the man pulling his legs in and slamming the door. The driver hit the gas and the car tore out of the parking lot, swerved through two lanes of traffic, cutting off a car that had to slam on its brakes to avoid a collision, and sped off down the road.

A splash of dried mud on the license plate conveniently obscured the number.

Alexa stopped, breathing hard. She looked around and found everyone staring—Mason's dealers, pedestrians, passing motorists, everyone.

"Damn it. This stakeout is ruined," she muttered.

She turned back to Mason, to find him popping up from behind a parked car. She got the impression that he had put something underneath it. Probably that illegal firearm he had been carrying.

He walked around the car to her, trying to look casual.

"Aren't you going to pursue him?" Mason asked.

"We got bigger fish to fry, plus they got too much of a lead on us."

"And you're not even going to radio it in?" Mason cocked his head, studying her. "Are you even on duty?"

Alexa looked away, suddenly embarrassed. This guy was smarter and more perceptive than she thought. Looking around to assess the situation and avoid his question, she saw several people still staring.

Damn, word will spread on the street like wildfire. If Pérez has any contacts left at all he'll hear about this for sure.

We've failed.

Stuart came storming back to them, not even winded by his sprint across the parking lot.

He frowned at her. Alexa took half a step back, shocked by the level of his sudden anger.

Stuart turned to the drug dealer. "You. Stay put. Alexa, we need to talk."

They stepped a few paces away. Despite Stuart's instructions, Mason moved a bit to the side to stand next to another parked car. No doubt to distance himself from the gun he had ditched.

"What the hell are we doing?" Stuart growled, keeping his voice low. "We nearly got this loser killed."

"We took a calculated risk, maybe too much of one, but we did it to save lives," Alexa replied, trying to sound conciliatory.

Stuart shook his head.

"This wasn't right, and you know it."

Alexa flushed with shame. Until Stuart had put it in words, she had been able to push it to the sidelines, explain it away as necessary.

But now?

Before Alexa could respond, Mason shouted, "It's cool! Go back to your posts."

Alexa looked around. Mason's three dealers had closed in, each approaching from a different angle. They hesitated. The looks they gave Alexa and Stuart were not kindly.

"Go on!" Mason repeated, waving his arms.

Reluctantly they turned and went back to their accustomed spots.

Alexa walked up to Mason.

"You all right?" she asked.

"Yeah, no thanks to you."

Alexa cringed.

"Look, this didn't work and now word is out. Pérez is still gunning for you, so if you're smart you and your buddies will take a holiday. Get out of town for a while."

"I got work to do."

"Work that should get you arrested and might get you killed. Get out of town. That's the best I can do for you. I'll ignore the drugs we confiscated, and I'll ignore what you stowed underneath that car over there." Mason's eyes got shifty. "You just get out of town. And once this is all over, I'll be checking on you. If I find you peddling drugs around here again, it'll be open season."

"But you promised immunity."

"If we caught Pérez."

Alexa turned and walked away, ignoring the string of Spanish and English curses hurled at her back. She and Stuart headed back to her Jeep on the other side of the road.

"Now what the hell do we do?" she grumbled.

"What do you mean?" Stuart asked.

"What should our plan of attack be? I'm all out of ideas."

She had to make this good, turn her failure into success.

"Here's an idea," Stuart said with cutting sarcasm. "How about we follow orders and take the next two days off instead of breaking several different regulations and endangering the public?"

"We can't leave this case, Stuart," she said, flinging her hands above her head. "Rebstock is good, but he's saddled with some civilian advisor breathing down his neck. He needs our help. If we—"

Stuart threw his hands in the air. "Jesus Christ, Alexa! Do you think you're the only capable cop in the whole damn state? We're off the case. Yes, for the wrong reasons, but that doesn't change the fact that we're way overstepping our authority here. Let them handle it."

Alexa stared at him. "What are you saying?"

"I'm saying we're done. I should have never agreed to this in the first place. I'm going home, and so should you."

"But …"

"Go HOME, Alexa."

He stormed off. Alexa followed at a distance.

"Wait!" she called after him. It was all falling apart. "At least let me give you a ride."

"I'm taking the bus."

He kept on walking. Alexa stopped and watched him go, wondering if her relationship with her partner had been broken forever.

In many ways, he had been right. The fiasco with Mason had been a serious error of judgement, and it had been wrong to pull Stuart into it too.

But all those bodies … the senator's daughter …

She couldn't just let those people down, couldn't stand by while the body count rose and rose and rose.

Damn, Alexa thought, heading back to her vehicle. *Maybe I'm as big of a junkie as Brianna Silverman.*

* * *

Back home at her little ranch, Alexa sat in her office, listening to the police scanner and scouring what little records they had of Vicente Pérez. She kept having to fight the urge to look over her shoulder, half expecting to see Stuart standing there, glowering his disapproval. That argument with him hurt even more than the ugly purple bruise on her chest from Vicente's bullet.

She forced herself to focus on the records.

There wasn't much to go on. He had managed to avoid trouble with the law. Of course, he had not been entirely under the radar. There was an extremely thin file on him because of his association with Los Diablos Auténticos, but it didn't even have a photograph.

It was enough to get started, though.

Vicente had come up from Mexico, presumably sent by the Pelayo family, the narco organization that supplied most of the drugs to central Arizona. It wasn't the biggest family in the Mexican drugs business, or the most successful, but it had staked a claim in the profitable business by being more brutal than its rivals.

And in the vicious drug wars of Mexico, that was saying something.

Little by little, it had solidified its position in central Arizona and was now slowly expanding throughout the rest of the state. Alexa wondered how many hits Pérez had made outside of the territory run by Los Diablos Auténticos. While he had been part of the gang, he still answered directly to the Pelayo family, and might have done some extra work for them on the side for one of the other gangs or distributors the Pelayo family worked with. Someone at his level didn't simply work for just one fairly large stateside gang.

But other than that, the police file didn't tell her much.

Except for one detail—that Pérez had come to the United States on a marriage visa.

He had married an Anglo woman named Theresa Palmer, a resident of Phoenix.

A check of state records revealed that they had gotten divorced five years later and she had moved out of the state. This was standard practice for the narco families. Bribing a government official to fake citizenship was chancy and expensive, and always ran the risk of later discovery. Far better just to pay some desperate woman a few grand to marry a narco representative who would give them a comfortable lifestyle and a steady supply of drugs until they had been "married" long enough that they could get divorced without suspicion and the narco rep got to keep their citizenship.

Alexa did a national search for Theresa Palmer and found she now lived in California and held a job as a waitress at some place by the beach called the "Sex n' Surf." Alexa didn't have to think very hard to figure out what Palmer's waitressing duties might entail.

She Googled the business and noted down the number. She doubted Theresa was still in contact with her former husband, but if Alexa kept hitting dead ends it wouldn't hurt to reach out to her. She might have some insight into his character and what he might plan to do next.

Alexa went back to the marriage license and discovered an interesting detail. One of the witnesses was named Erasmo Pérez. A relative?

Erasmo had been born in Phoenix and had quite the criminal record. Starting with shoplifting and affray, he graduated to drug dealing and grievous bodily harm. He had spent six of the past twelve years inside. He had left prison for the last time five years before and was still on parole.

A search of parole records revealed that he still lived in Phoenix, in the worst barrio in the city.

That struck her as odd. First off, the barrio was not in the territory of Los Diablos Auténticos, so it wasn't like he was the gang's local organizer. Secondly, if Erasmo Pérez was a cousin, that meant he'd be close to Vicente. The last name Pérez was reasonably common in Mexico, but it was too much of a coincidence to think the best man at Vicente's wedding of convenience just happened to share the same name. And family ties were just important in the Mexican crime organizations as they were in the Italian Mafia. Erasmo should be part of the organization, living in Diablos' territory or at least some nicer part of town his position would mean he could afford.

So why the bad zip code?

Alexa could think of three possibilities.

One, Erasmo worked for the narcos but not Los Diablos Auténticos. Perhaps he worked higher up in the organization, acting as distributor or perhaps a liaison to or enforcer for another gang.

Two, he really did work for Los Diablos Auténticos and they were trying to stake a claim in new territory. If so, the police hadn't caught wind of it.

The third possibility intrigued Alexa the most—Erasmo and Vicente had a falling out and Erasmo had left the organization. It would explain why he was hiding out in enemy territory. It would be safer. It would also explain why he had to live in such a poor area.

Fallen out about what? Alexa had no idea. And how could Erasmo have avoided his cousin? If Alexa could have tracked him down so easily, Vicente must have known where he lived. So why not kill him?

Did he have orders from on high not to? Could he not bring himself to point a gun at family?

Or maybe, and this made Alexa shiver a little, maybe Erasmo Pérez was even more dangerous than his cousin.

There was only one way to find out the answers to all these questions.

Alexa needed to pay this man a visit.

This time, she'd go it alone. She wouldn't put anyone else's life or career in danger.

Maybe if she could get a breakthrough in the case, maybe if she could find a line of inquiry that stopped the killing, Stuart would forgive her.

And she could forgive herself.

CHAPTER FIFTEEN

Alexa had been to the southeast side before, and it always affected her with a powerful mixture of sadness and fear. Sadness for the many decent people forced by circumstances to live in such squalor, and fear for the human wolves who preyed on their despair and desperation.

As she drove along the grim streets, litter scattered on the sidewalks as a mute testament to the fact that the city authorities overlooked this part of town and even the garbage collectors feared coming here, she realized she had something new to worry about. Her Jeep stuck out like a sore thumb. While it wasn't the latest model and had more than a few scrapes and dings from frequent off-roading, it was way better than anything else she saw on the road. People were going to notice her, and on the southeast side getting noticed was a bad thing.

The strip malls were run down, many of the shops boarded up. There were few standalone homes, and those looked near to collapse. Most people here lived in ugly concrete apartment blocks. She'd been in some of them on raids. Broken elevators, peeling paint, cracked windows, graffiti and trash in the stairways. It was amazing that anyone could live a decent life in such conditions.

And yet some did.

She saw a black woman in a nurse's uniform, eyes exhausted, head held high, leading three small children back from school through a gauntlet of prostitutes and drug dealers. She saw an Asian man standing behind bulletproof glass at his convenience store. She saw an elderly Hispanic man cleaning a spray-painted drawing of a penis off the side of a building.

Alexa wanted to put every one of them in her Jeep and drive them all back to her ranch.

She got to Erasmo Pérez's address, a five-story apartment building that, if possible, looked even worse than the buildings around it. A heap of trash bags, their sides split open, sat out front. Several windows were broken, their cracks taped up or their panes replaced with cardboard.

The parking lot contained very few cars, and none of them looked like anything anyone would want to steal. Alexa drove into the lot, swerving to avoid an empty beer bottle, and parked her Jeep. She locked her doors and set her car alarm, not that it would make much difference. The public ignored car alarms even more than Stacy's parents ignored their child.

As she walked toward the building, already worried about the safety of her vehicle, she noticed a black man in his thirties, wearing old jeans and a muscle t-shirt with stains on it, walking toward her with obvious intent. He looked well built, the kind of person who could hold his own in a neighborhood like this. Alexa tensed, her hand straying to her gun where it was hidden underneath her shirt. Her other hand moved toward the pocket where she kept a bottle of pepper spray.

He stopped in front of her, blocking her path. Alexa stopped too, just out of reach.

"Get out of here," he said.

"Excuse me?"

The man looked around, then waved a hand at her. Alexa was reminded of Pablo Mason waving off his customers. It was the exact same gesture.

"Get out of here. You don't belong here."

"I need to visit someone."

The guy shook his head. "This place is too dangerous for you. You come in here wearing those clothes and driving that Jeep? Everyone is scoping you out. You're not safe here. Go on."

He waved her off again.

"I need to visit someone in this building," Alexa explained.

The man looked over his shoulder at the building and then back at her.

"No drugs are worth what you risk by going in there."

"I'm not going in to buy drugs."

The man snorted as if that was the worst lie he had ever heard.

"Want to make twenty bucks?" Alexa asked.

He frowned. "I don't have nothing to sell you."

"Guard my Jeep. If someone comes that's too much trouble, leave. But you could just stand there and glare at the less serious criminals. If my Jeep is still in one piece when I get back, I'll give you twenty bucks."

"All right," he said doubtfully. "But no guarantees."

"I understand." Alexa stepped around him.

"I'm telling you: you don't want to go in there."

"You're right. I don't."

She walked to the front doors, a pair of battered wooden ones with meshed windows. Glancing over her shoulder, she saw the man standing close to her Jeep, arms crossed to show off his impressive muscles, looking all around him.

Alexa nodded at him. Her Jeep was as safe as it could be.

But what about her? She didn't have her partner, didn't have any backup. She had come here all alone. No one even knew she was here.

Heart hammering in her chest, making the bruise from Vicente's bullet hurt with every beat, she swung open the doors.

No one was in the lobby. The place was bare of furniture, just an expanse of cracked and dusty tile. The only paint on the concrete walls was graffiti. To the left ran a row of mailboxes, some of them forced open. At the far end of the lobby, she saw a lone elevator with a faded sign reading "Out of Service."

Alexa took the stairs, and immediately wished she hadn't. It smelled of beer and stale urine.

Erasmo Pérez lived on the fourth floor. She huffed up the steps, trying to block out the stench.

She made it just past the second floor when she came around the landing and stopped short.

A man stood just around the turn of the stairs. He was a bit older, with watery blue eyes; a soft moist, mouth; and a blonde bouffant that looked like a cheap imitation of a Las Vegas Elvis impersonator. His impressive gut told of a diet of cheap beer and fast food, but was massive. In an arm-wrestling match, he would give the guy guarding her Jeep a run for his money.

And he just stood there.

"Hey," he said, giving her an arrogant smile.

"Hey."

Alexa did not try and pass him. He took up most of the stairway, and she did not want to get within reach.

They stared at each other in silence for a moment.

"Mind getting out of my way?" Alexa asked.

"I'm not stopping you." He stared at her breasts. "Of course, if you want to stay a while, I can show you a good time."

Alexa glowered at him. "I'm going to walk down to the next landing. Then you are going to pass me at a safe distance and go down to the ground floor. Is that clear?"

The man cocked his head, his eyes taking in her body from her boots all the way up to her eyes. "And who the hell do you think you are?"

Alexa considered her options. Leave. Show her badge. Show her gun. Give him a dose of pepper spray.

She decided on none of those things.

"Who am I? I'm the woman who is going to kick your ass if you don't get out of my way."

The huge man took a step down toward her. "Bitch, who the fuck do you—"

Alexa gave his groin a hard right jab, his chin an uppercut as he bent over from the pain, and then flipped him past her so he slammed hard against the wall. He ended up in a heap on the floor.

"Don't call women bitches."

She walked up the final flights of steps and went down a dingy hallway. An old woman, her hair in curlers, opened a door just ahead, took one look at Alexa, and slammed the door. Strangers weren't welcome here. Alexa wondered what she thought Alexa was. A bill collector? A process server here to hand over court documents? A bail bondsman?

Whatever she thought, she sure wouldn't welcome a U.S. Deputy Marshal.

She got to Erasmo's room and knocked on the door.

Silence. She noticed no light shone through the peephole. Then for a fraction of a second a bit of light winked on before it went dark again.

An old trick for the paranoid and necessarily cautious. Unwelcome guests might watch your peephole for signs that you are looking out, giving them proof you are home, and a general idea of where you are standing in case they want to shoot through the door. So you avoid showing any light by hanging something over the hole, then replacing it quickly with your eye.

Erasmo, or whoever was behind that door, was paranoid, perhaps with reason. He or she also moved incredibly silently. Alexa hadn't heard a thing.

And she continued hearing nothing. Either the person behind the door had managed to replace the cover without revealing any light, or they were still watching her.

"Erasmo Pérez, I need to speak with you about Vicente."

Silence.

Alexa took a shot in the dark. "Vicente has gone rogue and you're in danger of your life. I'm trying to stop further bloodshed."

More silence. Alexa let out a sigh. She hated it when she tried to help people who refused to be helped.

"Erasmo Pérez, I'm going to count to three. If you don't open this door, I'm going to kick it down."

Silence.

"One."

"Two."

"Th—"

The door flew open, and Alexa found herself staring down the barrel of a revolver.

CHAPTER SIXTEEN

It was a cheap revolver, with a worn handle and a couple of chips on the metal. The kind you might buy for fifty bucks at a pawn shop or in a back alley. Still, Alexa didn't underestimate it. It was barely two feet from her head and the hand that held it did not waver a millimeter.

Alexa looked beyond the gun, a hard thing to do when one is pointed at you, and focused on the man behind it.

Right away she knew she had come to the right place. The man looked in his forties, haggard with deep worry lines, but the family resemblance to the man she had briefly glimpsed in the firefight was obvious.

As was his fear.

"Who are you?" Erasmo demanded.

Alexa lowered her voice. "Deputy U.S. Marshal Alexa Chase. I'm hunting for your … cousin?"

Erasmo nodded. His lips twisting as if he had tasted something sour. "My cousin. How I wish that demon seed had never been born."

"Could you stop pointing your gun at me?"

The mention of her job hadn't moved his hand at all. Now he lowered it.

Erasmo jerked his head. "Come inside before anyone sees you. Did anyone see you?"

"A big guy on the stairs and an old woman three doors down."

"Pervy Charley and Ms. Bennett."

Alexa entered a small apartment. A windowless bedroom was just left of the front door, a tiny bathroom beside it. To the right was a kitchen and ahead she saw a living room. Alexa was struck by two things. First, the poverty. Everything seemed to have been bought at Goodwill or a flea market. Second, the cleanliness. It was spotless.

Alexa sat on a lumpy couch facing a small TV. Erasmo sat cross-legged on the floor since there were no other seats. He still held his revolver.

"Show me your badge," he demanded.

Alexa did so.

Erasmo nodded and placed the revolver on the coffee table.

"Are your neighbors going to be a problem?" Alexa asked. "What were their names again?"

"Pervy Charley and Ms. Bennett. Pervy Charley is on welfare and spends most of the day and night standing on the landing, hoping to cop a feel. We've beaten him up a bunch of times, but he never seems to get the message. The fathers in the building take turns escorting the schoolkids up and down the stairs."

"He tries for the schoolkids?" Alexa asked, disgusted.

"He's never tried but we're not about to give him the opportunity. Did he try to grab you?"

"Tried. I think I killed his mood."

Erasmo's eyes twinkled. "Yeah, I bet you did."

"And Ms. Bennett? Is she going to call anyone that you or I should worry about?"

"Nah. The apartment gossip. If she doesn't find something juicy she makes something up. No one pays any attention to her, not even Pervy Charley."

"Nice neighbors you got."

"An improvement over the last place."

"Living with Vicente?"

Erasmo nodded, his face grim.

"You were a witness when he got married to Theresa Palmer at the Phoenix Courthouse."

"I was. You know about Theresa? What kind of person she is?"

"Tell me."

"Opioid junkie. I arranged for her to marry Vicente for a steady supply of what she needed."

"I take it they weren't close?"

"Financial arrangement. I don't think Vicente ever slept with her. He liked higher-class women and had the money to get them."

"Do you know where he might be?"

"No. I haven't spoken with him since I got out of prison."

"What happened?"

Erasmo shrugged. "I wanted out. Got tired of the killing. Tired of constantly having to look over my shoulder. Got really tired of my cousin."

"Tell me about him," Alexa asked, surprised at how candid Erasmo had become.

"What do you want to know?"

"Anything. We know almost nothing about him."

"He's always been careful that way. Didn't even get a record back in Mexico. back when he was young and naïve."

"Naïve?"

Alexa remembered him at the safehouse and had a hard time picturing that.

"Just a hyped-up kid trying to make a name for himself like thousands of others. Got tricked into joining a gang called Los Verdugos. It means—"

"The executioners, I know."

Erasmo nodded and went on. "They saw his potential. He was fast and smart and learned real quick to be vicious. Had to because he was small for his age. Always trying to prove himself, although I don't think he was naturally bad. They sure made him that way, though."

"How?"

"Played him. Built him up and knocked him down, only to build him up again. They could tell he was an insecure little kid whose family didn't want anything to do with him. He always tried to please. So they would build up his ego, saying he was tough, saying he was smart, then get him in some situation he couldn't handle. Then he'd end up beaten up or robbed and they'd laugh at him."

"He's lucky to be alive. Why did they do that?"

"To make him their slave. Here. In the mind." Erasmo tapped the side of his head. "You have to remember he was just a kid, barely into his teens, and living with a bunch of adults who were all hardened criminals. He wanted to impress, be one of them. And every time he messed up, he'd try harder to please."

"Sounds like an abusive marriage."

"In a way it was. Oh, not like that. They didn't use him that way. But they treated him real bad all the same. It twisted him inside. He got so determined to be the best and baddest that he became exactly what he wanted to be, God forgive him." Erasmo hung his head and continued in a quiet voice. "God forgive me too."

"Why?"

"I was … involved in the business. I knew some people. A family. Well, you know …"

"I'm not here to investigate you, Señor Pérez. I'm here to find your cousin."

Erasmo studied her for a second. “All right. And if you do send me back to prison, I’d only be getting what I deserve. I got him into the cartel. I told them that although he was young, he was plenty tough and that his youth was something in his favor. Made him more malleable. So he worked in Mexico for a few years until they wanted to send him up here to replace a guy that got shot. I arranged a marriage for him so he could get a visa. That’s when the real trouble started.”

“Sounds like it started a lot earlier than that.”

Erasmo reached for the table. Alexa tensed, ready to spring. While this man had been cooperative, he had a whole string of offenses to his name.

Her host noticed her reaction as he picked up a pack of cigarettes near his gun.

“Don’t worry. Yeah, I’m dangerous, but only to people like Pervy Charley.” He lit a cigarette, took a long pull, exhaled, and continued. “You think things couldn’t have gotten worse? They did. Remember a few years back some of the gangs had a war?”

“Yeah. Between those supplied by the Pelayo family and those supplied by the Urgel family.”

Erasmo studied her through a blue haze of smoke. “You’ve done your homework. Yeah, it was all about territory and which narco family would get it. What do they call it on the news when foreign countries do that? A proxy war. The Pelayo family has a reputation to uphold, and they had Vicente uphold it.”

“They got as vicious as they get down in Mexico?”

Alexa had seen some of the photos from south of the border. Dead men hanging from bridges. A tidy line of bodies, each shot in the back of the head, lying in a roadside ditch. Corpses half dissolved in acid, with evidence that they had been alive when they had been drenched. A cruelty unimaginable outside of a Middle Eastern terror cell.

“We couldn’t be as public about it, but yeah. A lot of bodies deep in the desert you never found.”

“We?”

Erasmo hung his head. “We.”

“I thought Vicente didn’t use assistants,” Alexa prompted, remembering something the leader of Los Diablos Auténticos had said.

“He doesn’t. He did the actual killing unless we got into a gunfight or something and we all had to throw in. But even with the executions that were all his work, I have to take responsibility. I vouched for him with the Pelayo family. Vouched for him with Los Diablos Auténticos. I was there all the way, and that blood is on my hands as much as it is on his."

Alexa leaned forward, looking past the firearm that, for a man on parole, could send him to prison for another ten years. "Let's put a stop to the bloodshed. Vicente has gone rogue, killing without orders and without reason. Cortez and his men burnt him on the altar. We nearly caught him, but he got away. I need anything, absolutely anything you might know about his present whereabouts."

Erasmo shook his head and took another long drag from his smoke. "Sorry, but I just don't know. I swore to the parole board that I'd put all that behind me, and I was telling the truth. I'm done with that stuff. I haven't talked to my cousin in years."

"Anything. Anything that might help."

"I don't even know where he lives anymore. And I don't know any of the gang these days. You know how quickly all that stuff changes. Any names I can give you are either in the pen or in the graveyard."

"Vicente is killing all the mid-level dealers, and he's taking out a lot of innocent bystanders as he does so. Once he runs out of dealers, there's no telling who he'll go after next."

Erasmo gave a helpless shrug. "I'm sorry. I simply don't know. Oh wait, I remember Los Diablos were setting up a safehouse a few years back. It's somewhere on West Palm Street. I can't remember the number."

"387."

"That must be it. So you been there?"

"Vicente was hiding out there. Me and my whole team nearly got killed."

"Yeah," Erasmo said with a sigh. "That's sounds like my cousin."

Alexa stood. That tip about the safehouse proved Erasmo wasn't leading her on. But he had been out of the loop so long he didn't know anything. Erasmo escorted her to the door.

"So what are you doing these days?" Alexa asked.

Erasmo shrugged, looking around his little apartment. "Whatever I can. Hard for an ex-con to get work. Luckily I got a friend in a temp agency. He gets me work sometimes. Landscaping for office buildings. Cleaning up garbage. That kind of stuff."

"Good luck to you." Alexa handed him one of her cards. "Call me if you can think of anything."

"I will. Feel free to hit Pervy Charley on your way out."

"That won't make me feel better."

Erasmo cracked a grin. "You'd be surprised."

Alexa went down the stairs, not finding the oversized pervert. Just as well; she had some thinking to do, and too little to go on. Where could she look for Vicente next? She could call his ex-wife, but she doubted she'd find much of anything from her. Other than that, who could she talk to?

Out in the parking lot, she spotted the man who had warned her to leave the neighborhood, still standing by her Jeep, arms crossed and scowling at a group of teenagers lounging conspicuously across the street in a pose a lot of street cops called "lounging with intent."

Alexa handed him a twenty.

"Thanks," he said. "You find what you want?"

"Not at all," Alexa grumbled. "In fact, I'm even more in the dark than I was before."

CHAPTER SEVENTEEN

Vicente felt more at home now that he had gotten to the southeast side. It was a rough neighborhood, the roughest, and that made Vicente feel safer. The street thugs he could handle. It was the cops he worried about.

But cops didn't come here much.

No one to stop him from what he needed to do.

Still, he kept sharp. He might have been followed, and if he hadn't been followed, he still had to keep alert for the wolves that hunted in these parts.

Just as he made it to Erasmo's old building, he saw a Jeep pulling away down the street. Too nice and too new for this part of town. Maybe a process server or a parole officer. The Jeep rounded a distant corner and was gone.

Vicente cut across the street past a group of teenagers who were just getting up from the curb to move on somewhere else, not that there was anywhere to go in this neighborhood. A muscular black man walked away down the sidewalk. Otherwise, Vicente saw no one nearby and no one paid him any attention.

He passed through the dingy lobby of Erasmo's building. Vicente had been keeping track of his cousin since he had gotten out of prison. Although the guy swore that he didn't want anything to do with business anymore, it was good to keep tabs on people.

At first, he had done so because Erasmo was family, even if Erasmo had turned his back on him. Vicente had hoped Erasmo would get back into the gang. They had always left the door open. Sometimes guys coming out of prison swore they would go straight. They rarely did. It was best to just nod and pretend you believed them and wait for them to come around.

Judging from this building, Erasmo had kept his word.

It didn't matter. Vicente wasn't here to get him to rejoin Los Diablos Auténticos.

Now he had other reasons to look him up. Better reasons.

The elevator was broken, so he took the stairs, seeing no one. As he got to the fourth floor and strolled down the hallway, an old woman with her hair in curlers peeked out of her door, glared at him, and slammed it shut. Vicente made note of the apartment number.

He got to Erasmo's door and paused. The peephole was dark. He must have it covered. If Erasmo had been looking through, a bullet would be coming through the wood right now.

How to do this? Erasmo would look before he opened the door.

Vicente stepped to the side, out of view of the peephole, pulled out his gun, and knocked.

Not that he expected Erasmo to open the door; he merely wanted to see if the guy was home. If he was, Vicente would leave and come back in an hour once Erasmo had figured the mystery knocker had gone away for good, and then kick the door in, guns blazing.

Vicente nearly dropped his gun in shock when Erasmo opened the door.

"I told you I don't know—"

Erasmo froze, staring at his cousin.

Vicente jerked his gun toward the interior of Erasmo's apartment.

Erasmo licked his lips, eyes darting to the left and right. Vicente jerked his gun a second time. Erasmo, hands wide where Vicente could see them, backed into the apartment. Vicente followed, closing and locking the door behind him while not taking his eyes off Erasmo. The guy may have left his criminal life behind, but he was still very dangerous.

"Face the wall with your hands on top of your head. You know the drill."

Erasmo did as he was told.

Vicente spotted the knife on the cutting board in the kitchen, the baseball bat leaning on the wall behind the front door, and most of all the cheap revolver sitting on the coffee table in the living room.

Vicente pressed the gun against his cousin's back as he edged past him. He grabbed the revolver, emptied out the bullets on the floor, and tossed it aside.

"What do you want?" Erasmo asked, still facing the wall.

"Justice."

"I'm not in the game anymore. I saw the news about the bust. I didn't have nothing to do with that."

"Didn't say you did, cuz. This is about something else."

Erasmo turned to look at him, but he didn't move. He didn't dare. "What do you mean?"

Vicente looked him in the eye. He saw fear there. He had never seen fear there before. "You gotta pay for what you did."

His cousin looked baffled. "For what?"

If you have to ask, you have to die.

"For bringing me up here. For making my wedding day be with some crack ho whose name I kept misspelling. For putting me in a war with the Urgel family. For making me do Cortez's dirty work."

"B-but … you wanted to do all that!"

"Did I?" Vicente snarled. "Or was it just more manipulation like with Los Verdugos? They took me away from my family, away from my brother and sisters!" Vicente, realizing he was shouting in a building that probably had very thin walls, lowered his voice. "They took me away from everything. *You* took me away from everything."

Erasmo shook his head. "I didn't take you away from your family, Vicente."

"No, Los Verdugos did, and soon I'll be going down to Mexico to take care of them, if I can find any of them left alive. What you're guilty of is making it all complete. Taking me away from my country, putting me in a foreign land where all I do is the same shit I did back in that slum. That's why you got to die."

Erasmo paled. "Cousin. You can come clean, like I did. Give it all up, Vicente. You got money; you don't even have a record. You can just walk away."

"Walk away? You think I can just walk away? After all I've done?"

"I did, Vicente. So can you. I'll help you. We're family."

Vicente shook his head, disgusted with the weakness and cluelessness his older cousin was showing. To think he had once looked up to this guy!

Well, Erasmo was right about one thing. He was family, so he'd give him a chance. More of a chance than any of the others. Erasmo deserved that at least.

Vicente flicked the safety of his pistol back on and put it in the holster hidden beneath his vest. Then he drew his knife.

Or at least, started to draw his knife, because as soon as his hand moved away from the holster, Erasmo bolted for the door.

Erasmo just managed to grab the baseball bat, turn and bring it up for a swing when Vicente's knife rammed into his throat.

The blade cut the larynx in half, passing on through the windpipe and into the spine. Erasmo froze, eyes going wide. He let out a wet, choking sound, shuddered, and the bat fell with a clatter onto the floor. Vicente grabbed him with his free hand just as his knees buckled and pulled him into the bedroom, where he lay his cousin on the bed. With practiced care, he wiped the knife clean and returned it to his sheath.

Then he turned to Erasmo, who still twitched a little as the light went out of his eyes.

"I forgive you, cousin," Vicente said. "You paid the price and now you are forgiven."

Vicente walked out of the apartment and down the hallway to knock on the door three doors down. He still had to take care of that nosy old lady.

CHAPTER EIGHTEEN

Alexa got the call just as she was getting back to the ranch. The sun was slanting low over the desert to the west and Alexa looked forward to a relaxing cup of coffee on the back porch before getting back into it with her online research.

She fumbled for the phone while keeping an eye on the dirt road. It was from Marshal Hernandez.

Her heart did a flip flop.

Had he found out about what they tried with Mason? Stuart wouldn't tell, would he? But what if Mason had filed a complaint? Or some passing patrol car had recognized them? What if someone saw her on the southeast side?

All these questions went through her head as she answered.

"Hello, Marshal Hernandez. How are you today?" Alexa gritted her teeth at the overly chipper tone she had put into her voice. It sounded so fake.

Hard to act relax when your job was on the line.

"Hello, Deputy Marshal Chase. Are you ready to come back to work?"

Alexa had just slowed to a stop underneath the open roof that sheltered her Jeep from the sun. She saw Stacy come around the corner of the house, smiling and waving. She had probably been out back with the horses.

"Come back to work?" Alexa asked, confused.

"Detective Rebstock talked with the mayor, who talked with the senator. He managed to make him see reason. You and Special Agent Barrett are back on the case."

I never left it.

Out loud she said, "Really? Thank you, sir."

"Can you come in to headquarters right now to catch up? Special Agent Barrett is on his way."

Alexa turned her Jeep around, the wheels spitting gravel. Stacy's shocked face swung into view in the rearview mirror and Alexa slammed on the brakes.

She closed her eyes for a moment. *Damn.*

Her brother's words came back to her.

You spend most of your time running around the entire Southwest chasing killers, drug dealers, and escaped convicts. How can you raise a kid, especially a needy one like her, when you're doing all that?

She opened her eyes. Stacy walked up to her window. Alexa let out a slow breath and hit the button to make the glass roll down.

"You are such a spaz!" Stacy laughed.

And you are far too forgiving.

"How are Smith and Wesson?" Alexa asked, trying to ignore her impatience to get back on the road. Stacy didn't deserve that. Everyone else could just live with it, but not Stacy. Never Stacy.

"Good! I took Wesson out along the wash to see the petroglyphs. Kokopelli gets lit up this time of day."

"I bet the Hohokam did that on purpose," Alexa said with a smile.

"Sure! So, um … are you leaving already?"

Alexa bit her lip. Her eyes strayed to the Carpenter trailer across the open stretch of cacti and rock and hardpack.

"Sorry. Got called in. I'm not sure when I'll be back. Sorry."

Stacy slumped. "But I was making ravioli."

Stacy Carpenter's ravioli walked the line between unappetizing and inedible. The last time she made it Alexa snuck to the fridge and ate five handfuls of lettuce just to ensure she wouldn't be in the bathroom for an hour the next morning. But Stacy's lack of culinary skill wasn't the point.

Alexa reached out of the window and took her hand. "Sorry."

"It's that psycho that killed the senator's daughter, isn't it?"

"Yes."

Stacy looked at the ground. "Well, you got to catch him."

"I do. He's on a killing spree."

"Jesus Christ! How many killing sprees is this state going to have?"

Alexa didn't have a response to that. It seemed like everyone was cracking up. And how to explain that to a needy thirteen-year-old when she couldn't explain that to herself, when the only reason she could give was that society was breaking apart at the seams, that her parents, dousing the fires of their self-rage in alcohol every night, were the norm and not the exception?

She had no answers for this kid. Alexa couldn't even explain why Stacy never got mad at her constant absences. Disappointed, yes, but the kid only ever blamed the job, not her.

Why was that? Stacy had every reason to be mad, and yet she was endlessly forgiving. Was it simply because Alexa offered her a clean house where there was food in the fridge and no vomit on the floor? Where there was no shouting, no embarrassing incidents, where the only disappointments came because the adults in the room were trying to save lives?

Alexa had no idea.

Maybe she actually understands that you need to do all this, even though it hurts her to see you leave.

Alexa gave her hand a squeeze.

"I'll text you if I'm going to make it back at a decent hour." *Which I'm sure I won't.*

The kid was instantly happy again.

"OK," she chirped.

Alexa remembered hearing Stacy's dad creeping around the place the other night. Shifting in her seat, Alexa went on.

"If I don't get back and things aren't … too bad, I think it would be better for you to stay at the trailer tonight." Stacy's face fell and Alexa hurried to continue. "If things aren't too bad. Your parents are still a bit sore at me."

Stacy nodded. Even this she understood.

"Gotta go," Alexa said.

Stacy made a few air punches. "Knock 'em dead."

"Save me some of that ravioli," Alexa added against her better judgement.

"OK."

Alexa drove off as Stacy waved into her rearview mirror.

Sorry, kid. I'd stay if I wasn't trying to save lives.

* * *

Alexa met the rest of the team in a conference room at one of the larger police stations, where Rebstock ruled supreme. He'd outlasted everyone else on the force at that station and most others, and had several mayoral commendations and favors. The brass plaques he had tucked away in a closet somewhere. The favors he used when the time was right. Alexa felt honored she had been the recipient of one of them.

Alexa wasn't surprised the mayor had gone to bat for him. Probably a few previous mayors had too. The big surprise was that the senator listened. The mayor must have convinced him that the best way to catch Vicente was to let Rebstock do whatever he wanted.

Wise idea.

Rebstock sat at the head of the table, blissfully ignoring the No Smoking sign above his head, Alexa and Stuart flanking him and several other officers and detectives taking up the rest of the seats. The old homicide detective got straight to the point.

"Let's get you two up to speed and think of a plan of action. First off, there's very little in the police records about Vicente Pérez. He was an enforcer for the Pelayo family from a young age. Our sources south of the border tell us that before that he was a runner and a fighter for a Mexico City street gang called Los Verdugos. Our man is extremely careful. He never got a criminal record there or here. A few years back he married an American named Theresa Palmer and got U.S. citizenship."

Alexa bridled with impatience. She had already learned all this in her own private investigations, not that she could mention that.

Rebstock went on, and things got more interesting.

Way too interesting.

"We checked up on Theresa Palmer. She's a stripper in California now. Hasn't seen Pérez in years. She didn't come out and say it but reading between the lines, I could tell the marriage had been set up to get Vicente a visa. She had no other useful information. The marriage license did, though. One of the witnesses had the same last name as Vicente, a guy named Erasmo."

Alexa's heart skipped a beat. So they had found out about Erasmo too. Hardly surprising.

"With a bit of digging," Detective Rebstock said, "we discovered he was Vicente's cousin. Erasmo Pérez has a whole heap of priors, but his parole officer says he's kept his nose clean the past few years. So we went to see him."

Alexa tensed. "What did he say?"

I'm not fired yet. Maybe he didn't say anything about me. But he would, wouldn't he? I never told him I was there unofficially, so there would be no reason for him not to come out with it. Oh, damn, I'm sunk.

Detective Rebstock looked right at her. Alexa resisted the urge to cringe.

"He didn't say anything. He's dead."

CHAPTER NINETEEN

Alexa surveyed the humble but clean apartment she had visited only a few hours before. Ducking under the police tape, she edged around a large bloodstain taking up half the floor of the hallway, saw a bit of spray on the wall near the door, and noticed the baseball bat lying on the floor in the middle of the pool of blood.

Stuart edged past her and into the living room while the officer on guard remained in the hallway, shooing away curious neighbors.

She looked into the bedroom and saw Erasmo laid out on the bed, body straight, hands folded over his chest, eyes shut. Only the garish puncture wound in his throat showed her he wasn't playing dead.

"Annette says he was killed almost instantly," Stuart said. "No other wounds. No gunshot wound to the back of the head as usual."

"Maybe because he was family. He never laid out anyone with so much respect before."

Stuart went into the living room. "If he respected his cousin, he shouldn't have killed him. I'm thinking he didn't shoot because he was in the middle of a busy apartment complex. He's not as psycho as we thought."

Alexa nodded. Vicente may or may not have been psychotic, but he showed self-control when he needed to.

"Here's the gun Rebstock told us about," Stuart said from the living room. "Reported stolen five years ago. Ballistics will probably link it to all kinds of crimes. Probably Erasmo's considering the quality. Bullets all over the floor. Vicente must have gotten the jump on him. Emptied the gun and had a little chat with his cousin. No need to empty the chambers unless he wanted to feel safe talking to Erasmo before he killed him."

"I think you're right. I wonder what they talked about?"

Stuart emerged from the living room. "If we knew that we could crack this case. Shall we go see the other victim?"

Alexa sighed. "Sure."

They went three doors down to another taped off apartment with another local cop trying to shoo away curiosity seekers.

Alexa looked in and saw Ms. Bennet sprawled out in her own front hallway, stuck like an insect in a pool of her own blood. Her throat was slit. Her eyes were open in a look of surprise.

Of course. She must have seen him. Erasmo said she kept tabs on everyone who went along the hallway.

The cop at the door spoke.

"The neighbor who found the bodies is here."

Alexa stepped out into the hallway and stopped short.

Pervy Charley stood there. When he saw her, his eyes bugged. Alexa held his gaze and he looked away, growing pale.

See this uniform? That's right, you tried to sexually assault a Deputy U.S. Marshal.

While he looked cowed, he was still unintentionally dangerous. If he mentioned anything about her previous visit, her career might be finished.

Alexa decided to cut him off by questioning him.

"So how did you find the bodies?" Alexa asked. She was acutely aware of Stuart's presence beside her, and that of the cop. If his answer strayed from the topic, that could spell some serious trouble.

"I was walking along the hallway, I live just at the end there, and saw blood coming from beneath Ms. Bennet's door. I knocked and called out but there was no answer. I found the door unlocked and went in."

I bet you check all the doors to see if they're unlocked.

"So you called 911?" Stuart asked.

"Yeah," Pervy Charley said, still looking at Alexa. She could tell he was wondering what to do. She gave him a hard look.

"Did you touch anything or move anything?" Stuart asked.

"No. I ran right out and called the police."

"You sure you didn't take anything?" Alexa said in a firm tone. Stuart looked at her, obviously wondering about the strange question.

Pervy Charley blanched. "No! Why would I do that?"

"So how did you find the second body?" Stuart asked.

The police officer cut in. "He didn't. Since the records showed a known felon lived on this floor, we knocked on his door, found it unlocked, and found him."

"I don't know anything else, and I didn't see no one," Pervy Charley said. "Sorry."

He looked at Alexa when he said it, and she could tell he was apologizing for the incident on the stairs.

Are you sorry you tried to cop a feel or are you sorry you tried to feel a cop? I don't need to ask because I can answer that myself.

"Annette says she got fingerprints off Erasmo's gun and a few other places."

Pervy Charley's eyes sparkled. "Is Annette the CSI woman?"

"Yeah," Stuart said.

Oh, Stuart, if you only knew what was behind that question.

"Let's get out of here," Alexa said.

"Yeah," Stuart agreed.

They walked down the hallway, leaving Pervy Charley and the rest of the sad scene behind.

"You know," Alexa said. "Those fingerprints won't mean a damn thing. Sure, they can convict if we capture him alive, but that's not going to happen."

"We should try," Stuart said, putting enough emphasis on the words to point out yet again his disfavor at her overly zealous treatment of suspects. Then came the concession. "But you're right. He'll want to go down guns blazing."

Once they started down the stairs, the same stairs where Alexa had her run-in with Pervy Charley, Stuart asked, "So what did you do after I left?"

Alexa paused. What to say? She didn't want to lie to him but telling him the truth might make him angry again. Especially since she had failed to mention that she had seen the murder victims just before their time of death.

How soon after I left did Vicente arrive? If things had gone a little differently, I could have run into him without any partner or any backup.

Alexa realized that her answer was late in coming. She decided on a half-truth.

"I did some background checks, hoping to find out more about Vicente and the gangs he was in, first in Mexico and then here. I looked at the P.D.'s file on him. Pretty slim."

"Did you find the marriage license?" Stuart asked.

Another pause as they walked through the grubby lobby. "Yes."

Stuart muttered something under his breath but didn't ask the obvious question.

They stepped out into the early evening. With two police cars parked out front and a hearse from the city coroner pulling up to take the bodies away, the scene had attracted a small crowd. Alexa felt a sudden fear that someone—the man who guarded her Jeep or the kids who had been lounging across the street—might call out to her. No one did.

Her phone rang. Detective Rebstock. She turned it to speaker so Stuart could hear.

"You at the murder scene?" he asked.

"Yeah."

"I'm arranging a meeting with Cortez again, but his lawyer can't do it until eight tomorrow morning."

"Tomorrow morning? That's too late! We're at a dead end. We can't let Pérez remain free another night."

"We got all available units looking for him. We got a good sketch of him on every media outlet. He can't hide forever."

"He seems to be doing a good job of it," Alexa grumbled, then looked around as if the narco enforcer would suddenly pop out from behind a cactus or parked car. "Where the hell *is* he?"

* * *

Vicente Pérez sat in the living room of the Delany home, trying to relax and plan his next move.

Delany. That was their last name. Jeff, the nine-year-old son, had told him that. The younger sisters were Elaine and Rianna, eight and five. They had been quiet for a while.

He made sure they remained quiet.

This was a pretty safe place for the moment. Like many middle-class people, the Delanys didn't seem to know any of their neighbors. None had come over, anyway. You could never take over a home in the barrio for a whole 24 hours without a dozen people noticing. Why would people want to live cut off from their community like this?

You do. You're cut off from everyone.

I'm different.

I was MADE different.

The only problem was the wife, away in Los Angeles on a business trip. He didn't know her name. "Mom" was all the kids ever called her. She had called the dad several times, but that hadn't taught Vicente her name since the contact number was listed as three hearts. Luckily it turned out that Jeff knew his father's phone code. A little convincing got him to unlock it and Vicente sent a text to her saying he had lost his voice and the kids were "just fine."

That led to a romantic little interchange full of hearts and emojis. Vicente even chuckled a bit over it, something he hardly ever did about anything.

That had been last night. The next day the messages grew more pressing, more curious. She had asked to speak with the kids, and he had ignored the question, which got her suspicions up. Plus, she wasn't buying that laryngitis story anymore. "What's going on?" turned to "What's wrong?" turned to "What are you hiding?"

At last, he had to cut her off with, "I've been thinking about us and our future. We'll talk when you get back. I don't want to talk right now. The kids are fine. Please don't text me again."

That had been a mistake. You can't land a bombshell like that on a woman and expect her to remain silent. The phone got flooded with desperate messages and missed calls. Finally, he switched it off. It was a distraction and he needed to think.

Sooner or later this place would become unsafe. The wife wasn't due back for another two days but after all that she might come back early. Plus, the husband, whose body was stuffed in the laundry room with the pizza guy and was already beginning to stink, had missed work today. Vicente had sent a text calling in sick and ignored a call in return.

He needed to move.

Vicente checked the flesh wound on his side, bandaged with the First Aid kit the Delanys kept in their bathroom. The bleeding had stopped long ago, the pain was nothing to a man like him, and the wound didn't interfere with his movements. He was ready to go.

But something made him linger. This house was comfortable. Food in the fridge. Nice furnishings. The kids' drawings on the refrigerator. He didn't even mind when he stepped on some Lego. It would be nice to live in a house like this.

You could have, if they hadn't ruined you.

Yeah, people like Erasmo.

He had thought he might feel a pang of regret for killing his cousin, but he hadn't. They say killing family is the hardest, and he supposed it was. Except Erasmo wasn't family. He had lost the honor of being called that when he had helped in Vicente's corruption. Anyone who did that was no longer family.

No, Erasmo wasn't family like the Delanys were a family. The Delanys were the real thing.

Vicente looked around the well-appointed living room with its pictures of family vacations. DisneylLand. The Grand Canyon. A beach somewhere. The family all smiling, comfortable with the camera and with each other.

He could stay one more night. It would be worth the risk.

And then?

Then he'd have to find another safe place to hide while he continued his work.

Because he had so much more work to do. They all had to pay.

He got up and checked the fridge and cupboards. The food would hold out until tomorrow. He couldn't risk going to the supermarket, not with that sketch all over the news.

Frightening how good a sketch the police made of him when they had only seen him for a few moments, and then only in a gunfight. He wondered if Jeronimo or one of the others had helped with that.

He left the kitchen and went down the carpeted hall to the walk-in closet, untying the rope securing the double doors, and opened them.

Three startled little faces looked up at him.

He had been kind. He hadn't gagged them or tied them up, and he had left the light on. He had even brought in some pillows and blankets and toys. The kids were smart enough not to make a noise. Even though they hadn't seen the corpses in the laundry room, they knew what had happened. They didn't dare defy him.

Vicente smiled. Their eyes widened. Rianna, the youngest, hid her head under a blanket.

"We'll have dinner soon, kids. What would you like, spaghetti or pork chops? Extra portions. It's a special dinner. I'll even let you watch some TV if you promise to be quiet."

And then it's back in the closet with you. I have to go out. Sneak out, so you think I'm still here and don't cause trouble. But I'll be back.

Yeah, a special dinner. Your last dinner with me.

CHAPTER TWENTY

By the time Alexa got back to the ranch, it was pitch dark. A new moon cast no rays and other than a few distant lights in the Carpenter trailer and some neighbors further off, the desert lay swathed in darkness. The lone porch light Alexa always kept burning looked like a star that had lost its galaxy.

Other than the porch light, no lights shone in the house. It looked like Stacy had listened and stayed at her parents' trailer.

As Alexa got out of her Jeep into the warm Arizona night, she cocked an ear. No sounds of partying over at the Carpenter trailer. Sometimes, if they were really hungover, they took a night off.

So Stacy wouldn't be at Alexa's place. She'd stay home as Alexa had asked her to earlier in the evening.

A sudden stab of loneliness hit her. Without entering the house, she walked around the side to the back to see Smith and Wesson, her horses. They always cheered her up, just like they cheered Stacy up.

Two horses and a messed-up kid. That's all I get to come home to, and sometimes I don't even get the messed-up kid.

She pulled out her phone as she walked. No calls from Stuart. Was he still angry at her? She guessed he was. She felt tempted to call him and apologize, but she had apologized before and that had only seemed to make him angrier. Best to let it lie.

Just as she got to the back corner of the house, something made her freeze. It had sounded like a footfall, a stealthy one of a man trying to move silently.

Just like she had heard the other night.

But why would Mr. Carpenter be skulking around her house when she wasn't here?

Or could it be someone else?

She stood just at the back corner of the house, just out of sight of the backyard. As quietly as she could, she eased her gun out of its holster.

Silence. But a *full* silence, as of someone standing close.

Alexa leaned to the right, to bring part of the backyard into view without exposing herself around the corner. In the starlight and the few distant lights of her neighbors, it was little more than shapes in the shadows. She saw Smith and Wesson standing at the back of the corral, as far from the house as possible, standing completely still and staring at some point out of her line of sight.

Horses had a sense for strangers, and a sense for unusual occurrences. They were staring at something they didn't trust.

Some*one* they didn't trust.

And that person stood just around the corner.

The softest crunch of a boot on gravel, almost inaudible beneath the beating of Alexa's heart. It did not repeat.

Alexa summoned her courage to swing around the corner when a sound far to her right made her stop at the last moment.

A girl humming to herself.

Stacy.

While Alexa couldn't see her, she knew the girl was walking the path between their houses. She had done it so many times she didn't need a light to find her way. The kid must have seen Alexa's Jeep come up and immediately ditched her parents to come over.

What to do? The humming drew closer. The prowler must have been able to hear it too.

She needed to end this while Stacy was still far enough away to not be a target.

Because she didn't believe it was Stacy's dad anymore. She didn't know who it might be, but she had to assume he had come with no good intentions, and she had to assume he was armed.

She swung around the house, crouching as she did so and leading with her gun. A dark figure stood there, further away than she had estimated. Maybe six feet. It jerked and swore. A male voice.

Not seeing a weapon, Alexa hesitated, for just a half second, her mouth opening to order him to get on the ground.

A blinding flash and the roar of a gun. Alexa felt the heat and wind of the bullet as it shot less than an inch above her head.

The horses whinnied and reared, and behind her she heard a scream.

A girl's scream.

Alexa fired.

A groan. The shadow crumpled and fell.

Keeping her gun trained on the target, Alexa moved back to get as much behind the corner of the house as possible. She needed cover if this guy tried to fire again.

"Stacy, are you all—"

The man fired again. The bullet smacked off the corner of her house. Alexa fired the next instant. The shadow jerked, and Alexa saw the gun fall away.

"Move a muscle and I'll shoot to kill!" Alexa shouted. She grabbed the Maglite off her belt and flicked it on, praying it wasn't her neighbor.

It wasn't. It wasn't Vicente Pérez either.

She had no idea who this man was.

Short and stocky, about thirty, with dirty blonde hair framing a wide face. That face contorted in pain, pale in the harsh beam, teeth gleaming. He had a bullet to the gut and another to his thigh. The bloodstains spread out along his shirt and jeans.

Alexa rushed him, kicked the gun out of reach and shouted, "Stacy, are you all right?"

Stacy said something but Alexa couldn't make out the words over Smith and Wesson neighing and galloping in circles around the corral.

"What?" Alexa shouted.

"I'm fine. What's going on?" she said, her voice cut with panic.

"Get down on the ground and stay there." Alexa stepped out of reach of the man sprawled out before her. He didn't look like he had any fight left in him, but it paid to be cautious. She glanced around, her flashlight beam darting to every corner of the back lot. No one. She ran it along the back of the house and didn't see any signs of forced entry.

Then she focused it back on the man in front of her.

He groaned, his eyes screwed shut and brows knitting. The initial shock was wearing off, and the terrible agony of a gut shot was all but paralyzing him.

"Who are you?" Alexa demanded. "Is anyone else with you?"

"You bitch!"

"Who are you? Stacy, call 911!"

"I already am!"

Alexa leaned closer, both to threaten the man with her gun and to get in close in case some unseen sniper in the darkness of the desert might be considering a shot. If she got close to the intruder, anyone else might reconsider firing.

"Who are you?" Alexa demanded. "Damn it, answer me!"

"I … I'm Joe Richardson."

Alexa blinked. That name did not ring a bell.

"Who?"

He opened his eyes, fixing her with a heated gaze. Sweat beaded on his face but his gaze was firm.

"I came to avenge Drake Logan."

Alexa's jaw dropped. "D-Drake Logan sent you?"

The prowler spat at her, a gob of blood landing on her boot.

"He didn't need to. I've read his masterpieces, and I read the news. I knew you put that great man in jail. You fixed it so I could never meet him." The man groaned as another wave of pain washed over him. Then he rallied and tried to spit again, only managing to dribble on his chin. "I can do the next best thing, though. I can continue his work. There will be more of us, bitch. Just. You. Wait."

* * *

The police and ambulance had finally left. Stacy was back at the trailer, her parents too shocked by what had occurred to even complain.

That would come later, though. Oh yes, Alexa knew that for a fact.

Alexa slouched on her sofa. Stuart sat in an armchair nearby. He had come as soon as he had heard, driving at his usual insane speed and making it almost before the first responders.

Together they had checked the entire area and found no sign that the intruder had come with anyone else.

"He said he came to avenge Drake Logan," she said, trying to keep the fear out of her voice.

"That psycho has a lot of fans," Stuart replied. "He's like a serial killer rock star. I guess we should have assumed it would happen sooner or later." He paused, and then in a quieter voice added, "I could be next."

Alexa gave a little shrug, staring at the floor. "I don't understand it. My number is unlisted. My address is private. How did he find me?"

"You know there are ways. A friend in a utility company. Or a credit card company. Lists on the Dark Web. Someone with a bit of knowhow could do it easily enough."

Alexa shuddered. "His first bullet could have hit Stacy. Oh my God, what if Stacy had come over before I got back, and he had been lurking around? Wait, does this guy have priors?"

Everything had been such a blur she hadn't even had the presence of mind to ask while the police had still been there.

Stuart got on his phone, using it to log onto the police database. After a moment, he nodded.

"Yeah, he's got priors. Spent a lot of time inside."

"For what?" she asked, dreading the answer.

Stuart scrolled down.

"Drug dealing. Assault and battery. Illegal discharge of a firearm. And … sexual assault."

Alexa buried her face in her hands. "Oh my God. Oh my God. Oh my God."

She felt the sofa shift a little as Stuart sat next to her. His strong arm went around her shoulders.

"It's over now."

His soft tone and reassuring arm loosened something in her, and suddenly she found herself weeping for the first time since her partner had been killed. She cried for a long time, Stuart gently rubbing her back and whispering to her things she couldn't hear over the sound of her own misery.

"She could have been assaulted and it would have been my fault!"

"It wouldn't have been your fault. It would have been his fault. And Drake Logan's fault."

"What difference would that have made to her?"

Stuart didn't have an answer to that.

Alexa trembled, trying to wipe away her tears. "He won't be the last. Even if he acted alone, more will come. He said so."

Her partner paused, then let out a sigh. "I guess he's right. I should be expecting a visit too."

"Should I move? How can I move? I have horses! And Stacy … "

"Moving won't help."

Alexa winced. He was right. If some twisted fan of that serial killer could find her here, they could find her in her new place just as easily.

"What do I do?" she said, not expecting an answer.

Because there was none.

Her phone buzzed. She checked it, thinking it was Marshal Hernandez calling again, or maybe Stacy.

Melanie.

"Ugh!" She tossed the phone back on her coffee table.

Her sister-in-law worked for Action News in Phoenix and would have heard about the attack at the ranch. She heard about everything.

Melanie was the last person she wanted to talk to.

"You should call your father," Stuart said. "She'll tell him if she hasn't told him already."

Alexa didn't want to explain that she didn't want to. Dad would be concerned, of course, but there'd be that undercurrent of disapproval she always heard when she got in danger. An old-fashioned rancher, he didn't think women should go into law enforcement or the military, especially not his little girl. Riding horses? Herding cattle? Fixing trucks? A rancher girl could do that, but chasing criminals was crossing the line.

But she couldn't ignore him.

She texted instead.

"I'm sure Melanie has told you I caught a prowler on the ranch. I had to shoot him. I'm fine. He's wounded and in custody. I'll call tomorrow."

She hesitated then added, "Love, Alexa."

She pressed send and leaned back on the sofa, suddenly exhausted. Stuart's hand, which had been still rubbing her back, got caught between her body and the cushion. He didn't object or try to pull it away, and it felt reassuring there, so she didn't move.

Alexa let out a breath and closed her eyes.

"You should try to get some sleep," Stuart said.

"Not sure I can."

He pressed his trapped fingers against her back. "You can. You're tough and you can. You've been through it all before. When I started my first tour of duty, we got into three firefights in the first week. Talk about being thrown into the deep end of the pool to learn how to swim! I don't think I slept more than two hours that whole week, I was so jazzed up. But then … it was weird … I sort of got used to it. I found I could sleep the whole night through if they didn't launch rocket attacks on our base. Even when they did, I'd go right back to sleep after we got the all-clear. You've been through this all before, and a lot worse. You're going to be just fine."

Alexa looked at him.

"Could … could you stay tonight?"

Stuart nodded. "Of course. I'll even pull sentry duty all night if you want me to. I've done that more times than I can count."

Alexa looked around. "Oh, but you don't have anything. You don't even have a toothbrush."

Stuart managed a smile. "You serious? Ever since I became your partner I realized the value of having an overnight bag in my trunk."

Alexa leaned forward, finally freeing Stuart's arm. He pulled it away.

"Thanks so much, Stuart. You're a good friend."

"No problem."

"But you don't need to stay up all night. We need you fresh for tomorrow. We're still hunting Vicente Pérez."

Stuart chuckled and shook his head. "I think you're better now."

CHAPTER TWENTY ONE

The next morning, Alexa felt more composed. Just as worried, just as angry, but more in control of her emotions.

Melanie had called her twice more the previous night but hadn't tried to call in the morning. Her husband Wayne, Alexa's brother, had probably told her to stop.

Stacy had texted too, saying she was all right. She had even sent a selfie of her on the school bus, smiling and waving.

Now Alexa and Stuart were back in the jailhouse heading for the interrogation room to hopefully get more information from Jeronimo Cortez.

She sure hoped he'd offer something. She'd been trying to get into Vicente Pérez's head this whole investigation and failed. What were his motivations? None of it seemed to make any sense. He wasn't totally insane. The care with which he had killed his cousin and Ms. Bennett had proved that. He had stopped his traditional routine of shooting his victims in the back of the head so that he wouldn't be detected in a crowded apartment building. He had known he could get away with it in the drug house that he had attacked because in that kind of neighborhood, people didn't get involved. But even in a crappy building like the one Erasmo lived in someone was bound to call the police. People lived too close together to assume they'd be safe just by looking the other way.

So he had changed his M.O. Your standard serial killer was very much married to their method. They didn't like to switch up. It was a compulsion for them.

And trying to destroy the drug distribution network didn't seem to be his motive either. If it was, why kill Erasmo? He must have known his cousin had quit the game.

All these questions swirled around her head as they walked down the corridor and entered the interrogation room. Rebstock was already there, along with that civilian sent by the senator, sitting at the table across from Cortez and his lawyer. The civilian looked distinctly uncomfortable to be in the presence of a gang member.

Probably never seen the inside of a jail, either.

But that suit wasn't the only one who looked uncomfortable. Cortez fidgeted, eyes a little wide.

"About time you got here," he said, the words coming out in a rush.

"People like you aren't usually anxious to see people like us," Alexa replied.

"Detective Rebstock told me about Erasmo."

"Did you know him?" Alexa asked as they sat down.

"Never met him. Heard of him, though. A legend. That man helped build a damn empire."

"He went straight," Alexa said.

Cortez nodded. "Rebstock told me that too. Vicente's gone totally nuts. Killing family? What the hell was he thinking?"

"We were hoping you could give us a little insight on that," Stuart said.

Cortez shook his head, one leg bouncing up and down from a bad case of nerves. "Sorry, gringo. I got no idea. But I do got something for you."

"What?" Detective Rebstock asked. "And why did you make me wait to hear it?"

Cortez grimaced. "I wanted you all to be here, so I only have to say it once. I don't want to snitch twice."

"Snitch?" Alexa asked.

"There's a meeting today."

Alexa cocked her head. "What kind of meeting?"

"You heard of the Wickenburg Warriors?"

"No," Alexa said. She looked at Rebstock.

"A motorcycle gang," the detective told her. "We suspect them of trafficking in narcotics like a lot of the motorcycle gangs, but we have nothing on them. They're real careful. We've barely been able to give them a speeding ticket."

"They do a hell of a lot more than that," Cortez said. "They're dealing meth here in Phoenix. That started a war because they muscled in on a bunch of people's territories. They backed off and said they wanted to negotiate. They don't got the numbers to win a war, so they want to buy their way in."

"That doesn't happen too often," Rebstock said, obviously intrigued.

Cortez shrugged. "Business is business."

“So how does this relate to Vicente Pérez?” Alexa asked.

“There’s supposed to be a meeting today between representatives of all the gangs and some people from the Wickenburg Warriors. We were supposed to go. I can give you the details. Vicente knows about it.”

Alexa leaned forward, interested. This might be good. If it happened.

Stuart gave voice to her doubts.

“With so many dead, will people even show?” he asked.

“It’s been in the works for a long time, and with all the trouble no one wants to deal with a war as well. People will show.”

“All right,” Alexa said. “Tell us.”

“There’s a place called the Roadhouse Diner on the northwest side.”

“I know it,” Alexa said. An old-school place that had been around for decades. She’d eaten there once or twice but it hadn’t stuck in her mind as particularly memorable except for a jukebox that played Ska.

“The owner acts as sort of a middleman with the gangs. Any time a message needs to be passed, he’s the one to do it. Nobody touches him, like an ambassador.”

“A well-paid ambassador, I bet,” Rebstock said.

“Hell, yeah. Nobody going to do that job for free. Anyway, he agreed to have the meeting at his diner. Neutral ground. He’s done stuff like that before. The head of the Wickenburg Warriors will be there. Tall gringo. Wears all leather. He’s an older dude and he’s losing his hair in front but keeps it long in back. Goes by the street name Diamond, because he’s got an Ace of Diamonds tattooed on the side of his neck. Don’t know his real name. He’ll come first, and then the reps for all the other gangs will come. Each rep gets two guys as muscle, but no one is supposed to come with guns. They meet at nine-thirty this morning.”

Alexa glanced at the clock. “Jesus! That’s an hour from now. With morning traffic, we’ll barely get there in time.”

Cortez shrugged. “Put on your sirens.”

Rebstock snorted. “And announce to the whole neighborhood we’re coming? Come on, Jero, you know better than that. And why the hell didn’t you tell us this earlier?”

Cortez looked at the floor. “It’s no easy thing to snitch. I’m only doing it because it’s saving their lives.”

“We won’t be saving their lives if we don’t get there on time,” Alexa said.

“I wasn’t going to talk to you without my lawyer here.”

Alexa stood. “We got to get going if we’re going to get there before Vicente Pérez does.”

The others stood up too, and they practically raced down the hall and out into the parking lot.

* * *

At such short notice they couldn’t set up any sort of proper raid. Alexa let Stuart drive, hitting the siren until they got within a few blocks of the diner before shutting it off. Rebstock followed Stuart’s crazy driving as best he could in an unmarked car with another plainclothes detective. The guy actually worked vice, not homicide, but was the only one available as they ran out of the station. Rebstock had literally grabbed him by the collar and swept him along. Two local patrol cars had positioned themselves nearby as backup.

The plan, as much as there was one, was to scout the area first to see if more backup was needed. If nothing had kicked off by the time they had gotten there, they would hang back and wait for Vicente. If he didn’t show, then at least they could bag a bunch of gang members. Cortez was getting to be pretty useful.

Alexa worried he might recognize them. Hopefully not. The one time they had met it had been dark and he had been running and shooting. Plus, they had been in uniform and now they wore street clothes.

But Rebstock … he was so distinctive in appearance.

Well, Vicente had only glimpsed him for a moment when he had popped out of the front door of the safehouse, found it blocked, and ran back inside. They’d have to hope Vicente didn’t get enough of a look at the homicide detective to recognize him in daylight a few days later.

Hopefully Vicente wouldn’t. Hopefully he hadn’t shown up already and gunned down everybody in the diner. Hopefully they’d get there first, and he’d fall into their trap.

Too many hopes, not enough foundation for any of them.

Some of those hopes had better pan out, because this slim lead was the only lead they had.

The first hope rose in Alexa as they drove past the diner, a decent-looking place with big windows and an old neon sign that looked like it had been there since the Sixties. No gunshots. No heaps of dead bodies. Peering through the diner windows as Stuart drove past, she saw only a couple of people seated at a booth, and a couple more at the counter.

Then they had passed, and the diner interior went out of sight.

While the glare of sunlight on the diner windows as the car passed at thirty miles an hour kept her from making out anything more than shapes, Alexa had seen enough.

The fight hadn't kicked off. In fact, the meeting didn't seem to have started yet.

She checked her watch. Twenty minutes after nine. It was supposed to start at nine-thirty.

They parked out of sight around the corner, looking in all directions before opening the doors. They were in an open area of shops, a gas station, and a few restaurants. No suspicious characters and certainly no one who looked like Vicente Pérez.

Stuart checked his gun where he kept it hidden beneath a loose shirt. "He'll probably come in a car, drive right up, and start shooting up the place."

"Patrol car 434. Nothing to report," a female voice said over the police radio. Stuart had lowered the volume to keep anyone outside from hearing. His had a methodical caution that tried to think of everything, borne from his two tours of duty.

"Patrol car 87. Nothing to report," a male voice said.

Feeling edgy, Alexa got out of the car. Stuart joined her and they met Rebstock and the vice detective a few paces away on the sidewalk.

"Me and Chuck will scope out the back," Rebstock said. "You guys scan the front. Try to keep out of sight."

Alexa nodded. "Sounds like a plan."

A thin plan, but the only plan we have open to us.

Well, I guess we could warn the motorcycle gang and whatever other thugs are in there.

Should we?

Alexa remembered Pablo Mason and how she had left him dangling as bait. That lapse of judgment still bothered her. And yet what choice did they have? If they cleared out the diner now, assuming the criminals went quietly, Vicente would never show. Instead, he'd proceed to hunt them down somewhere the police wouldn't know about. Warning them wouldn't save them; it would only give them a stay of execution. The only way to ensure their safety, ensure everyone's safety, was to leave them unaware while she and her colleagues sprang the trap.

You just keep telling yourself that, Alexa, she thought bitterly.

You know, maybe Stuart's right. Maybe I really do think more of the job than other people.

"I'm sorry for looking into your past," she said quietly as she and Stuart walked toward the diner.

"Not now," he muttered. "Let's make an initial pass."

To her surprise, he took her hand. For an instant she thought he had forgiven her but then realized it was part of their disguise. Husband and wife looking for a place to eat. Alexa felt like curling up in embarrassment.

As they passed the diner, Stuart pointed to it. "How about this place? The sign says they got cheese steaks."

"Yeah, maybe. I'm hungry," Alexa replied.

Only a couple of people were within earshot, and walking away from them, but the playacting was just as much for their own benefit as anyone who might be eavesdropping. Getting into character makes you look more the part, and makes you feel the part.

She looked through the window. A hulking man in a sleeveless t-shirt stood behind the counter, his arms covered in tattoos. Leaning against the counter, looking out the window, was a guy who fit Cortez's description of Diamond. His gaze briefly settled on Alexa and Stuart before moving away to check out the rest of the street.

Besides Diamond, a couple of more bikers sat in a booth eating breakfast. One or two more people sat near the back, half hidden in the shadows and obscured by the glare of sunlight on the windows.

The last thing she saw was the Closed sign on the door, at odds with the sight of people eating inside.

I guess they don't want innocent people interfering with their meeting.

After they passed, Alexa looked around to make sure no one was within earshot and spoke in a quiet voice. "Now what?"

"Not sure. Looks like everybody's late."

That didn't sit right with her. If this had been in the works for months, wouldn't everyone be on time? Unless something scared them off. The bikers didn't seem scared, though.

Stuart still held her hand. They paused at a Burger King just down the road.

"Should we eat here?" he asked, still in character.

"Burger King for breakfast? No thanks." Alexa didn't have to pretend with that line.

"After a couple of years eating K-rations in the field, you'd appreciate a BK burger."

"I'll take your word for it."

"Actually, I'd like a breakfast burrito. Never had one of those until I moved here."

Alexa chuckled, hoping this joking meant that the air was clearing between them.

Don't get your hopes up. You screwed up big time in the past few days. Not once, but twice. He's not going to forget that anytime soon. He's just being professional.

Alexa's phone buzzed inside her pocket. She had put it on vibrate but had turned off the ringer so as not to attract attention.

Pulling it out, she saw a text from Rebstock.

"One of the units reports a known drug mule approaching the diner. Thin Anglo male, about sixteen years of age, 5'10", brown hair, green eyes, wearing shorts and a Phoenix Suns t-shirt. Carrying a dark green school bookbag."

Alexa showed the text to Stuart, and they looked at each other curiously. Why would an underage drug mule come to such an important meeting? Come to think of it, Cortez had said each gang could only bring one representative and two guards. There had been more than that inside.

Then Alexa saw the time on her phone. Twenty to ten.

What about the meeting? It looked like everyone was late.

An older woman passed by.

"Maybe we can find something on the other side of the street," Alexa said, turning a bit so she could glance down the road at the diner. Sure enough, a lanky kid matching Rebstock's description was coming up the other way. A moment later he turned and entered the diner. Despite the sign saying "closed," the door was unlocked.

Stuart glanced around to make sure no one was close.

"Damn," he said under his breath. "Shall we risk another pass?"

"I think we need to. Rebstock and the other guy are out back, and we don't have any other plainclothes officers."

"Diamond scoped us before."

Alexa sighed. "Yes, he did."

They turned and, hand in hand, walked back toward the diner. Scanning the street, she didn't see any other suspicious characters watching or approaching the place. Traffic passed by in both directions, but no vehicle slowed or turned into the narrow strip of parking spots in front of the place.

Alexa tensed as they walked within view of the diner's windows.

The two guys at the booth by the window hadn't moved but had stopped eating and looked out at the street and sidewalk. They saw Alexa and Stuart, then their eyes kept moving to take in the rest of the area. Alexa relaxed a little. The two bikers had been eating before and so hadn't seen them the first time.

The kid stood by the counter, his bookbag open. Diamond pulled out a large brown paper bag that looked like the kid's lunch but almost certainly wasn't. Two more bikers had appeared at the counter, and the owner busied himself at the far end of the counter, cleaning the soda machine, his back to the scene.

Diamond nodded to the kid, gave him a playful punch on the shoulder, and looked around.

His eyes went right to Alexa's. Before she could turn her gaze innocently away, she saw a look of recognition.

Diamond reached inside his leather vest. Sunlight glinted off metal.

CHAPTER TWENTY TWO

Alexa hesitated for a fraction of a second too long. Diamond could have been pulling out a lighter, or a flask, all sorts of things. She did not want to be the first to draw because then the sting would be ruined.

A moment later she realized it had been ruined anyway. Diamond pulled out a .357 Magnum that looked as big as his beefy forearm.

Actually, only half pulled it out. Unsure what these two strangers on the street wanted, if they were cops or simply lost, he didn't pull out the gun and fire, he merely showed it, hoping to intimidate and, if the man and woman who had passed the diner twice did turn out to be cops, he'd have reasonable deniability. He could claim he thought they were about to get robbed.

But it didn't work out that way.

Instead, several things happened at once.

While Alexa reached for her gun and stopped when she saw Diamond hadn't fully drawn but only presented, Stuart dropped prone behind the concrete curb and pulled out his gun.

The veteran hadn't seen the hesitation, or if he did his combat training overrode any caution he might have had. In Iraq, a threat was as good as an attack.

Alexa dove for the right as Diamond yanked out his gun. She saw movement from the others too, and the underage mule standing, mouth open, staring.

Diamond fired first, the .357 Magnum round punching a hole in the diner window and spiderwebbing the glass. Stuart fired an instant later.

Then Alexa got into the game. The two bikers at the booth were closest. One rose, banged into the table and didn't get ready in time for the first exchange of shots.

The other calmly pulled a sawed-off shotgun out from under the table and leveled it at Alexa.

Alexa fired. Another devastation of glass. From behind a curtain of cracks she saw her target fall.

Then, confusion. Diamond lurched to the left, flailing as he moved, no longer holding his gun. Two more rounds came from unseen figures through the glass, one ricocheting off the pavement near Alexa's boot, the other taking out a sideview mirror of a car Stuart rolled behind for cover.

The window was more cracks than glass now, and Alexa could only see vague figures moving about. The presence of the kid made her hesitate. She couldn't fire in and risk hitting him. They could fire out and wouldn't care who they hit.

Stuart solved that problem with three tidy shots along the top length of the weakened windows, causing a waterfall of shards that left the diner interior open to the street and fully visible.

That led to a fusillade on both sides.

Diamond had disappeared, and so had the proprietor. The guy with the shotgun lay sprawled over the table, bleeding into his Denver omelet. The biker who had trouble extricating himself from the booth now had an UZI in his hand, while two more bikers crouched behind the counter with revolvers.

The kid still stood paralyzed in full view, hunching his shoulders a bit with his hands in front of his face.

Mr. UZI screamed and sprayed. Alexa got behind a telephone pole. It turned out she didn't need to. Mr. UZI was doing what Stuart always referred to as "spray and pray," a nearly blind waste of ammunition with the hope that quantity would compensate for accuracy.

It didn't. Stuart took him out with a single shot.

The two guys behind the counter were more cautious and more experienced. They kept up a steady, precise fire that made Alexa squeeze behind her telephone pole and Stuart curl up behind the engine block of the car.

Then came a lull. The bikers couldn't hit them, and they couldn't show themselves. Police sirens wailed in the distance.

Then there was a flurry of gunshots on the other side of the building.

Diamond and maybe some others must have tried to get out back. I hope Rebstock and the other detective are all right.

Her worries eased a moment later when she heard Rebstock's voice boom out, "You're surrounded. Come on out with your hands up or we'll toss in the tear gas."

Alexa didn't remember packing any tear gas, but she wouldn't put it past Rebstock to make a habit of carrying a couple of tear gas grenades in his jacket pocket.

His command was greeted with silence. Alexa peeked out …

… and found the whole situation changed.

One of the guys from behind the counter had slipped around to the front and put his gun to the teenager's head. His other arm gripped him around the shoulders. The second gunman stood where he had before, staring in shock.

"All of you back off or the kid gets it!"

"Mike, what are you doing?" the second gunman said.

"Shut up! Cops, I'm coming out. Don't fire. I'm serious."

Alexa stood up, keeping behind the telephone pole as much as she could.

"Let him go," she demanded.

The biker shifted, pulling the boy along with him, glass crunching underfoot.

"Just ease back," the biker said. "Ease back and let me get into a car, and I'll drop him off down the road."

Alexa got the man's head in her sights. "Let. Him. Go."

A gunshot. The man jerked, then crumpled forward, leaving the shivering youth standing on his own.

The biker behind the counter stood with his gun pointed at his former companion, smoke curling out of the barrel.

He stood stock still for a moment, then seemed to wake up to what he had done. The last remaining biker dropped his gun and slowly raised his hands into the air.

Stuart and Alexa rushed the diner.

They found everyone dead except the boy and the man who had saved him.

No, not everyone. They found the proprietor curled up behind the dishwasher. She cuffed him after she cuffed the biker.

"Main room of the diner clear!" she shouted.

Rebstock appeared, squeezing his bulk through the narrow doorway leading to the kitchen. "So's the rest of the building. Chuck's got Diamond and another goon cuffed and is giving Diamond some First Aid. I'm afraid I ruined his day even more than one of you did." He looked around. "Damn, you made a hell of a mess in here."

Alexa took in the carnage. More bloodshed, this time of people they had actually intended on protecting, and they hadn't seen a trace of Vicente. He sure wasn't going to show up now.

They had screwed up. Big time.

Alexa slumped. Everything seemed to go wrong with this case.

The teenager still stood in the middle of the ravaged eatery, his head and left shoulder covered in blood, none of it his own. Alexa noticed he had peed his pants.

Stuart walked over to him. He put a hand on his chin, getting some blood and brain matter on his fingers, and turned the boy's face up to look at him.

"You are not a gangster," Stuart told him. "This was a mistake. Nearly a fatal one. You've been given a second chance. You won't get a third."

The boy gave a quick little nod, shivering all over.

Alexa nudged her two prisoners.

"What happened to the meeting?"

"Meeting?" the man who had saved the underage drug mule said. "This wasn't no meeting. This was a pickup."

The paper bag still sat on the counter. Alexa peeked in and saw a heap of small packages containing a crystal substance. Most likely meth.

"No meeting with other gangs?" she asked.

The biker looked confused. "Why would we do that?"

Alexa let out a sigh.

That kid with the wet pants wasn't the only one to make a bad decision today. Cortez didn't want us to bag Vicente, he wanted us to take out a rival gang.

He played us like a fiddle.

* * *

Vicente Pérez needed to leave the Delany home. He had enjoyed another relaxing night in a King-sized bed in a safe house with plenty of food in the fridge. Time was ticking, though. He had things to do, and he could not stay here indefinitely. He was leaving in the father's car.

But first there was one last loose end he needed to take care of.

He walked over to the closet where the kids were kept, untying the rope that secured the doors.

He opened them. The boy and two girls stared at him, frightened as ever.

Vicente crouched down so he could talk to them on their level.

"I need to leave now."

Jeff, the nine-year-old son, went pale. His younger sisters Elaine and Rianna looked relieved.

Vicente addressed the boy. "Don't worry. I'm not taking you with me and I'm not going to hurt you. I'm going to close this closet door and leave it untied. Then you are going to count to one thousand. You can do that, can't you?" All three nodded. "Count out loud. Really loud so I can hear you. Once you get to a thousand you can come out and go to your neighbor's house. Don't come out until you get to a thousand, or I'll be waiting, and things will go very bad for you. Do you understand?"

They all nodded.

"We … we won't call the police," Jeff said. "We promise."

Vicente smiled. "Of course, you'll call the police. Don't worry. I won't be mad. You'll only be doing what you have to do, just like I do what I have to do. And when you talk to the police, tell them my name is Vicente Pérez, and that I don't kill children and I don't break up families."

Except for their dead father in the laundry room.

That was necessary. He got in my way.

Quiet. Get on with this.

"So count to a thousand, all right? And then go straight out of the house to the neighbors. Don't go anywhere in the house or I might be hiding there. Just straight out the front door and to the neighbors. Can you do that?"

All three children nodded.

Vicente smiled. "Good. You're a brave boy, Jeff. Like I was when I was your age. You'll do well in this life. Just remember that family, real family, is what matters most in this world. Start counting."

The kids hesitated, then Rianna started reciting, "One … two … three …"

The other kids joined in. With a final nod to Jeff, Vicente stood, closed the closet doors, and walked down the hall, pulling their father's car keys out of his pocket.

As soon as those kids call the cops, they'll put out a search for that license plate. I got twenty minutes, maybe half an hour before the car gets too hot.

Time enough to get where I'm going.

The last death on this side of the border, then I can go down to Mexico City, clean up things there, and retire.

I'll be done.

Yeah, right.

No, I'll be DONE.

CHAPTER TWENTY THREE

Alexa didn't know what to do next. Cortez's tipoff led to a major bust but a dead-end in the Pérez case. That maniac was still out there somewhere, hunting whoever he was hunting for whatever reasons he was doing it.

Damn, we're no closer to understanding him than when this all started.

They were just driving back to the station when a call came over Stuart's police radio.

Alexa listened in shock as the dispatcher outlined a home invasion, double murder, and kidnapping by a man who identified himself as Vicente Pérez.

As soon as the dispatcher gave the address, Stuart punched it into the GPS and peeled out for the location. He didn't even need to ask.

"Could this be a trick?" Alexa wondered.

"You mean that it isn't really Pérez and that someone is helping him lead us the wrong way? Maybe. Cortez seems good enough at that, though."

"Big time. If he hadn't been the one to tell us about him in the first place, I'd suspect him."

Stuart grunted. "He's yanking our chain so much we could charge him as an accessory."

Assuming we could even prove he lied. But it doesn't matter if we can't pin it on him. He's going down for so much already, he'll never see the light of day again.

At least some justice is coming out of all this.

They ended up in a normal, middle-class neighborhood in front of a normal, middle-class house. The only thing abnormal about it was the swarm of police cars and ambulances parked in front of it.

Alexa sighed. How many times had she seen this? How many times had she seen the dull, seemingly safe routine of modern living shattered by a sudden intrusion of violence?

It had happened at her own home just the day before.

At least the local police station had promised to keep an eye out, on both her ranch and the Carpenter trailer. They knew her there and were always glad to help. Law enforcement was like a large tribe. Individual families such as the local P.D. or the BATF or the U.S. Marshals might have their rivalries and petty squabbles, but when one officer goes down or gets threatened, the whole phalanx closes ranks.

They got out of the car. The lead officer, a tall, thin cop whose deep worry lines showed he had endured years of hard service, walked over to them.

"Owner of the house and a pizza delivery guy dead in the laundry room. Throats slit. Three kids were locked in a closet for the past two days. No signs of abuse or neglect. Looks like the kidnapper fed them."

He turned to where three small children—a boy and two smaller girls—sat in the back of an ambulance getting their vitals checked by a pair of female EMTs.

Alexa felt her stomach clench. Kids. Vicente had actually involved kids. Even most drug gangs were above that, an unspoken rule that kept their own children and younger relatives safe.

I'm going to kill him. I'm not going to arrest him; I'm going to kill him.

"Can we talk to them?" Alexa asked.

"You're leading the Pérez hunt, right?"

"Us and Detective Rebstock."

"Sure. The general description they gave matches Pérez. They seem OK considering what they've been through. Poor kids."

"Thanks."

"Oh, and we haven't told them about their dad yet. The mother is landing at the airport in an hour. We're waiting for her."

"All right. Did the two victims have gunshot wounds to the back of the head?"

The older cop shook his head. "I heard about that. Vicente shoots his victims in the back of the head even after they're dead. Not this time. Maybe afraid of the neighbors hearing? Or the kids? I don't know."

He's adapted.

The cop went on. "Just make sure you don't let on about the murders, OK? I think they suspect but it's better if the mom breaks it to them."

"OK. I'll just ask them about Vicente Pérez."

"Go easy," Stuart told her.

Alexa felt a spike of irritation. Did he think that she would just rush up to a trio of traumatized kids and start cross-examining them?

Considering how I've treated Stuart, can I really blame him for thinking that?

"I will," she promised. "Or … maybe you'd like to take the lead on this?"

He had done well with that drug mule, and with a couple of younger boys they had caught buying drugs in Benson during a previous investigation.

"No, I think you'd better," Stuart said. "Small kids like that will talk to a woman easier."

She nodded and walked over to the ambulance. The pair of EMTs looked at her warily, as if to silently express the same "Go easy" Stuart had said. These kids had probably been questioned several times already.

Alexa took a deep breath, put on a smile, and leaned into the back of the ambulance.

"Hi. My name's Alexa. Are you guys feeling better?"

They all nodded, downfaced.

"You guys sure were brave to put up with all that. I'm proud of you."

"That's what Mr. Pérez said," the boy replied. "He said I was tough and was going to grow up to be just like him."

Alexa's stomach churned. "I think you'll be much nicer than him."

The boy nodded, eyes straying from her back toward the home that would never again feel safe.

"Did he say anything else?" Alexa asked.

"He told us to count to a thousand before we came out of the closet," one of the girls said. "I think we did it right."

Alexa nodded. "He did that to give himself time to get away. He was afraid of you."

The boy said, "He knew we'd call 911. And he even gave us his name. It was like he wanted you to know."

I've been wondering about that. Why would he want us to know? He's always acted on the down low. Why make a show of himself now?

"Did he say anything else? Anything unusual that stuck in your mind?"

The kids shrugged. Then the older girl spoke up.

"He said he wanted you to know he doesn't kill family and that family is the most important thing in the whole world."

Alexa blinked. An odd thing for someone to say after killing their cousin.

"Thank you. You three have been very brave and very helpful. We're going to catch him. I promise. My partner and I are really good at catching bad guys and when we catch him, we're going to put him away in jail forever and ever and he'll never hurt anyone again."

"You're not going to catch him," the boy said.

"We will. We've caught people just as bad as he is. Worse, even."

The boy shook his head. "He won't let you catch him. He'll shoot at you and make you shoot him."

Alexa paused. That was probably true, and this kid had spent way more time with the guy than Alexa had.

Taking a deep breath, she said, "Don't worry. You're safe now. Your mom is coming real soon."

The boy spoke up. "What about our ..." He gave his sisters a sidelong glance. The older one's eyes filled with tears, but she gave a significant look at the youngest, then back at her brother and shook her head. The boy slumped.

Alexa didn't know what to say, so she said nothing. She found herself walking away.

She felt gutted. And angry. Not just at Vicente, but at herself for bumbling this case so badly. How many more people would get hurt before they finally tracked him down?

Probably a lot, Alexa thought grimly. *He's harder to catch than a mirage.*

Stuart stood not far off talking on the phone, his face red with anger.

"What do you mean they let him out on bail?" he growled.

"Let who out on bail?" Alexa asked, coming up to him.

Stuart hit speaker. "Rebstock, repeat what you just told me. Alexa isn't going to believe this."

She heard a deep breath on the other end of the line, then Rebstock's gravelly voice said, "They let Cortez out on bail."

"What? That's crazy!"

"That's more than crazy," Rebstock replied.

"What idiot thought that was a good idea?" Alexa demanded.

"An idiot named Senator Silverman. He got the governor to let Cortez out on bail in exchange for a bunch of information on the other gangs."

"What, we got to do his dirty work for him while he scoots off south of the border? No way!"

She glanced over her shoulder, suddenly self-conscious. Had the kids heard and thought she was talking about Vicente?

In a lower tone, she went on. "Don't they understand he's a flight risk?"

"Considering how much dirt he gave on the other gangs, I don't think they care much. They did put a tracking anklet on him, but you know those aren't foolproof."

"Rebstock, this is insane. You can't let them do this."

"It's already been done. I objected, but the governor and the senator didn't want to listen. We got a tail on him. Want to pick it up?"

"Hell, yeah!" Stuart said. He sounded just as angry as she did. He'd been shot at too, after all.

"Let's go," Alexa agreed. "There's nothing more to do here. We already know who did it and Vicente is too smart to leave any clues behind."

"I'll get you in touch with the unmarked car and you can sync your GPS," Rebstock said.

Alexa and Stuart hurried to the car. The unmarked car was already signaling their GPS and with the touch of a couple of buttons Alexa synced it.

They saw two dots, one in front of the other, on the east side of town.

"They're way ahead of us," Alexa moaned. "We'll never catch up."

"How long have you known me?"

Stuart hit the gas, shot out between two police cars, swerved through a red light, nearly taking out a delivery van, and roared down the street.

"Let me get my seatbelt on!" Alexa yelped.

"No time," he said, hunched over the wheel, eyes focused on the road.

She struggled to clip the belt around her.

"Put yours on too!" Alexa ordered.

"No time."

Alexa's phone rang. She pulled it out, looked at the screen, and her heart clenched.

Stacy.

Was she in trouble? Had there been another follower of Drake Logan prowling around the ranch? Had someone come to Stacy's school? Or, and she remembered the report of Pérez pretending to be Mrs. Delany's husband on text, could this not be Stacy at all?

She fumbled with the phone in her hurry to answer.

"Who is this?" she demanded.

Stacy's voice came on. "Um, who do you think?"

Alexa let out a gust of air. "Oh, Stacy, how are you? Is everything OK?"

"Fine. Maybe I should be asking you."

Stuart took a corner on two wheels, swerving between a gas truck and a city bus.

"Sorry. Just a stressful day."

"Like always." Alexa could practically hear the teenage eyeroll.

"So everything's OK?"

"Yeah. So you won't be home tonight?"

Stuart wove between three lanes of traffic and blew a red light. "No, I don't think so."

"All right. Have fun chasing bad guys."

"Fun isn't exactly what I'd call it. Love you."

"Love you too. Bye!"

Stacy hung up.

"That sounded like Stacy," Stuart said, still hunched over the wheel.

"That kid requires so much attention."

"Name a kid who doesn't."

"I just wish I could give it to her."

"You give her what you can. You're doing a good job."

Alexa wasn't so sure, but she didn't have time to ponder that question right now. As they sped through Phoenix at a terrifying speed, Alexa tried to think through what they had learned.

"So why do you think Vicente would tell us he never kills family? He used those kids to send us a message."

"Is he claiming he didn't kill Erasmo?"

"He must have killed him. Who else would have?"

Stuart shrugged, weaving between traffic. "Maybe he's just trying to throw us off the trail."

"What trail?"

"Maybe he's overestimating how close we are behind him."

Alexa grunted. "Flattering but unhelpful. And why stay here so long after killing Erasmo? Why not run for the border like Cortez is doing?"

"Cortez is heading east, not south," Stuart pointed out.

"He'll get rid of his anklet, switch cars a couple of times to shake us off and go for Mexico."

"Maybe. The question is, what is Pérez planning? He must have someone else in Phoenix he wants to kill. Maybe several someones."

"But who?" Alexa asked, not expecting an answer.

"Damn good question. None of this makes any sense. First, he goes after drug dealers, then he goes after his cousin … who's next?"

They drove in frustrated silence for a time. Alexa watched the two dots on the GPS, the first being Cortez driven by whoever had picked him up from jail, the second the car trailing them.

Whoever drove the second car was a pro. Thanks to the GPS anklet, they could hang back a couple of blocks, staying out of sight but close enough behind to catch up if Cortez stopped or the signal disappeared.

Meanwhile, Stuart continued his manic drive through Phoenix. In only a matter of minutes, they got right beside the unmarked police car. Alexa glanced over and saw two detectives she didn't recognize.

Cortez led them to the fringes of the city and then out into open desert marred here and there by housing developments or light industry.

"He's not supposed to leave the county," Stuart said. "Let's bust him."

"Maricopa is a big county. He's still inside it."

Stuart grunted. "Let's bust him anyway. He should have never been let out."

Now that they drove on an open road, they could see Cortez's vehicle, a souped-up Camaro painted a brilliant red. Not exactly subtle, but he knew he was being tracked, and Alexa felt sure he knew he was being followed. Neither Stuart nor the unmarked Phoenix P.D. car made any attempt to hide. They were still a good quarter mile behind Cortez and the other traffic on the road partially obscured them.

Cortez slowed, then turned down a gravel road that ended in a chain link fence and an iron gate. Beyond Alexa could see a ranch house. The fence enclosed several acres of bare scrub and rock.

The car stopped at the gate. Already two figures were running out of the ranch house to open it. Even driving by at a distance Alexa could see they were armed.

"Looks like a better safehouse than the last one," Stuart said. "No way we can approach without being seen."

"Yeah, but they can't get out without being seen."

"Unless they have a tunnel. Remember the narco tunnels going under the border? I read the report on those."

Alexa nodded grimly. "I've been in them. Yeah, we're going to have to do a stakeout here."

"Phoenix P.D. can handle that," Stuart said. "We need to go after Pérez."

They had driven past now, going over a small rise, the ranch disappearing.

Their radio crackled. "Surveillance unit here. We'll loop around. I'm alerting other units to form a stakeout."

"Thanks," Alexa replied, and put the radio back on the dashboard. "Stuart, I think we need to stay. I think Vicente will hear Cortez is out and come for him."

"We can't be sure of that."

"We can't be sure of anything! I know what you're thinking. If he wanted Cortez, he'd have had a million opportunities before he went rogue. So yeah, we're grasping at straws here." Alexa looked out at the stretch of barren desert. "But straws are all we got right now."

CHAPTER TWENTY FOUR

Vicente was frustrated, and seriously worried. His next target wasn't where he was supposed to be.

After leaving the Delany home, Vicente had driven the father's car for as long as he dared before ditching it. Sporting a pair of sunglasses and one of the dad's Hawaiian t-shirts and feeling like a fool, although marginally safer for the disguise, he had boarded a bus and took it to an eastside barrio. In his hands he carried a small briefcase with several changes of clothing. He'd go through them all today, making sure anyone who noticed him would give the police a different description than the last. A good thing Mr. Delany was the same size as him. He had picked the most distinctive items of clothing from his wardrobe.

A good thing, too, that the guy had favored loud clothing. As terrible as his tastes were, it helped with the disguise. A lot of amateurs think you should wear nondescript clothing. That was all right for the day-to-day, but not when you're being hunted. Wear something so loud that they look at that instead of your face. He even knew a hitman in L.A. that wore a clown costume, changing into street clothes right after making the kill.

Vicente allowed himself a smile. That was real class, making a hit with giant shoes, a big red nose, and orange hair. If he had done that, the Delany kids would have had a complex for the rest of their lives.

You scarred them enough already, Vicente. They're going to grow up damaged or twisted.

He found himself thinking about them again and again on the drive and the bus ride. A boy and two younger girls, just like Luis, Concepción, and Inez.

And Jeff was nine, just as Luis had been when he had stupidly boasted he had joined Los Verdugos.

The little idiot. He had always tagged along when Vicente had been trying to work. Standard little brother stuff, but you can't have that when you're running weed for a street gang or acting as go-between delivering messages between the distributor and the local vendors.

Couldn't have some snot-nosed kid following him when he had man's work to do.

Luis had begged Vicente to let him into Los Verdugos. No way. Luis had been too young and too foolish. And after the fourth or fifth "no," Luis had acted like the stupid kid he was and went behind his back.

And that had led to disaster. The guys had said no, but Luis had bragged he had been initiated into Los Verdugos anyway.

What had he been thinking? That if he said it, the guys would simply accept him? And he said it to their parents!

Luis had gotten him kicked out of the family, kicked out of the one thing that mattered to him.

So he had to find a new family in Los Verdugos. And that new family had slowly withered his soul.

Luis had killed him.

But although he was dead inside, Vicente still walked this earth, and he would avenge himself.

First, he had to find Luis, and his next target, Luis's childhood friend Angel Gonzalo, would know where he was.

The problem was, he had gone to Angel's address, only to find he had just moved, and the new tenants had no idea where he had gone.

This could be the end. With the cops closing in, he didn't have time to scour the barrio for Angel. Vicente went into a gas station bathroom and changed shirts, throwing that ugly thing he had worn for the past couple of hours in the trash where it belonged. Now he wore a t-shirt saying, "My Wife Went To Paris And All I Got Was This Lousy T-Shirt."

Can't blame her for going to Paris without him, if he'd actually wear a shirt like this.

All he knew about Angel Gonzalo was that he ran a hunting and fishing supply shop. He had wanted to break into his residence and wait for him to come home, nailing him in private. Now it looked like he'd need to take the riskier option.

A quick Google search found only two shops on the east side that catered to the hunting and fishing crowd. Vicente picked one at random and headed to it, hoping the cops didn't spot him on the way. He took the smaller roads and alleys as much as he could, hand poised over his hidden pistol.

By some miracle he made it. As soon as he got there, he knew he had picked the right shop.

He could see Angel through the window, standing behind the counter of his mid-sized shop showing some guy the specs on a hunting rifle. The wall behind him contained a rack of guns, and two aisles were stocked with fishing poles, tackle, and various other gear. A middle-aged couple looked through some of that.

Vicente wondered how much business he got from the working-class residents here. The nearest fishing was far away in Lake Havasu, a resort for old gringos. The hunting made sense, though. Lots of Mexican-Americans had been raised on desert hunting, even if they lived in the city. Rabbit was good meat, and so was javelina if you cooked it right.

Vicente strolled past the shop and kept on going. He took a slow walk around the block, nervously scanning for police cars. The more time he spent out on the streets, the bigger the risk, but it would be even riskier to deal with a shop full of customers.

I'll go around another block, and if there are customers still there, I'll just have to chance it.

To his surprise, when he came back to the shop a few minutes later, all three customers had left. Angel stood behind the counter texting. With a final look around the street, Vicente walked inside.

An electric bell rang a cheerful two tones as the door opened, and Angel Gonzalo looked up from his phone. First his gaze settled on the words on Vicente's t-shirt, and Vicente made it two steps inside the shop before Angel registered his face.

Then his jaw dropped, and his eyes widened.

He ducked to the left, but by then Vicente's gun was in his hand, drawn faster than the *vaqueros* could manage in those Mexican-made Westerns he had loved as a kid.

Angel froze.

"Back away from the alarm," Vicente ordered.

Angel's arms raised in slow motion as he stood up and took a step to the right.

"Put your hands on the counter. I don't want you signaling to the street."

Angel did as he was told. Vicente kept his gun low and in front of his body to keep any passersby from spotting it through the window.

“Where is he?” Vicente asked. He noted a security camera above Angel’s head. He paid it no attention. Vicente wouldn’t be around long enough for it to make any difference.

“Where is who?” Angel said, struggling to keep his voice from wavering.

“Don’t play with me.”

“I’m not playing with you. You’re killing everybody! How the hell am I supposed to know who you’re killing next?”

“Luis. I’m looking for Luis.”

Angel gaped. “Your brother?”

“You’re his oldest friend. You know. Even though you immigrated here years ago you must have kept in touch.”

Angel got a set look on his face and didn’t reply. Vicente ground his teeth. He’d have to do this the hard way.

“Move over to the door, lock it, and put the closed sign up. If you try to run into the street, I’ll gun you down and then kill the next man I see.”

“Even if I do as you say you’ll make me give you innocent blood,” Angel grumbled, but he did as he was told. Once he had finished with the door, he turned, looked Vicente straight in the eye and said, “I’ll never tell you where your brother is.”

Vicente smiled. Still had the *cajones* he had when he lived in that slum down in Mexico City. He had to, to get out of there and end up running a business in the States.

“I saw a door behind the counter. That lead to an office?”

“Yes.”

“Let’s go there. Walk in front and don’t try anything.”

Angel moved toward the counter, slowing a bit as he walked past a display of fish gutting knives.

“You won’t grab one in time,” Vicente told him.

Angel’s shoulders slumped a little and he walked to the office, opening the door.

They entered a tiny office with a desk, an old PC, and a filing cabinet.

Of most interest was what covered the walls.

Dozens of photos of Angel on hunting and fishing trips. Three of them, just under an image of the Virgin of Guadalupe and situated opposite the desk so someone sitting there would face them, caught his attention.

Two were in the desert, with Angel and a few other men posing with guns. The third was of Angel and another man in a boat off the coast of what looked like Baja, holding up a huge swordfish.

Luis was that other man, and he was in the two hunting groups as well.

Vicente's breath caught. Luis was so much older, having reached a filled-out middle age. The smooth, skinny face had filled out and become crisscrossed with wrinkles. The narrow shoulders had broadened.

Luis was a man now, and even though Vicente hadn't seen him in decades, he recognized his little brother immediately.

A lump rose in Vicente's throat. He pushed it back down. Then he noticed something. In all three pictures, Luis wore a military cap. Something about the way he wore it, the care with which it was maintained, and his erect posture, told him it was not bought at a surplus store.

"Did Luis join the army?"

"He's an officer."

That spelled trouble. "Does he live on a base?"

"No."

Good.

"Where is he?" Vicente demanded.

"I won't tell you."

Vicente picked up a framed photo from the desk showing Luis with a woman and two bright-eyed girls. He turned it so Angel could see and tapped on the glass with the barrel of his pistol.

Angel slumped.

"Where is he?"

"He lives in Nogales. The Mexican side."

"Address?"

Angel didn't speak.

Vicente threw the photo on the ground. The glass shattered. Angel flinched.

"Address?"

"Number 24 Ignacio de la Torre. It's near the base."

Vicente nodded. "You did the right thing, Luis. Friendship is important, but family first."

The shop owner's lips curled into a snarl. "You talk about family when you want to kill yours?"

Anger rose in Vicente's gut like battery acid. He struggled to control it. After a moment, when he was able, Vicente explained in a reasonably calm voice. "Luis stopped being my family when he betrayed me. He, not me, is the one who broke up our family. Do you remember?"

Angel stared. "What are you talking about?"

"It was so long ago, maybe you don't remember. But I do. Oh, I do. He bragged that he had joined Los Verdugos. Remember that? And my parents blamed me for that. They disowned me. I never got to see them again, or my sisters."

"You're not going to kill Concepción and Inez too!"

Vicente groaned. Even though Angel had grown up in the same slum, he had grown up to become a civilian.

"You understand nothing. Concepción and Inez are innocent. They didn't break up the family. Even my parents are innocent. They kicked me out, yes, but they had been lied to. I am no longer angry with them. Luis, on the other hand …"

"He was a boy! A little boy!"

"Who never admitted his lie. He broke up a family, a family I was in a position to help. I started making good money, Angel. You know that. I could have gotten shoes and proper dresses for my sisters. A doctor for my father so he could get his health and pride back. Then my mother wouldn't have had to clean the houses of rich people. She wouldn't have been exhausted at the end of every day. We could have had happiness."

Angel looked at him with—what? Sympathy? Understanding? Vicente wasn't sure. Then his features hardened.

"Luis gave them all that. He became an officer and the pride of the family. He helped them out with money, put your sisters through university. Each of them has a picture of Luis in their house, and they never mention your name."

Vicente raised his gun.

Angel swung around, raising his hands toward the picture of the Virgin of Guadalupe.

"Oh Virgen Inmaculada, Madre del verdadero Dios—"

Vicente shot him in the back of the head. Blood sprayed all over the pictures of Luis and the Blessed Virgin. Angel fell hard on the floor.

Vicente pursed his lips, looked around the office, and spotted a box of Kleenex on the desk. Taking some, he carefully wiped the holy image clean.

Mexico. He had assumed Luis was still in Mexico. That would not save him. Vicente had already made arrangements.

* * *

Night had fallen, and Alexa crouched in a drainage ditch half a mile from the ranch where Jeronimo Cortez had holed up. The ditch was between a cotton field—a terrible waste of water in such a dry climate—and an open stretch of unirrigated desert. No one was around to spot them, and she could get a good view of the ranch through her binoculars.

Not much sign of life. Cortez had gone straight into the ranch house, and other than a couple of guys going out to fiddle with the engine of one of the cars parked out front or to feed the half a dozen Rottweilers that prowled the grounds, she hadn't seen anything.

Cortez must think he's safe. I can't see how even Vicente Pérez could get in there.

A movement to her right made her look. In the dim light of the distant road, she recognized Stuart's short, stocky frame. He walked near the bottom of the ditch, straddling the narrow trickle of wastewater, instinctively crouching even though he could walk erect and still have his head below the top of the ditch. It reminded her of those grainy black and white films of soldiers in the trenches in World War One.

Why does he do it? All those hard years in Iraq and he gets out of the military, comes home, and takes on a job like this. And he seems to enjoy it, even thrive on it.

But he hates it too. I can see it in his eyes when we come across a murder scene, or the shakiness that comes into his hands when the shooting stops and it's all over and he's safe enough to have time to think what he's just been through.

He's caught up in it. He can't leave it.

Like me.

Stuart crouched down next to her, and even though there wasn't anyone within half a mile, he spoke in a whisper.

"Talked to dispatch. Got some information on this house."

"Yeah?"

"It's owned by someone who had no criminal record and no known association with Los Diablos Auténticos."

"Hardly surprising. They like to keep their records clean, like Cortez said with that safehouse. They simply paid some civilian to sign the papers."

"Sure, but get this. I also ran the license plate of that car we followed, and one of the other guys on stakeout brought along a good enough pair of binoculars to make out the license plates of the cars parked in front of the ranch house. None of them are associated with Los Diablos Auténticos. None of the owners have any criminal records at all."

"Maybe this is a local safehouse for the narcos?" Alexa wondered out loud.

Stuart nodded, the movement barely visible in the dark. "That's what I'm thinking."

Alexa looked out across the dark stretch of desert at the well-lit compound. A pair of Rottweilers paced along the inside of the chain link fence.

"Why would they let Cortez come here with a GPS anklet?" she wondered aloud. "That's like handing us insight into their operations."

"I've been wondering about that," Stuart replied, "and I don't have a good answer. Maybe they think we already knew about this place. Or maybe they're so desperate to take out Vicente they're willing to run the risk."

"That's a hell of a risk. You think they're so scared of him they'd do this?"

"They brought him up."

Good point.

"Well, if it does kick off, we'll send in all units and scour the place," Alexa said.

"We won't find anything. If they had anything incriminating here, they cleared it out before Cortez showed up. It was easier in Iraq. The terror cells were never careful that way. If we got intel about a group, we'd bust in and find RPGs, bombmaking materials, cell phones full of numbers, all you could ask for. When you don't care about dying, you don't worry so much about incriminating evidence."

"You're not fighting terrorists anymore," Alexa said.

Stuart looked out at the ranch, its lights glittering in his eyes.

"Aren't I? These people plot to hook innocent civilians on substances that will ruin their lives and eventually kill them. If anyone gets in their way, they get taken out. They twist people like Vicente, kill women and children, and destroy communities. Oh yeah, I'm still fighting terrorists."

Alexa's phone buzzed. She checked it and her heart leapt.

Captain Filipe Santos, in charge of the precinct in her neighborhood. After she had caught that follower of Drake Logan, he had promised to keep an eye on the place.

He wouldn't have called if there hadn't been trouble.

She picked up.

"What is it?" she demanded without even saying hello.

"Not sure," he replied. She could hear he was in a car. "The Carpenters reported a prowler. We're in route."

"Oh my God! I'm coming."

"You close?" he asked.

"No. But I'm coming. Any details?"

"No. Just that they saw someone creeping around the trailer."

"I'll be right there."

She hung up.

"Prowler at my place," Alexa told her partner.

Stuart looked at her, then the distant ranch they were staking out, and back at her.

"I can't leave. Take the keys and go."

Alexa was about to object when she realized he was right. Both situations were equally dangerous with potential loss of life. But she knew which one she had to choose. Alexa grabbed the keys from his outstretched hand and without another word sprinted down the drainage ditch.

It was a long way to get from here to her ranch, but at least she could go on little-used county roads.

If Stacy was in danger, she'd get there so fast she'd make Stuart look like a Sunday driver.

CHAPTER TWENTY FIVE

After five blown traffic lights, three near-collisions, and calling off two pursuing police vehicles by radioing in that she was a cop and not a joyrider, Alexa made it to her ranch.

As she approached, she got a radio call from Captain Santos.

"We've apprehended the prowler, a teenage male near the Carpenter trailer."

Alexa drove up the gravel drive toward the Carpenter trailer, visible in the distance. She could see a police car parked there, as well as the Carpenters' battered pickup.

"A teenager? Was he armed?" Alexa asked.

"No. I, um, don't think this was the threat you were expecting."

"What do you mean?"

"Just come on up. It's easier to explain."

"Coming."

A minute later she pulled up in front of the trailer. Before she had even come to a stop, she could hear Mr. Carpenter shouting and swearing. Alexa parked not far behind the police car, switched off the engine, and got out.

Captain Filipe Santos came to meet her. He was a weather-beaten man with short hair graying at the temples, a lean figure, and hard eyes that could turn kind when they needed to be. He was close to retirement and Alexa hoped he'd forget that fact. He was the best cop in these parts and knew everyone.

"Thanks for coming personally," Alexa said.

"Anything for my favorite U.S. Marshal."

"Deputy U.S. Marshal."

He cocked his head. "Only deputy? They haven't made you commander-in-chief yet?"

Alexa smiled, not only at the tired old joke he'd been saying for years but for the fact that he was joking at all. That meant the situation wasn't serious.

And yet he hadn't told her to turn around and return to the stakeout.

"You little slut! What the hell's the matter with you!" shouted Mr. Carpenter from the trailer. Alexa heard someone crying. It sounded like Stacy. Alexa moved toward the trailer, but Captain Santos stepped in her path.

"Just an angry father, Alexa. And he's got a right to be angry. Don't interfere with the first real bit of fatherhood that guy has shown in ages."

"What happened?"

Captain Santos jerked a thumb in the direction of the squad car, where Alexa could make out a blonde head wearing a baseball cap.

"When Carpenter called in to report a prowler, I figured it was someone like the last one. You missed it, but I had three other squad cars here as backup. I was even wearing Kevlar. Damn, that thing makes my lower back hurt. Anyway, turns out it wasn't a Jack the Ripper, but a wannabe Casanova."

"Huh?"

"A teenaged boy, Alexa, coming to visit Stacy."

"What?"

"She told her parents she was going to go to your ranch to check on the horses, but her dad decided to check everything out because of that guy you caught the other night. Well, he didn't get far before he found our Romeo hiding behind a rock. Poor guy nearly had a heart attack. Good thing he forgot to load his gun, or we'd have even more trouble than we already do."

"So she's was going to meet some kid in the desert?" Alexa couldn't believe it. Stacy? Her little girl?

In the trailer, the shouting had died down. Alexa ducked around Captain Santos, who protested but didn't try to stop her, and headed for the trailer. As she passed the squad car, she glimpsed a wide-eyed boy in a baseball cap. She glared at him.

Hope Santos scares some sense into you if Carpenter hasn't already.

Just as she approached the trailer, the door popped opened and Stacy's dad stormed out. He was a messy man in every way—unshaven chin on a thin face, unkempt brown hair that needed a trim, a checkered lumberjack shirt buttoned the wrong way, and dirty jeans and boots. At least he didn't look as boozed up as usual. The latest drama had disrupted the evening's drinking. That probably didn't help his mood.

“There you are!” he barked. “It’s about time you got here. So this is what you’ve been letting her do when she’s over at your place?”

Alexa looked him in the eye. “You know that’s not true.”

Carpenter looked hesitant. Even his addled mind realized he had said something stupid.

Not one to back down, he puffed up his chest. “Well, it’s no surprise this happened, what with her not being around her father. A girl needs a father and a mother, not some neighbor.”

Carpenter said “neighbor” like an insult. She had been raised to help and respect her neighbors. Obviously, he hadn’t.

Had he even been raised at all? Maybe he was just continuing the cycle he had grown up in.

“So what happened?” Alexa said, trying to get the conversation onto a useful track. She had heard from Santos but wanted to hear his version of events.

“We’d just had dinner when Stacy says she has to go over to the ranch to feed the horses. Said she forgot. That struck me as funny because she never forgets anything with those damn animals.” Alexa’s fists clenched at that, but she kept her mouth shut. “But I didn’t think nothing of it. I took my gun and went out to check everything was OK. After that psycho you caught, I’ve been patrolling the area. Keeping the neighborhood safe.”

Alexa resisted the urge to laugh. “And that’s when you saw him?”

“Yeah. He was hiding behind a rock on the path to your place. Must have known she was coming.” He looked past Alexa at the squad car, shaking his fist. “My daughter is only thirteen, you freak! You try that stunt again and I’ll blow your damn brains out, you hear me?”

“Relax, he’s only a kid.”

“Kid my ass, he’s eighteen years old!”

Alexa’s jaw dropped.

“Not for another two months!” Stacy’s voice protested from inside the trailer.

“Stacy, get out here!” Alexa and Carpenter shouted at the same time, then looked at each other.

Pause. The door creaked open. Stacy, slumped and sullen, stepped out of the trailer, walking with the unmistakable gait of a kid who knows they’re in serious trouble.

Stacy walked up to them, eyes on the ground.

Mr. Carpenter turned to Alexa. "I'm going to talk to Captain Santos about pressing charges. You try and talk some sense into her."

That took Alexa by surprise. Was this a tacit admission that she had more influence over her than he did?

Maybe some sense of reality breaks through the alcoholic fog. Maybe that's why he keeps drinking.

Carpenter stormed off. Alexa turned to the girl she thought told her everything, the girl she thought was still more child than young woman.

"An eighteen-year-old boyfriend? Are you freaking kidding me?"

"He's still seventeen."

"Don't even start. He's old enough to go to college and he's sneaking out to see a kid in ninth grade? What do you think he's after?"

"We're both in high school."

"So what?"

"We didn't do anything."

"Yet."

Even in the half light, she could see Stacy blush.

"He understands me," Stacy said in a quiet voice.

"You have your friends. You have me. If you want a boyfriend too, pick someone in your grade."

"All the boys in my grade act like little kids. I'm an adult."

Alexa took her by the chin, lifted her face so that she'd look in her eye, and said, "No. You. Are. Not."

Right away she knew she had said the wrong thing, because she saw something in Stacy's face she had never seen before.

Anger and defiance, directed not at her parents, but at her.

"Yes, I am! I cook and I take care of Smith and Wesson and I do all sorts of stuff here too. And it's not your business anyway. You think I just sit around when you're out on your cases? I got a life, you know!"

And there it was. Alexa had just gotten lumped with all the other adults in her life. The adults who were too wrapped up in their own affairs to give her enough attention. It wasn't fair, Alexa cared and did her best, but from Stacy's point of view Alexa was only a nicer and more sober version of her parents. When a case called, she disappeared. When the bottle called, her mom and dad disappeared. One was legit and the other wasn't, but the result was the same. Stacy was a kid of convenience. Attention to her took second place.

Her brother's words came back to haunt her yet again.

How can you raise a kid, especially a needy one like her, when you're doing all that?"

"I'm sorry I can't be around more," Alexa said.

"I don't need you all the time! I got my own life."

Alexa took a deep breath, tamped down the anger she felt rising in her, and said, "This boy is far too old for you. What do you think a seventeen-year-old is going to want from a thirteen-year-old?"

"It's not like that! He's nice. He thinks I'm interesting," Stacy preened.

"You're too young and he's trying to take advantage of you."

Her teenage eyes rolled. "Like you know anything about relationships. You're always single."

Alexa frowned. "This isn't about me. It's about you, and I'm trying to help you. Did you call me earlier to make sure I wouldn't be home? Were you planning to take him to my house?"

Stacy evaded her eye.

"Jesus, Stacy! You know what could have happened?"

"It's not like he would have made me do anything! What kind of a guy do you think he is?"

"The kind of guy who sneaks around a thirteen-year-old girl's house. He should be going out with girls his own age but they're probably all too smart for him."

"Whatever!"

With a swish of her blonde ponytail, the girl stormed off to her trailer.

"Stacy, wait!"

Alexa walked after her, but the girl didn't turn around, opening the screen door to the trailer and slamming it behind her. She rushed through the tiny living room past her mother, who sat placidly in a lumpy armchair, a large glass of cheap scotch in hand, watching television.

Stacy disappeared into her room, slamming the door behind her. Her mother continued to watch TV.

"Aren't you going to say anything?" Alexa demanded.

The woman gave a little shrug, not taking her eyes off the screen. "She's got her own life."

"Ugh!" Alexa threw up her hands in despair.

As she turned, she saw Stacy's father approaching.

"Thanks for talking to her," he said with apparent sincerity. "I don't know what's gotten into her."

Bad parenting, that's what's gotten into her. Maybe this will wake you up.

"I'm not sure I did much good," Alexa said and sighed.

"I'm going to keep her on a tight leash from now on. I think she was going to meet him over at your place, so from now on she can't go over there unless you're there."

"I think that's a good idea for the time being."

With a curt nod, he went back into the trailer.

Alexa felt gutted. Betrayed. She had provided a safe place for Stacy to get away from her parents, a place with food in the fridge and two wonderful horses to ride and fuss over. And Stacy had abused her trust.

And now what? Where could the kid run to when her parents got drunk?

She walked over to Captain Santos, who stood by the squad car.

"So what's going to happen with him?" Alexa asked, gesturing toward the terrified kid in the back seat. He looked younger than his age, but that made no difference to Alexa. He had no right to be catting around after Stacy.

Captain Santos replied in a low voice so the kid couldn't hear. "Other than criminal trespass there's no evidence of any crime. Carpenter wants to press charges on the trespass. The kid will probably get some community service. I've talked to his parents and they're furious. They said to keep him down at the station until morning to teach him a lesson."

Alexa grinned. "The old 'sit and stew,' eh? Good idea."

"I'll stick him alone in a cell and give him a chance to grow up a little."

Alexa shook his hand. "Thanks."

"Well, I best get going."

"I need to go too," Alexa said.

This had all been a grand distraction at the worst possible time. She checked her phone and saw she had missed a call from Stuart a few minutes ago. She had been so distracted speaking with Stacy, she hadn't even heard it ring.

She called him back. He picked up on the first ring, as if he had been sitting with his phone in his hand waiting for her to return his call.

“There’s been another murder,” he said before she could speak. “A Mexican-American male in his thirties. We don’t know if it’s connected to the others, but we’d better treat it like it is. Rebstock’s giving me a ride. Get over as fast as you can. The other units can watch Cortez. I don’t think he’s the target, at least not yet.”

“I’m on my way,” Alexa said, already running for the car.

CHAPTER TWENTY SIX

The man who Detective Rebstock had already identified as Angel Gonzalo, lay face down in the office of his shop. Alexa could see he had been shot in the back of the head. Execution style.

Alexa stood in the doorway. Annette bustled around the room, peering and prodding at everything, and it was best not to get in her way. Stuart, being the eager-to-please boyfriend, had run off to find her a coffee.

But Alexa didn't need Stuart here. She didn't really even need Annette. The murder scene said it all. Another Hispanic male killed with a shot to the back of the head.

Rebstock sat at the desktop computer, ignoring the blood-soaked wall, the dead body, and the CSI expert busy at her job. His eyes were fixed on something on the screen.

"Alexa. Come here."

"Got him on security footage?" she asked, edging her way along the wall of the small office. She had noticed the camera behind the counter on her way in.

"Yep. It's him."

"Hardly surprising. Let me see."

The security footage that Rebstock had retrieved showed Vicente Pérez entering the shop. Angel Gonzalo was visible from the back and above. The camera was located right in the top corner of the room behind the counter.

As they watched, Angel looked up and jerked in surprise.

"He knew Vicente," Rebstock said. Alexa nodded.

Angel ducked for an alarm button visible behind the counter but froze as Vicente drew a pistol out of seemingly nowhere, and so fast that Alexa would have had to slow down the video to see how he managed it.

"Damn," she muttered.

"Narco hitman," Rebstock grunted. "What do you expect?"

"I expect we need backup."

The two talked for a moment before Angel locked the front door and the pair disappeared into the office.

One detail stuck out. Instead of his usual stylish black, Vicente wore cargo pants and a t-shirt that said, “My Wife Went To Paris And All I Got Was This Lousy T-Shirt.”

“I bet he got that t-shirt from the Delany home,” Alexa said. “He probably got a bunch of other clothing as well.”

“Yeah. Probably changed outfits three or four times by now.”

“No car keys in the pocket or on the desk,” Annette said without turning around.

“I’ll put out a search for Señor Gonzalo’s vehicle,” Rebstock said, getting on the phone.

Alexa turned to Annette. “Anything else of note?”

“Nah. We already know who the perp is and how he made the approach. Nothing interesting in this place.”

She sounded bored and irritated. Annette liked a challenge.

Alexa looked at the blood pattern on the wall. She didn’t need a ghoulish genius to tell her Angel had been standing when he got shot.

“No second gunshot wound to the back of the head,” Alexa said.

“Nope,” Annette replied, studying the man’s hands. “No signs he got a chance to fight either.”

Vicente had switched it up. No more *coup de grace* once the victim was down. He had done that with all of the early ones.

Because all the early ones were connected with illegal drug distribution, either as sellers or buyers. This guy had no connections. Neither did Mr. Delany or that pizza delivery guy.

So ... a coup de grace for a fellow soldier? They often call each other that. they’re in a war with each other and with honest society. A war with us.

I’m going to win this war, Vicente. I’m a soldier too, and so is my partner.

Her gaze followed the trail of blood up to its spattered source about six feet from the floor … and her eyes froze on a photo.

It showed Angel Gonzalo and another man in a boat somewhere in glittering water with a rocky, desert coast in the far background. Both smiled for the camera as they held up a large swordfish. There was something about the face of the man in the military cap that drew her. She stared at those smiling features, the glass in front flecked with Angel Gonzalo’s blood.

Alexa peered closer, eyes going wide.

It couldn't be ...

She tried to speak, but her voice came out as a rasp. Clearing her throat, she managed to say, "Rebstock, could you pull up the best image of Vicente's face from the security footage and zoom in?"

"Sure."

They had never gotten a proper look at him before, and while the police sketch that they had created from hers and other officers' eyewitness sightings was good, the security footage was far better.

"Here we go," Rebstock said.

Alexa went around the desk and peered at the image, a slightly grainy closeup of Vicente, mouth open in speech, facing his latest victim.

She didn't even need to look back at the photo to know the truth.

"That man with Angel Gonzalo in the fishing photo," Alexa said. "What do you see?"

Rebstock looked at the photo and his breath caught.

"Holy moly. They're related."

"What do we know about Vicente's family?"

"Nothing."

"We need to talk to the Mexicans."

"Yep." Rebstock got on his phone and began to punch in a number. "I got an *amigo* in Nogales who can help me out. High up in the *federales* until that outfit got replaced with the National Guard. He's good at digging, digging deep and digging fast."

"Good. Fast is what we need. Because I'm thinking Vicente came to Angel because he knew he was friends with his relation. Where that guy is, brother I'm thinking, is where we'll find Vicente. And hopefully this time we'll find him before it's too late."

CHAPTER TWENTY SEVEN

The *coyote* was a lean, weather-beaten man in leather, straddling an all-black Kawasaki dirt bike. Vicente noted the powerful engine and extra fuel tank.

They had met, as previously arranged, at sunset in a poor and dusty suburb at the end of the bus line where the cheaply made homes looked out on the fringe of the desert.

Vicente had changed back to his traditional black and had a small carrier bag strapped to his back.

"Got the money?" the *coyote* asked instead of hello.

Vicente pulled out a wad of a hundred-dollar bills. "Half up front, half when you get me across the border."

The *coyote* took it and counted. He gave a curt nod, stuffed the money in the pocket of his leather jacket, zipped it up, and gestured to the back seat.

"Hope you don't mind riding in the bitch's seat."

"Careful who you say that to. Some guys might get angry," Vicente said as he swung his leg over the seat.

"Not you. You're too in control to get angry over a little joke like that."

"I guess you don't take many people from north to south."

The *coyote* barked out a laugh. "You'd be surprised. You know, the price to go north to south is higher than the usual way. That's because people going south are richer and more desperate."

Vicente smiled. This man was a pro.

The *coyote* revved the engine and headed off along on a dirt county road. After a few miles, the *coyote* cut off into the desert to link up with another county road a few miles to the east. Vicente had to keep a firm grip on the back bar to keep from falling on the bumpy ride.

"We got enough fuel to make it to the border?" he shouted over the engine.

"I got fuel dumps."

Vicente nodded. Yes, this guy was a pro. He'd get him across the border and into Nogales with little or no trouble. As long as he didn't try and betray him. The *coyote* must figure he was carrying a lot of cash. That could prove tempting.

A long ride in the night down county roads and across the more level stretches of desert. When overlanding, the *coyote* didn't turn on his headlights and yet barely slowed down. He moved by a combination of instinct, good night vision, and an intimate knowledge of the land. Vicente hung on to the back of the dirt bike and admired him. He always had respect for fellow professionals. It would be a pity to kill him at the end of this trip.

Once, in the middle of the night, in a spot in the desert that seemed like every other they had passed, the *coyote* stopped and shut off the bike. Vicente's hand moved close to his gun, worried the man might cheat him, but he simply hopped off, went over to a patch of dirt and felt around for a moment. Then he stood with a grunt, lifting up a rope that pulled up a wooden hatch. Curious, Vicente walked over.

In the starlight he could see several jerry cans in a concrete-lined pit. He also saw a can of motor oil, a toolbox, and a few plastic packages.

"How the hell did you find this all the way out here?" Vicente asked.

"I'm good at what I do," the man said with a shrug.

"You got a lot of these?"

"Trade secret. I'm sure your trade's got secrets."

That came out as a statement, not a probe. The *coyote* had no interest in knowing anything about him. He hadn't even asked for a name, because he knew whatever one Vicente gave would have been false.

The coyote hauled out a jerry can and filled the tank.

"Will we need to make any more pit stops?" Vicente asked.

"Not with the extra tank I fitted on here."

He finished filling the tank, returned the jerry can to the pit, and closed the hatch. Vicente helped him spread sand over the lid.

Then they were off through the desert again. The *coyote* took them on the most rural route possible. Only a few times did they see the distant lights of towns or lone ranches.

At last, in the early hours of the morning, his guide parked the bike and switched off the engine.

"I thought you said we don't need to refuel before the border."

"We don't. The border is just a mile over that hill."

Vicente looked around, as if he could get his bearings in this dark desert. The moon was a crescent as thin as a fingernail and its faint light seem to obscure more than illuminate.

"I don't think we've come far enough to the east or west to get past the walled sections."

Most Americans thought the wall ran along the entire border. It didn't. At least not yet.

"We haven't. Don't worry. I'll get you across."

The coyote started walking south. Intrigued, Vicente followed. The *coyote* didn't seem worried about having a fugitive at his back on a dark night.

And why should he? If Vicente killed him now, he'd never get to Mexico and the *coyote* knew it. The real showdown would come once they got to Nogales.

They walked for a time in silence until they came to a low ridge. His guide got down on his hands and knees and Vicente followed suit. They crawled up the ridge. Twice Vicente pricked his hands on cactus thorns. The *coyote* seemed unaffected. The man really did have remarkable night vision. From beyond the ridge Vicente could discern a faint glow. Nogales? It didn't seem bright enough for that large city that straddled the border.

The *coyote* got on his belly, worming his way forward soldier style.

Like Luis.

Vicente put that from his mind and imitated his guide. Whatever was beyond that ridge posed a danger, and he needed to stay alert.

An officer. Little Luisito got out of the slum and made something of himself.

Pride mingled with hatred. He shoved both emotions from his mind.

After a few more scrapes from sharp rocks and another prick of a cactus thorn, Vicente got to the top of the ridge and lay beside the *coyote*.

Beyond, the ridge descended as a steep slope to a flat area about a mile wide, cut off by a high wall of steel bars that looked like the wall of a prison cell door. The bars were close enough together to make it impossible to pass through, but wide enough apart to give American patrols a good view of anyone approaching from the Mexican side.

A two-lane road ran along the American side, and Vicente watched as a white and green SUV four-by-four drove along it. A U.S. Border Patrol vehicle. A common sight on the highways and back roads of southern Arizona. This was why the *coyote* had taken him across the desert. If they had taken roads to the border, they would have run into at least three or four of them.

Vicente's gaze ran along the wall. At this distance, he could just pick out the cameras set on high poles to give maximum visibility. All, he knew, were equipped with night vision optics. In the distance to his left rose a watchtower manned by some Border Patrol officers who probably had even better equipment, not to mention a camera bank to monitor all the cameras for their section.

The *coyote* opened up a satchel he carried at his side and pulled out a pair of night vision goggles. Putting these on, he watched the desert a minute, slowly moving his head back and forth.

"No horse patrols," he said, pulling them off and putting them away.

Vicente smiled, something he rarely did. "Fighting technology with technology, eh? So what kind of technology are you going to use to get us past that wall?"

"No technology at all, just the oldest trick in the book."

The *coyote* wormed his way back out of sight from the wall. Vicente followed.

Once they got far enough back to rise, his guide led him at an easy jog about a quarter mile to the east, where the ridge was cut by a ravine. The narrow cleft ran at an angle, so they remained invisible to the watchers on the wall.

They scrambled down this for a time, Vicente nearly losing his balance in the dark while the *coyote* acted more like a mountain goat, springing from rock to rock and having to stop several times to wait patiently for him.

Once when Vicente caught up, he asked, "What about the drones? I heard the Border Patrol uses drones with infrared."

"Only to scan the Mexican side and the wall itself. Drones are expensive. Don't worry, we're almost there."

Where? Vicente knew better than to ask.

He got his answer another hundred yards down the ravine, where the *coyote* stopped at a little crevice to one side. He felt around for a moment, then pulled up a hatch much like the one he had used to get his gas.

"There's a vertical shaft here with metal rungs," he said. "Climb down about twenty feet and you'll come to a floor. You'll have to do it in the dark. Once you get down, wait for me. I can't turn on the lights until I've closed up."

"A tunnel?" Vicente asked, amazed. "And the gringos don't know about it?"

The *coyote* chuckled. "Bribery works on both sides of the border, bro."

Vicente climbed down, breathing stale air and sensing the tunnel close around him. It didn't take long to get to the bottom, where he bumped his head against the low ceiling of a tunnel that led off somewhere. Vicente was completely blind.

He heard his guide close the hatch and climb down, then feel along the wall for a second before his clicked a switch.

A lightbulb in the tunnel next to them turned on, making Vicente blink and cover his eyes.

Once his eyes adjusted, he uncovered them and gasped.

A square tunnel about five feet to a side, its walls of hardpacked dirt reinforced with beams at regular intervals, ran off into the distance. Lights were strung every hundred feet or so, and on the floor ran a narrow-gauge electric railway track complete with a flatcar.

Vicente laughed. The *Guardia Nacional* had busted one of these tunnels a year ago. Presidente Obrador got on television and bragging about how good his new police force was. Looks like they weren't as good as they thought.

Better than the Americans. They hadn't found any tunnels.

"That's right, bro," the *coyote* said with obvious pride. "I'm taking you for a ride. Don't touch the third rail and we'll be in Mexico in two minutes."

They sat down on the flatcar. The *coyote* pushed a button and the electric railway car hummed along at a steady speed. Vicente shook his head in wonder. This man was sure earning his fee. Yes, it had been high, higher than the cost of killing a man, but Vicente was getting first class service.

Vicente noticed the ceiling up ahead was spray painted red. As they drew closer, he could see it was a crude sketch of a hand, middle finger raised.

"The fence is just overhead," his guide told him.

After another minute the car began to slow. Vicente could see where the tracks ended at another small room with a ladder like the one they had left.

As the car stopped and the *coyote* switched off the current, he said, "Once we get to the ladder we have to switch off the light. Security. You understand. I'll climb up first and open the hatch. You come right after me."

Vicente didn't feel nervous. If this guy wanted to turn on him, he would have done so before revealing the location of the secret tunnel.

Now all Vicente had to do was find the best time to turn on him. It wasn't about retrieving the first half of the fee, although of course he'd do that; it was about cleaning up anyone who might talk about where he had gone. He was on the verge of retirement, and he wouldn't let anything endanger that.

They climbed in darkness, the only sound their labored breathing. A creak of hinges, a gust of fresh air, and Vicente saw starlight overhead. Once out, he looked around. All he saw was desert. The border wall stood out of sight beyond a hill.

"Welcome to Mexico," his guide whispered.

Vicente was about to ask which direction lay Nogales when the *coyote* gave a low whistle. A bush rustled not far off. Vicente put a hand on his gun.

"Relax," his guide said as a young man, barely out of his teens, emerged from the gloom. "This guy will take you the rest of the way. It's only an hour through the desert to Nogales. Once you can see the lights of the suburbs, you give the other half to him."

Good. I'll kill you, force this guy to tell me how to get to Nogales, and kill him too.

To keep up appearances, Vicente asked, "He gets half the payment even though he's only taking me through a bit of Mexico?"

"He's my little brother."

Something inside him turned over.

"Family business, huh?" he asked in a quiet voice.

"Nothing more important than family." The *coyote* put an arm around the younger man's shoulder. "Me and my bro been working together since he got out of school. We do everything together. The two of us against the world!"

For a moment, Vicente only stared at them. Two brothers, arms around each other. Smiling.

"That's a good thing for you," Vicente said, and meant it.

Yeah, I mean it. Because I had planned on killing you to hide my tracks, but now ... now I can't. Now you and your little brother can go on loving each other the way brothers should.

I wish I had what you have.

CHAPTER TWENTY EIGHT

Half an hour later, Vicente strolled through the outskirts of Nogales. The cantina stood up ahead, its neon sign of a shapely woman dancing with a giant bottle of beer flickering in the night.

He felt frustrated and impatient. All he wanted to do was to track down Luis, but he had gone too far to not be cautious now. This had to be done right. He had to pay a certain cantina a visit. Not because he wanted a drink. He had business to do.

Los Amigos Borrachos was a place he had often heard of but had never been to. His work had never kept him long in Nogales, and as an enforcer with a major narco family he had never required what the bar's clientele offered.

Now he did.

A few tough-looking young guys hung out in front, leaning against cars and talking about nothing with a great deal of swagger. Reggaetón filtered out from the bar, a thumping mix of dance music and rap that Vicente had never liked. A lot of the underworld liked it, though, a bit like some American gangs liked hip hop. Both styles had lyrics that strutted and bragged, singing about toughness in a fight and expertise in bed.

He didn't care about bragging. He wanted to see the man behind the boast, and he was a good judge of men.

Like this crowd lounging on their secondhand sports cars and drinking beer. Tough, but not the level of tough he needed. Good enough for a barroom brawl or to intimidate a shopkeeper late on his protection payment. Not nearly good enough to take on a soldier protecting his home with the help of the Mexican police and perhaps some gringo officers as well.

And how could he tell this? Their entire body language. The way they lounged too easily, in postures that could not immediately turn into a fighting stance. The way some had a hand in their pockets, delaying the use of that hand for a whole half second when every fraction of a second might mean the difference between life and death. The way a couple of them were nodding off, having drunk too much to be any use at all. The way they didn't even notice him until he walked right through their circle, an act of deliberate disrespect goons like this would be sure to notice.

They did.

"Hey," someone called behind him just as he passed through.

Vicente turned and walked back into the circle. Might as well even the odds a bit by letting them surround him. Besides, he needed to show no fear. The door and windows to the cantina were open to the warm night, and everyone inside could see out. The more sober and observant in that crowd had already turned to watch the brewing trouble. He must show certain members among those people that he did not feel fear.

Not that he ever felt it. That emotion had been gutted out of him years ago.

He faced the one who had spoken. He could tell he had the right man because he had pushed off from his seat on the hood of his lowrider and stood with his feet planted shoulder width apart. The hold on his beer bottle had reversed so that he now held it by the neck, low on his side and ready to swing up like a club. The others—all five of them—also had beer bottles they would not hesitate to smash into his face.

The man facing him was young, muscular, half-drunk, and stupid. Vicente didn't need to analyze the others. If this was their leader, the others would be the same.

"Hey," the man said again.

"Yes?"

"You don't got enough room to walk?" he challenged. Vicente heard shifting sounds all around him.

Vicente looked him in the eye. The man had not made an assessment of his opponent. Booze and superior numbers gave him a dangerous level of confidence.

Dangerous for him.

"I wanted to walk here," Vicente said.

All conversation died in the cantina. The Raggaetón continued, the party music somehow emphasizing the silence of the crowd.

The young tough looked around theatrically. He swept an arm around, the one that didn't hold his bottle, his weapon. "You could have gone that way. You could have gone *that* way. Instead, you walked right through our conversation."

“Is that a big deal?” Vicente asked.

A few chuckles from the others. More shifting. This was escalating and they knew it. They loved it.

“Yeah, it’s a big deal,” the guy said as if talking to a slow child. “It’s disrespect, man.”

Vicente gave him a long, steady look. “Well … maybe I don’t have any respect for you.”

The tough blinked. He had been expecting some banter as an attempt to cool the situation, or an apology about being drunk that would let Vicente get out while saving face, or maybe even for this lone man all in black to pull a gun, at which point the six friends could save face by backing off. Anything but this level-voiced defiance.

Vicente looked into his eyes and saw hesitation.

Maybe you’re not as drunk and stupid as I first thought.

“You crazy, man?” one of the others chimed in.

Vicente glanced at him. Bigger. Drunker. Thus, more and less dangerous. He, too, had reversed his hold on his beer bottle.

“You’re the people showing disrespect,” Vicente told him. “I came to get a drink and make friends, and here you are stopping me and squaring up.”

“What the hell? You—”

“Disrespect,” Vicente emphasized. “You’re the ones showing disrespect. You need to apologize, and you can do that by shining my boots. They got dusty in the desert.”

A sudden movement to his left. Vicente ducked, saw the onrushing body, scooped up the guy’s legs and used his own momentum to throw him against a man to his right. Both landed on the hood of a car with a loud bang. The guy that got hit landed on the back of his head and probably got knocked out cold.

Vicente didn’t have time to check. The drunker one he had addressed was raising his bottle, but too slowly. The man who had called him out, the wannabe leader, had quicker reflexes. His bottle was already swinging down on Vicente’s head.

He grabbed the guy’s wrist and pushed forward, elbowing him in the ribs and getting out of the way of another bottle that, instead of hitting him in the back of the head, only grazed his shoulder.

Like the previous two, the leader and Vicente ended up lying on the hood of a car. Vicente twisted, hearing the guy’s wrist snap. The guy shrieked and dropped his bottle, which Vicente plucked out of the air as he rolled off of him and ended up on his feet between two parked cars.

Only three to go, now all in front of him instead of surrounding him.

No, four. The guy he had thrown like a sack of corn was disentangling himself from his unconscious friend and would be back in the show in a couple of seconds.

Big Drunk Dummy let out a roar and charged, raising his bottle high. Vicente's bottle smashing across his face took care of him.

His two friends acted smarter. As the brute fell to the ground, screaming and trying to hold together his face, they came at him with knives. They came low and careful, spreading themselves out as much as the parked cars allowed.

Vicente could have drawn one of his knives then. He could have drawn his gun. But to do that would have been to lessen the effect, and he needed to impress.

He lashed out with his boot, kicking the knife out of the hand of the man on the left, then ducked back as the one on the right slashed at him.

Another slash, another little retreat. This guy was pretty good. Vicente had to get this timed just right.

A third attack. Vicente grabbed his wrist, almost too late, and with his other hand grabbed the man's lower arm. With a deft movement he made the guy plant his knife into his own leg.

The guy screamed, staring with disbelief at the knife sticking out of his thigh. He did not go down, however. A hard right hook took care of that.

The guy behind him, the one he had disarmed, was reaching behind him for something tucked into the waistline under his shirt.

Vicente made a flying kick straight to his sternum, knocking his breath out and laying him flat on his back.

Vicente was on him in an instant, smashing his nose and then flipping him over. A .38 revolver fell out of the guy's pants.

Vicente grabbed it and stood.

The last man standing other than Vicente, the idiot who had attacked first and ended up lying on his friend on the hood of a battered old Camaro, had gotten to his feet, a bottle in one hand and a knife in the other. He had made it two steps toward Vicente before Vicente stood up with a gun in his hand.

The guy froze.

Vicente held up the revolver, hit the cylinder release to make the cylinder swing out, then reversed the gun so the bullets fell out. Then he tossed the pistol aside, making sure to hit the windshield of one of their cars. It left a satisfying crack.

Vicente took a step toward his last opponent, empty hands spread wide.

The guy bolted.

Vicente looked around at the mess he had made. None of these idiots looked like they were getting up and challenging him anytime soon.

He walked the two steps up to the cantina door and entered. Everyone stared at him as he crossed over to the bar. All of the tables were full, and several men lined the bar area. There must have been at least sixty or seventy people inside, mostly men but a few women at work at the only job a woman would do in such a place.

It only took him the few moments he walked from the front door to the bar to scan the entire crowd for what he wanted.

Los Amigos Borrachos was a place to pick up guns for hire, and he saw plenty of candidates. Most could be dismissed without a second look—the ones who were high, the ones who got too drunk, the ones with madness in their eyes that spoke poorly of their reliability.

But he saw three who looked perfect.

One sat in the far corner, back to the wall. A lean, rangy Mexican with the look of a *vaquero* about him. Not just the boots and the hat and the faded jeans, but the face tanned and seamed by long hours in the sun. He had pushed back from the table and neither of his hands were visible. He studied Vicente with expert eyes. Vicente made brief eye contact before continuing his search.

Next was the gringo, the only foreigner in the room, a husky man with a brown buzzcut and erect bearing that spoke of time in the military. He, too, sat with his back to the wall, the girl who had been on his knee now plopped unceremoniously onto a nearby chair. As she slid closer to him, he pushed her away, keeping his other hand out of sight. He, too, watched Vicente with the eyes of a professional.

Ex-U.S. military, probably, veteran of one of America's endless wars, and with too much of a criminal record to get a job as a "security contractor" as the Yankees liked to call their mercenaries.

The third stood by the bar, unmoving as the rest of the men there parted for Vicente like the Red Sea. He was a big man, but that did not impress Vicente. Neither did the long scar down one cheek or the hair that reached his shoulders and was better kept than a woman's. What impressed him was the poise in which he stood, and how he held his beer bottle normally, but in such as position so that he could toss it in Vicente's face. And he held it in his left hand, his off hand, the one with which to make a distraction that would give him time to pull the gun that was no doubt hidden under that loose shirt the hem of which his right hand pretended to play with.

Their eyes locked. A glint of mutual recognition. The big man's mouth made a brief, tight smile of amusement. Vicente turned away from him.

"Negro Modelo," he ordered. The bartender brought the beer so fast Vicente was surprised he didn't rock the cantina with a sonic boom.

Vicente took the beer, said "Put it on my tab," and walked to a corner table occupied by a run-of-the-mill thug and his girlfriend for the evening. They left before he made it halfway there.

"Put their tab on my bill," Vicente called to the bartender. No reason to be a bully.

He leaned back in his chair, the corner of Nogales's deadliest cantina to his back, and flicked a glance out the window. The five remaining toughs were piling into their cars and getting out of there. Two had to be carried.

He looked back at his three candidates—the vaquero, the gringo, and the big man—and they all moved to join him.

"Looking for work?" he asked in Spanish as they came up to the table.

"Sure," the big man said.

"Always happy to work for a fellow professional," the gringo said in fluent Spanish as Vicente expected him to.

The vaquero only nodded.

"Sit down," Vicente said.

They sat.

Vicente leaned forward. "It's a standard hit at a domestic residence. There's a good chance that the man knows we're coming and has police protection. Is that a problem?"

The big man snickered. The gringo smiled. The vaquero shrugged as if it made no difference.

"Good. We have to bust in there fast, take out the protection, and get the target. Five thousand dollars cash for each of you."

Vicente had brought plenty of cash with him across the border. He had been amassing it for months and didn't even need to touch either of his secret bank accounts here in Mexico.

"Six thousand," the gringo said.

Americans. Always so greedy.

"All right, six. But there's a condition. You don't take out the target. I'll handle him. Any of you take him out and you have to deal with me."

They all nodded. It wasn't an unusual request. They assumed this was a personal vendetta. Good, let them have that assumption. He couldn't really explain the truth, not even to himself.

"We doing it now?" the gringo asked.

"No. I still need the address. I'll get that easily enough, but even so I want to wait until later tomorrow. I have a feeling this is a family man, and I want to make sure the kids are at school. We'll hit it in the afternoon, once we're rested and have the chance to buy some weapons."

The big man with the ponytail looked around at his two new coworkers. "I'm sure we're all prepared."

"We're going to need something special," Vicente said. "I know someone who can arrange it."

The men nodded.

"What does he look like? The man you want for yourself?" the *vaquero* asked, speaking for the first time. He had the accent of the southern provinces, Tabasco or Campeche. A long way from home. Probably couldn't go back. Vicente knew how he felt.

Vicente grinned. "What does he look like? Why, he looks like me."

CHAPTER TWENTY NINE

Stuart had always imagined that the first time he visited Mexico it would be to some nice resort where he'd drink margaritas and bask in the sun. He'd recently updated that to include a lithe Mexican-American CSI genius who would translate for him when they weren't holed up in their hotel room making love.

His fantasy did not include hunting for a killer in the noisy, bustling city of Nogales in the middle of morning rush hour.

But a case was a case, and this investigation had led them to Nogales because that's where Vicente's younger brother lived. The local police had already tracked him down based on the photo they had scanned and sent to every police department in the country.

Other than a border wall and checkpoints, there wasn't much to distinguish the Arizona and Sonora sides of the city. Both were predominantly working class, predominantly Mexican, and seriously hot as hell. The Man Upstairs seemed to have turned up the temperature as soon as He heard Stuart and Alexa had headed south.

As they parked in front of the police station just south of the border and got out, it felt like the sun pressed down on them like a pile of a hundred electric blankets.

"Is it my imagination or is it hotter?" he asked.

"Your imagination. Nogales is at a much higher altitude than Phoenix. It's probably a bit cooler here."

"Oh. More south, though."

"Stop wearing black suits. It might help."

The trio of Mexican officers approaching them all wore camouflage of a white and black pattern, probably good for blending in when the sun was high and the light blinding. Stuart recognized the uniform of the *Guardia Nacional*, the National Guard. A quick scan with his soldier's eyes confirmed what he had heard—these weren't simply cops, they were a paramilitary outfit with all the training, attitude, and equipment. Erect bearing, soldiers' boots, Heckler & Koch USP pistols in their holsters and MP5 submachine guns hanging from their shoulders with one hand keeping a firm grip. Slap some Kevlar and a helmet on these guys and they'd be ready for Baghdad.

The lead man was older, a tall man with sharp eyes who took in the two American law officers whose transfer south of the border had been fast-tracked by Senator Silverman and some political contact he had down here. The men behind him were shorter and were of obviously lower rank. There was a subtle deference of stance that privates and NCOs took around officers that was universal among armed forces.

The officer extended a hand and in good English said, "Welcome to Mexico. I am Chief Inspector Fernando Revilla."

His grip was firm, and he made solid eye contact. Always a good sign.

"Special Agent Barrett of the FBI," Stuart replied.

Chief Inspector Revilla turned to Alexa, who shook his hand.

"Deputy U.S. Marshal Chase," he said.

The National Guardsman smiled. "Ah yes, Detective Rebstock has told many stories about you. All the Mexican papers featured your hunt for Drake Logan."

Alexa's features tensed a little at the mention of the man who had killed her former partner.

"So what progress do we have so far?" Stuart asked, wanting to get the conversation onto something a little less sensitive.

"As I mentioned in my email, we forwarded the photo you sent us to the Mexican Army base here in Nogales and they quickly identified the man in it as Capitán Luis Pérez. Since he is an officer with a family, he is allowed to live off base. We now have men at his home. Come, I will take you there."

The officer led them to an armored personnel carrier. An Israeli-made Plasan SandCat, to be precise. Stuart got a strange prickling feeling as he saw it. He hadn't been in an armored personnel carrier since he left the armed forces.

His feelings must have registered on his face because Chief Inspector Revilla smiled and said, "You are surprised? This is narco territory, my friend, and the narcos have RPGs. Two such *Guardia Nacional* vehicles have been hit by them in the past year. Both. far from Nogales, I assure you. But we cannot afford to ride around in simple police cars when chasing a narco hitman. Come, sit up front so you can see our beautiful city. I do not want you to get a bad impression of it."

Stuart hopped in the passenger's seat. One of the privates or whatever they were called down here got behind the wheel, gave Stuart a grin and a nod that seemed to express that no English was forthcoming, and Alexa and the rest clambered into the back.

Stuart looked around. It was different than the various American models he was used to, with a high carriage that probably made it good for overlanding on rough terrain. The Kevlar plating looked good enough to stop any number and caliber of small arms rounds, but he wouldn't want to be in one of these if the narcos started firing RPGs. The armor looked too thin for that.

Notice how Revilla didn't mention what happened to those two SandCats that got hit? Damn, what if Vicente gets his hands on an RPG? Or grenades? He has all the connections he needs. Sure, he might be cut out of the organization by now, but he knows who to go to and just take what he wants. He's certainly capable.

They pulled out, driving along a main street through dense traffic of pickups, cars and motorcycles as Chief Inspector Revilla leaned over Stuart's seat from the back and pointed out various landmarks through the bulletproof glass—the high hills flanking either side of the city center topped with fine houses, the factory district for American companies hiring cheaper labor south of the border, some of the officer's favorite restaurants and cantinas.

Stuart merely nodded and made interested noises, not really focusing on any of these things. His mind cast back to different streets in different cities far, far from here.

The traffic was the same. While fewer Iraqis had cars, many of the streets had been sealed off by Coalition Forces or local militias, siphoning the vehicles into a few main avenues to create bumper to bumper backlogs.

The sidewalks were similar too. Densely packed storefronts and sidewalks filled with street vendors. At a red light, a boy in clean but tattered clothing walked along the rows of parked vehicles, holding a stack of newspapers in one hand and a cardboard box filled with candy in the other. Boys did that at the red lights in Baghdad and Karbala too.

And the alienness of it all. The signs he couldn't read, the conversation in the back he couldn't understand, just like when he rode with Iraqi troops. You never knew what they were saying about you. You never knew where you stood.

Stuart tried to shake off that feeling. This was Mexico, not Iraq. There were no blast walls, no terror cells, no suicide bombers. The streets were cleaner, and the civilians did not look at him with poorly masked hostility. Sure, there was crime here, and some seriously dangerous organized crime, but this wasn't Iraq. Not even close.

But riding in this military vehicle with an MP5 sitting on the seat between himself and the driver, it was hard for his head to tell his heart he wasn't in a war zone. He even noticed that he had taken up the proper stance, riding low in the seat, chin down to maximize the cover of a helmet he wasn't wearing, eyes taking in every detail around him—the windows, doorways, approaching vehicles, the faces of everyone who looked in his direction.

The driver lit a cigarette and offered the pack to Stuart. Absentmindedly, he took one, said *gracias* as the guy lit it for him with a silver lighter bearing the face of Jesus, and took a long drag.

Stuart was not a smoker, but a lot of nonsmokers in war zones needed an occasional hit of nicotine.

"We're almost there," Chief Inspector Revilla said.

"Good," Stuart replied.

The SandCat turned down a pleasant residential street lined with trees. Concrete walls with broken glass or razor wire set into the tops blocked access to two-story homes for the middle class. Stuart's skin prickled again. Same as the wealthier Iraqi homes.

It's to stop burglars, not Islamist militias, he reminded himself. *No one's going to blow themselves up in this neighborhood.*

Yeah, but Vicente Pérez is plenty dangerous, and I think Alexa is right. This will be his next stop. The local cops sure seem to think so.

They parked in front of one of the walled houses next to a couple of squad cars of the municipal police.

Two cop cars and now an APC? If Vicente is watching he's going to get scared off for sure.

They got out, Stuart letting out a long breath in relief. Riding that APC had been weird. It messed with his head. He had thought he had gotten a grip with his military service. Sure, he had dreams sometimes and sure, he got tense and choked up when he thought about the guys he had lost, but on that ride, he had almost felt like he was back there. Not a flashback, not really, but it sure made a hell of a lot of memories bubble up from his subconscious.

I'll take a squad car back, RPGs or no RPGs.

A hand on his arm took him out of his thoughts.

Alexa.

"You OK?" she asked.

"Yeah. It's just hot."

Alexa glanced at the armored personnel carrier and back at him. Stuart cringed inwardly.

"I mean, you acted really tense and were looking all over the place. And then the smoking."

For Christ's sake, stop being so damn nosey!

In as calm a voice as he could muster, he said, "Yeah. I'm fine. This case is just wearing on me. That's all. I'm fine."

You say fine more than once, and it means you aren't.

"Let's get this done," he grumbled, dropping the butt of his cigarette on the ground and crushing it with his foot.

A municipal cop in a black uniform opened the gate made of a sheet of black steel and saluted Chief Inspector Revilla. Stuart saw he only had a sidearm. Not enough to deal with Vicente. Everyone should have an MP5 at least. Speaking of, where was his? He supposed he couldn't ask. He had never worked a foreign case for the FBI before.

Well, if—no, *when*—the shooting started, he was going to grab whatever he could get his hands on. These National Police looked tough, but they'd never been to Iraq.

Passing through the gate, they saw a gravel front yard and a driveway leading to a garage, the door open to show a car and two motorcycles. The yard was enlivened by potted plants and shaded by a pair of palm trees leading up to the house. Luis Pérez stood at the door in a military uniform, waiting for them. After introductions, Luis said in heavily accented English, "I am so glad you call. Do you know where is Vicente?"

"We don't," Alexa said. "We think he will try to make for the border."

Luis's face turned grim. "He kill Angel, my great friend. A man I know my whole life. Vicente is an animal." He shook himself. "But I am being rude. Come. I make coffee."

He ushered them into the cool interior. The floor was of tile, and the whitewashed walls of the front hallway were adorned with a large crucifix and several family photos.

Luis gestured at one of the photos. "My wife and girls, they are on base. The police, they say I stay here to be, how do you say, like when you go for fish?"

"Bait," Stuart said. "Señor Pérez, if you don't feel comfortable doing this, you don't have to. We can catch your brother—"

Luis rounded on him. "Do not say this! He is not my brother! He is animal!"

"Sorry."

"He is devil in human skin."

Stuart could only nod in agreement.

The army captain made a gesture at the three National Guardsmen and the cop at the front door. "These, and the two more they send, they will not be enough. They say they cannot give more. Too much crime and too small number of police. But my brother, he come with big guns, and people."

Stuart looked him in the eye. "Captain Pérez, I am Lieutenant Stuart Barrett of the U.S. Army, and I served two tours of duty in Iraq. You and I will plan a defensive strategy that will take care of whatever he throws at us."

A grim smile spread across the Mexican soldier's face, and his eyes glittered with that battle lust Stuart had seen so many times before. Shocking to see that directed at a man's brother, but Luis had spoken the truth. Vicente was an animal. A devil in human skin.

Capitán Luis Pérez of the Mexican Army extended a hand to Lieutenant Stuart Barrett, U.S. Army retired. They shook.

"Yes, Lieutenant Barrett. We go to war."

CHAPTER THIRTY

Alexa watched in amazement as Stuart and Luis Pérez systematically transformed a middle-class residence into a fortress over the course of a few hours. The downstairs windows were already barred like in many Mexican homes. Stuart and Luis removed the glass so incoming bullets wouldn't send dangerous shards into the defenders. Then they took the potted plants and set them up behind all the windows. They looked ridiculous, Stuart explained, but the heavy ceramic with the earth inside would stop at least one bullet before disintegrating.

Next, they removed the glass from the upstairs windows as well as any furniture that was in the way of giving a man posted there a comfortable position to stand.

A heavy oak side table, which looked like a family heirloom from a time when furniture was built to last, got dragged right next to the front door ready to be put across it, once night fell. The two men sealed up the back door immediately, dragging the washer and dryer in front of it.

Next, they took all the interior doors off their hinges in order to clear the field of fire. They also packed away any glass or ceramic items that might shatter and send out sharp fragments.

Stuart and Luis went about all this work with a quiet determination, speaking little to one another and not at all with anyone else. Stuart's face had the same set concentration that it took on when he did one of his manic drives through downtown Phoenix. Alexa wondered if his face had borne that expression the entire time he had been in Iraq.

The three municipal police and two National Guardsmen stood sentinel at various spots in the large, two-story house. Chief Inspector Revilla spent much of his time on the phone, cursing their bad luck.

"There's trouble with some gang fights," he told her in Spanish, having learned to his delight that she was fluent in the language. "We can't afford any reinforcements. And the army is on maneuvers. While Señor Pérez's family is under guard on base, the military can't send anyone to help."

"It's OK," Luis said. "They sent me some extra weapons."

“Aren’t you worried all these preparations will scare him off?” Alexa asked.

“My brother doesn’t scare off.”

Alexa nodded. That was probably true.

“English, please,” Stuart said, passing through with a heavy rug rolled up around every metal curtain rod from the house. That would probably stop a smaller caliber bullet, or at least slow it down enough that it wouldn’t kill the man behind it.

“Sorry, my friend,” Luis said, switching over. “My English, it is no so good.”

“Better than my Spanish.”

“I just tell them the army, they give me some fun things. Come.”

Stuart set the rug down across an open doorway, making a barrier to lie behind to fire, and followed Luis to a back room. This looked like a bro moment, but Alexa followed anyway. She needed to know all their resources. Chief Inspector Revilla came along too.

A long, olive drab crate sat on the floor of the sewing room. The heavy, old-style sewing machine, being potentially bulletproof, had been shoved against the window. More cover. These two guys were obsessed with cover.

Luis opened up the crate and pulled out three helmets, three Kevlar vests, and a pair of assault rifles. He tossed one of the assault rifles to Stuart, who caught it deftly and began to examine it with an expert eye.

“A Fusil FX-05,” Stuart said. “Mexican designed and produced.”

“We call it the Xiuhcoatl, after the Aztec fire serpent.”

“Foldable stock, not too heavy, not too light. Fires 5.56×45mm NATO rounds from a 30-round box magazine,” Stuart said, still examining it.

“And an extra magazine for you, my friend.” Luis tossed him one. Stuart absentmindedly snatched it out of the air without taking his eyes off the gun. “But you no see what other thing I have.”

Stuart, Alexa, and Chief Inspector Revilla peered in the crate. Inside sat a grenade launcher with a six-round magazine that looked like a revolver on steroids.

“A South African built Milkor MGL-140 grenade launcher,” Stuart said. “Effective range of up to 800 meters. Sexy.”

“You can’t use that in a residential neighborhood!” Alexa cried.

“Why? You think it is, how you say in English?”

“Overkill,” Alexa said.

"It is no overkill. Only tear gas. No explosive."

Chief Inspector Revilla looked relieved. He moved to the door. "I'm going to get the vehicles away. I'll grab all the gas masks from the SandCat. There are plenty for everyone."

"Good idea," Alexa said, "but I doubt moving the vehicles will fool him. He'll know there are police lying in wait, even if he hasn't scouted out the neighborhood already. You clear out the neighbors?"

"Hours ago," the National Guard officer said, walking out of the room. Alexa heard him call to two of the municipal police to help him drive the three vehicles a few blocks away.

Alexa turned to see Luis and Stuart, chests puffed out, examining the grenade launcher.

Ah, testosterone. So annoying and yet so useful. Especially in situations like this.

"Um, guys?" Alexa said. "We should probably finish our preparations."

"Right," Stuart said as if he had just woken up. "We got to laying the spikes behind the front gate. Let's go."

Just then, a dog barking next door made them freeze.

Alexa moved to the window, drawing her gun as she did so. It was remarkable that she had even been allowed to carry a gun south of the border, but Senator Silverman had friends among the politicians here and it had all been cleared in record time.

She looked over the concrete fence separating the yard from the neighbor's. She couldn't see the dog in the yard or the house but judging from the slightly muffled sound of the bark, she guessed it was in the house.

"That dog, he always bark," Luis said.

True, he had been barking on and off all day, but this time it sounded more insistent, more anxious. She stood staring at the neighboring property for a full minute. No sign of movement. Eventually the dog stopped barking.

"Let's go deal with those spikes behind the front gate," Stuart said.

Luis clapped him on the shoulder, and they headed out, now fully armed with military gear. Alexa started to put on her Kevlar.

* * *

Vicente sat in the passenger seat of the car, safe and out of sight behind tinted windows. The big man with the long hair sat behind the wheel. The gringo in the back. He hadn't asked their names. Why bother?

The *vaquero* came around the corner, long legs eating up the distance as he walked with a casual air yet fast for the car parked only a couple of blocks away from the house of the Luis Pérez family. The *vaquero* had been out on a scout. The gringo, with his military training, would have been more qualified, but his skin made him stand out. No matter. He would have plenty to do soon enough.

The *vaquero* got in the back seat.

"The police cars and armored personnel carrier just drove off. Only a driver in each one."

Vicente nodded. "Just as I thought. They're going to park a few blocks away to hide the vehicles, thinking we will scout out in the afternoon and strike at night."

"Those three drivers will come back soon," the gringo said.

"Yes," Vicente agreed. "We will strike now."

An assault against a house in a residential neighborhood protected by several policemen who expected trouble. Not a single one of the mercenaries objected or hesitated. Instead, they picked up the helmets and Kevlar vests stowed at their feet and started to put them on, their movements quick and efficient despite the cramped interior of the car.

Besides the body armor, each man was armed with various guns of their own choosing. The big man had a pair of UZIs. The *vaquero* favored a hunting rifle with scope and a Glock as a backup. The gringo had an M16 and an RPG.

The gringo would take the first shot.

Vicente did not put on a helmet or body armor, and only carried his usual knives and guns. He felt more comfortable that way. Easier to maneuver.

"You men ready?" Vicente asked.

They all grunted their affirmation.

"Let's do it."

The big man drove through the quiet neighborhood. He had put his long hair in a ponytail to keep it from getting in the way during the fight. Vicente looked around. Yes, the police were waiting. This place looked dead. How many homes had they evacuated? And how soon could backup come? They had to hit the place hard, get in, and get Luis.

He had some things to say to his brother.

He turned around to address the gringo sitting right behind him.

"Remember, as soon as we get up there—"

"I'm ready," the gringo said.

The big man at the wheel rolled down the window a crack. Not so low as to reveal who sat inside, just enough to hear the noises of the neighborhood. Yes, very quiet.

They pulled down the final stretch. Vicente didn't see the three policemen walking back yet. Good. That evened the odds a bit.

Just as they moved toward Luis's house, he could hear the sound of voices and the rattle of metal coming from the front yard.

What are they doing in there?

I'll find out soon enough.

The gringo readied his RPG and opened the door on the opposite side from the house. Just a crack, just enough to be ready when the big man pulled the car to a stop.

"Blast that gate and we'll move in," Vicente said. "*Vaquero*, you stay behind as sniper. Watch those upper windows."

"Will do," the *vaquero* said.

"Everyone ready? Stop the car in three … two …"

CHAPTER THIRTY ONE

Alexa got her Kevlar strapped on and checked on the guards. Chief Inspector Revilla and the two municipal cops weren't back yet. That left a municipal officer posted at the upper story rear window, making sure no one tried to sneak up on the house that way, and the two National Guardsmen patrolling the grounds. Alexa moved to the front window on the second story. The guys had stuck a small side table next to the window and put a large potted plant to block most of the space. She smiled at how it looked but considering the heavy ceramic and the fact that it had a good two feet thickness of soil in it, the thing could probably stop a bullet.

Peering around it, she saw Stuart and Luis standing below, stringing out some spike strips the municipal police had brought, putting them across the inside of the outer gate that led to the garage. The idea was that if anyone busted through the gate, which looked like it couldn't withstand a truck coming at speed, it would get stopped by the strips and not be able to ram into the house or be used as a getaway vehicle. Despite the hot Mexican sun, both men worked in Kevlar and had their helmets on. Both men were used to it.

She looked out across the neighborhood, the homes half hidden by palm trees and their own tall fences, privacy and security both important here. The houses in the immediate area showed no sign of life, having been quietly evacuated by the municipal police that morning. The only sounds were the buzz of insects, the occasional cry of birds, and the low hum of distant traffic. Even that dog was keeping quiet for the moment.

Then she saw a red four-door with tinted windows pulling up in front of the house.

She grabbed a walkie-talkie she had in one hand while drawing her pistol with the other.

"Car pulling up in the street outside," she said in Spanish. Every guard was equipped with a walkie-talkie. "Could be nothing. I'm watching it."

They'd had several false alarms already. Alexa kept alert just in case.

The moment the car stopped, a man in Kevlar jumped out of the far side, wielding an RPG.

He's going to blast the gate, and Stuart and Luis are right behind it.

"Get back in the house!" she screamed out the window.

The two soldiers didn't even ask why. They dropped the spike strip they had just finished spreading across the back of the gate and bolted for the house.

The man with the RPG braced it against the front of the car, positioning himself behind the engine block to add to the protection of his helmet and Kevlar vest.

Alexa doubted she'd hit him, but maybe she could mess up his aim.

She fired three quick shots. One punctured the hood right in front of him. Another shattered the windshield. She didn't know about the third shot.

He didn't flinch.

The rocket whooshed out of the launcher and an instant later slammed into the metal gate, which shredded like paper.

Alexa stumbled back from the force of the blast. White dust and a few larger chunks fell from the ceiling.

She looked up and stared.

A twisted piece of metal the size of her hand was lodged in the ceiling, still vibrating after its flight. A piece of the gate. It must have flown in from the window.

Right past her head.

Gunshots made her shake off her shock. She could be traumatized later. Right now, she needed to get into the fight.

She rushed to the window, keeping low, peeking out between the big ceramic pot, which hadn't been hit at all, and the side of the window.

In just the two or three seconds she had been away from the window, the entire scene had changed. The man behind the engine block had tossed aside his RPG and was now firing with an assault rifle through the shattered gate.

Luis and Stuart and maybe the National Guardsmen fired back from the first floor, aiming for him and peppering the car with bullets.

Coming at an angle, she saw a big man with a ponytail coming out of his helmet rushing for the gate, an UZI in each hand. She fired at him. The guy jerked but didn't fall.

Damn, hit his Kevlar. He's a beast not to fall from the impact, though.

She aimed for his legs.

A bullet shattered the ceramic pot, which fell in a dozen pieces and a heap of soil.

That silly idea just saved my life. Gotta love a man in uniform.

She crouched lower. Another bullet splintered the windowsill.

That hadn't come from the guy behind the car, who still fired at the downstairs, and it hadn't come from the man with the two UZIs, who had hidden himself out of sight behind the wall. Where had it come from?

Then she saw a third man in Kevlar crouched behind a telephone pole and trash can a little down the street, aiming right for her.

She ducked just as his next bullet ploughed through the heap of soil on the side table, covering her with it.

He's too far for me to shoot at with just a pistol.

Nevertheless, she popped up again, just in time to see the guy with the UZIs charge into the breach, leaping over the spikes, bellowing and firing both guns at the same time as his backup behind the car let out a burst as well.

Alexa didn't hear the guys downstairs return fire. They probably had to duck for cover. She hoped they were still alive. They wouldn't be for long if that monster made it to the windows.

She fired down at the charging man, and saw him convulse, trip over his own feet, and fall flat on his face in the driveway, a bullet through his neck.

The next moment, the sniper behind the telephone pole fired at her again.

This time he hit.

Alexa felt her head jerk to the side, heard a loud *clang*, and suddenly found herself lying on her side.

Gunfire continued, increasing in strength and intensity. Alexa tried to rise, fumbled, head spinning, ears ringing, bile rising in her throat. She paused, took a few deep breaths and finally succeeded in getting to a sitting position. She felt her face. No blood. Removing her helmet, she found a small dent on the side. A glancing shot that would have knocked her out or killed her if the Mexican army hadn't loaned her a helmet. She made a mental note to apologize to them for the Mexican-American War.

Pushing the side table away, she moved up to the window and peeked over, showing only a narrow space between her helmet and the windowsill. To her surprise, no shot came.

An instant later she saw why. The sniper had shifted to a position behind the wall and next to the gate, where he could fire at the lower story, figuring he had already killed Alexa. The guy behind the car kept up a steady fire too.

Alexa waited, and when the sniper popped out of cover to fire his rifle again, she shot at him. Her bullet pockmarked the concrete wall and made him dive back out of sight.

Sirens wailed in the distance. Backup already? No, probably Chief Inspector Revilla and the other two cops rushing back to the scene.

And another question, a more pressing one—where was Vicente Pérez? He hadn't made an appearance.

Just then a pair of bottles flew out from a downstairs window, smashing on the driveway just inside the gate and bursting into flames.

Molotov cocktails? When did the guys have time to make those?

The flames covered the entrance, blocking any more charges. Two more Molotov cocktails sailed through the air and the flames rose up even higher.

For a second there was a lull in the fighting. The sirens grew louder. Both the sniper and the guy behind the car had ducked out of sight, probably reloading. Alexa took the chance to do the same.

Just as she snapped her spare clip into place, a sound upstairs caught her attention. What had that been? A thud? Her ears rang so much the noise had barely registered.

She crawled to the doorway of the room and peered out. It looked out on a hallway with doorways leading to several other rooms, all open since the guys had removed the doors and set them up as barricades.

She saw nothing, though.

Another burst of gunfire below, but beneath that, had she heard something else, something up here?

Alexa crept along the hallway, hugging the wall of a house that had suddenly gone silent again. The sirens grew louder. She came to the first open doorway on her left, ducked in, cleared the room in less than a second. No one. A soft sound, too much muffled by the ringing in her ears to identify, made her dart back into the hallway.

Something was moving up here. One of the municipal police had been positioned in the back, but she hadn't heard anything from him since the fight began. Had he gone downstairs? Gone to one of the other upper story windows facing the front and gotten shot?

No, the noise had come from the back of the house.

And there it was again. Alexa froze. Movement in one of the back rooms.

The staircase separated her from two open doorways. She needed to walk past the open doorway just ahead on her left, and move a little to the right, to the top of the stairs, before she could see into the first of those rooms.

A burst of fire down below covered her movements as she advanced. She dared a quick look to the left to check on the room there. No one, but someone could be hidden in the adjoining bathroom. Check that or keep going forward?

She darted across the open doorway and got a bit of a view into the first of the back rooms.

The municipal policeman lay on his back on the floor. Only his head and shoulders were visible, but Alexa could see enough. A knife was lodged hilt-deep in his throat.

Vicente.

Alexa ducked back into the room on her left, willing to risk exposing herself to an uncleared room now that she knew what was in front of her.

Vicente burst out of the room a moment later, firing several shots in quick succession. He was so fast, so accurate, all Alexa could do was leap backwards, allowing herself to fall in order to avoid the bullets that smacked right through the flimsy drywall.

She performed a backwards roll, her Kevlar hampering her, and ended up prone, facing the doorway. She crawled ahead, ready to fire, and only saw a blur as Vicente launched himself down the stairs. She got off one shot before he disappeared.

Desperate, she leapt to her feet and ran over to the staircase, leaning over the banister and dangerously exposing herself in order to get another shot at him.

Too late. He was gone. The gunfire below was steady now, and no one would hear her warning as the most dangerous man in two nations snuck up on her partner and colleagues.

CHAPTER THIRTY TWO

Alexa tore down the stairs, desperate to catch up with Vicente. She had noticed he wore no Kevlar, carried no heavy weapons. He had opted for stealth and speed, and that had helped him sneak around to the back of the house, get over the back wall, kill a police officer with an incredible knife throw, and then climb up the back of the house.

What had his brother said about him? A devil in human skin?

She took the stairs five at a time, risking her neck in a desperate attempt to get there in time. She slammed down on the landing, heading around the corner with no time to check. A glimpse of Vicente darting around the far corner of the hall, the hall that led to the front room.

She made it in time to see what happened, but not in time to stop it.

Vicente came upon the four men in the front room without their knowing it. One National Guardsman lay on the floor, seriously wounded. The other knelt over him, trying to staunch the bleeding. Stuart was firing out the window and Luis was changing the clip in his assault rifle, kneeling by the other window of his ravaged living room.

With two quick, casual shots, Vicente took out both the National Guardsman and Stuart.

"No!" Alexa screamed.

Luis whirled around and spotted his brother just as Alexa raised her gun to fire.

Luis threw his empty gun at Alexa, who was so surprised at the move that she didn't even have a chance to bat it away. The weighty chunk of steel hit her in the arm, and her bullet planted harmlessly in the floor.

Vicente whirled around, but before he could fire, Luis flew at him, landing a boot in the small of his back.

Vicente fell on his face. A shot came through the window from the street outside and smacked into the wall inches from her head. Alexa ducked into the hallway to get out of the line of fire.

What the hell? Luis saved him and then me.

Just as she got in position to go back around the corner and fire, she heard Luis shout, "Follow me, brother!"

Alexa dared a peek, just in time to see Luis duck to the right and through the open doorway to the garage. Vicente ran right after him, firing an unaimed shot behind him that made Alexa dodge and not get a chance to shoot him.

By the time she got to the window, Luis had peeled out of the garage on a motorcycle, hitting a large chunk of the front gate that allowed him to jump over the spikes he had laid out behind the gate. He flew through the flames that still burned there, hit the pavement, and took a right down the street.

The next instant, Vicente did the same. Alexa fired, missed, fired again, only to hear the click of an empty gun. Alexa cursed and slapped in another clip. Vicente took a right and disappeared after his brother.

With a terrible sense of dread, she turned to the two new casualties. The National Guardsman looked dead. Stuart groaned. Alexa rushed over.

"Are you all right? Where did he shoot you?" She didn't see any blood.

"Got me in the Kevlar," he moaned. "Where is he?"

Alexa let out a gust of relief. She put a hand on Stuart's cheek, and he smiled up at her, his knitted brow relaxing.

"Get the son of a bitch," he said.

Before she knew what she was doing, Alex was up and running. She angled to the left, where the flames had died down a bit and she could jump over them and get into the street.

What just happened? What the hell just happened?

* * *

What just happened? Vicente wondered. *Luis saved me, then saved the gringa Marshal I fought back in Arizona.*

He had no answer. He hit the crumpled metal of the gate and flew over the spikes and the flames, landing in the street outside. Luis was already half a block away.

Just then a police car screeched up to them. The *vaquero* leapt out of hiding, leveling his rifle, only for the man behind the wheel, wearing the uniform of a Chief Inspector of the *Guardia Nacional*, to run him over.

Firing from the left. The Chief Inspector leapt out of the car and bolted for cover. The gringo must still be in the fight and firing at him.

Fine, let them kill each other. He needed to follow his brother. He needed to catch up with him.

Another car with *Guardia Nacional* markings appeared, making for them.

He hit the accelerator and sped down the street in the other direction after Luis.

After his brother.

Luis was nearly a block ahead of him, and on a faster model than the one Vicente rode, and yet he didn't pull away, didn't shake him in the several side streets in this neighborhood. No, he kept a steady pace, not allowing Vicente to catch up but also staying in sight.

Where is he taking me? Why did he save me? He wanted to get me away from the fight, but why?

Briefly Vicente wondered if this was some sort of trap and discarded the thought almost as soon as his mind formed it. Making it out of the house had been a miracle. The *vaquero* and the gringo must have noticed it was his brother and held their fire, but Luis could not have known they'd do that. Luis had risked his life to take him away.

But where?

Down a residential street, weaving between the infrequent cars. It was a workday and most people were at the office or factory. Those few drivers they did come across screeched to a halt and got as far over on the curb as they could when they caught sight of a man in full Kevlar, an assault rifle strapped across his back, powering down the road on a motorcycle. One poor guy swerved so much he took out three garbage bins and a fire hydrant.

Vicente chuckled and put on more speed. Luis must have seen that in his sideview mirror because he put on more speed too. Vicente had barely gained an inch.

They wove through the residential streets, missing cars by a hair's breadth and screeching around the corners. Luis kept on, not slowing, not turning around to face him with his superior armor and firepower, instead keeping on a relentless path for the edge of town.

Vicente could see that now. His brother's house stood close to Nogales's southern city limits, and his flight took him further in that direction as the houses thinned and more and bigger empty lots appeared between them.

That brought up a memory. Luis had always been a bit of a wanderer, striking out on his own even at a very young age to explore the city. He'd sneak onto city buses in the rush hour press or hang onto the back, riding them to the end of the line. It drove his parents crazy, and Vicente was usually the one who had to hunt him down.

Once Luis got all the way out of the city riding buses for free. No small accomplishment. He ended up sleeping out in a farmer's cornfield and riding the buses back the next morning. He had only been eight years old.

Father beat him for that little stunt. Didn't stop him from doing it again, though.

Vicente smiled. Little Luisito always dreamed of travel. He remembered once they were dumpster diving behind one of the tourist hotels downtown and found a whole stack of *National Geographic* magazines. Vicente liked them for the topless ladies. Luis loved them for the pictures and articles of all those far-off places. He covered his bedroom walls with pictures of the Amazon and the Himalayas.

Vicente wondered if that's why he joined the army. Did he volunteer for peacekeeping missions overseas? Haiti or Afghanistan or someplace like that? He hoped so.

More empty lots than houses now. Forested hills in the distance, marred only by a few rich men's villas. He suspected his little brother knew this route well.

Through the onrushing wind and the whine of the motor between his legs, he could hear a police siren. So they had picked up a tail. Hardly surprising. Well, he could take care of that easily enough. The big challenge would be Luis.

They came to a long open stretch past a large house enclosed by a wall. The street turned to dirt past the last house, the terrain rising a bit and growing rougher. Agave, prickly pear, and jagged outcroppings of rock replaced palm trees and telephone poles.

Luis slowed, swerved, and jumped off his bike, turning to face Vicente, who slowed to a stop a couple of hundred yards from him. He shut off the engine, put down the kickstand, and dismounted.

"I want to talk to you," Luis called. "I have some things to tell you. Away from the others. You have spilled enough innocent blood already."

"It's been a long time, brother," Vicente called back, smiling.

"We are not brothers," Luis said, pulling the assault rifle off his back. He held it at the ready, not quite pointing it at Vicente.

Vicente kept his hands close to his pistol and one of his knives, walking slowly toward Luis.

"You have done well, Luisito. All grown up and an officer in the army. Mother and father must be proud."

"They were. Now they have both been taken to their rest."

Vicente stumbled a little. Hearing that felt the same as when Luis had kicked him in the back and knocked the air out of him.

He'd never see them again. So much wasted time.

"And our sisters?" Vicente's voice wavered.

The siren grew in volume. Still only one, but the police car would be here soon.

Vicente continued to walk slowly toward his little brother.

"They are doing well," Luis said. "But how they are doing is none of your business."

"I'm done with all that, Luisito."

"Stop calling me by the diminutive. I am no longer a child."

"I can see that, Luis. You've grown into a real man."

"I wish I could say the same of you. Look at your life."

Vicente shook his head. "I said I'm all done with that, Luis. I killed everyone who twisted me. You know, I was planning on heading down to Mexico City to hunt for any of Los Verdugos who might still be alive, but now I won't. I'm done."

"Except for me."

Luis's gun raised slightly. The police siren grew louder, an insistent wail that remind Vicente how little time he had to make his brother understand.

Vicente let out a long, slow breath, forcing his muscles poised to fast-draw his gun and knife, to relax. It went against every instinct bred into him ever since joining that two-bit street gang as a kid, but he did it.

He had to.

With an effort he put his hands on his head, interlocking his fingers like the policemen order you to do. The policemen who had never once caught him.

"I'm not here to kill you, Luis." Until he actually said the words, he did not fully believe it himself.

Luis snorted. "If you wanted me to believe that, maybe you shouldn't have assaulted my home with a group of mercenaries."

"I don't want to kill you, little brother," Vicente repeated, his voice cracking.

"Stop calling me your brother! You are dead to me."

"Please, Luis, I—"

"I've been following the news, and I figured out what you're doing. You didn't need to tell me just now. You're killing everyone who ever pulled you deeper into crime. All your bosses, all your coworkers, and whoever else gets in the way. Like Angel! What did he ever do to you?"

The siren grew louder, cut off as a car came to a stop somewhere behind him. Vicente didn't turn around.

"And I know why you came for me, Vicente! That stupid boast I made when I was nine. Mother and Father believed it, God forgive them, and they kicked you out of the house. I admitted my lie later, but they said it was for the best that you were gone, that you were no longer a Pérez. And they were right."

"Luis. Little brother. I forgive you for that. I should have never blamed you. You were only a child. None of that matters anymore. I'm back now. I no longer work for the narcos."

Luis looked him in the eye for the first time.

"Vicente, I believe you."

The sound of running feet behind him, a woman's voice shouted, "U.S. Deputy Marshal. Get down on the ground!"

Vicente opened his mouth, but Luis spoke first.

"I believe you, but you must pay for all the evil you did."

Luis fired. The bullet hit Vicente in the chest, puncturing his heart, and smashing into his spine. He fell hard on the ground. For a second, stunned confusion, then a growing despair as the light grew dim.

"But I was done," Vicente whispered.

* * *

Alexa returned to the Pérez home as quickly as she could, cursing herself as she temporarily got lost on the unfamiliar streets of Nogales. She had left a gunfight back there and she had no idea how it had ended.

A municipal police car with two officers in it had appeared shortly after Luis had killed Vicente. They took over the situation and got the soldier's statement. She wasn't needed there. She was needed back at the house.

As she rounded the corner and saw the house a hundred yards ahead, she saw it was all over. Several cars from the municipal police and Guardia Nacional were parked outside, lights flashing. A Guardia Nacional vehicle was parked across the road to block it, two men with MP5s standing behind. When they saw someone in Kevlar driving a bullet-riddled car, they leveled their guns at her.

She screeched to a halt, raising both hands as she did so.

"Deputy U.S. Marshal!" she shouted in Spanish. "I'm down here on the Vicente Pérez case!"

"Get out of the car!" one of the National Guardsmen ordered, aiming his gun at her head. The other guardsman circled around to the side.

Chief Inspector Revilla came running up. "Let her through! She's with us."

The two guardsmen sloped their submachine guns, and she ran right past them.

"Is Stuart alive?" she asked as the chief inspector fell in beside her.

"Yes. We lost a municipal officer and one of my own men. The other guardsman is seriously injured. An ambulance just took him away. One of the municipal police who returned with me also got shot in the arm. He is being treated right now."

"And the mercenaries?"

"All dead. Vicente?"

"His … his brother killed him."

That was all she could bring herself to say about the strange scene she had witnessed on the empty lot. Vicente hadn't drawn a gun, he had only walked slowly toward his brother, arms out and imploring, saying something Alexa had been too far away to hear.

And then Luis shot him in cold blood.

He would get away with it. After the attack on the house, after all of Vicente's murders, any Mexican court—any U.S. court—would rule it justifiable homicide.

And how did she feel? She didn't know. It didn't seem right to judge Luis, not in that situation.

As she and the chief inspector came up on the scene of the battle, Alexa suddenly felt hot, weary, and in pain from the shot to the chest

Vicente had given her only a few days before. And she'd developed a headache and neckache from the glancing blow to her helmet.

Strange, she hadn't felt any of those things before this moment, but now that the danger had passed, now that it was all over, regular human weakness returned.

Alexa stopped short. No, it was not all over.

Stuart stood, shoulders slumped and his helmet in his hands, standing over the man who had fired the RPG at them and had then proved so effective in the battle.

For the first time, Alexa noticed he was Anglo, American by the look of him. His helmet had fallen off in the fight to reveal a brown buzz cut.

Military haircut, military training, oh God he was a veteran.

One look at Stuart's face and she knew who finally managed to kill this man.

Alexa moved up to Stuart, who stood motionless over his fallen fellow soldier. He turned to look at her, his movements and face wooden, eyes dead. For a second Alexa hesitated, then a slight softening in his face made her move closer and put an arm around his shoulder.

Together they stood close, saying nothing, feeling far too much.

CHAPTER THIRTY THREE

The Chase ranch in northern Arizona, three days later ...

Alexa sat on the swing on the back porch of her father's ranch watching her brother Malcolm teach Stuart to ride. He wasn't having much success.

Malcolm had put him on the oldest, steadiest mare in the stable, and had been taking him around in circles in the corral. Once he got used to that, and it took a while, they had set up a tiny little jump. Stuart let out an amusing yelp every time he went over it, and looked ready to fall right off, one arm waving to keep his balance like he was breaking a bronco.

This brought him much teasing from both Alexa and Malcolm. He seemed to take it in good humor. Most men don't like being laughed at, but considering how much life had thrown at Stuart, a little laughter meant nothing. And he was improving. Slowly. Very, very slowly.

Things had smoothed over between them. They'd been through fire together and that made her slipups fade in significance, and for that Alexa felt deeply grateful.

The situation with Stacy was still patchy. Ever since that night she had acted sulky, withdrawn. Alexa had hoped an offer of coming up to the family ranch, with all its horses and rangeland to ride out on, would thaw her out. But Stacy had sulked and said she didn't want to come. That hurt Alexa more than she cared to admit.

Give it time. She'll come around.

The screen door slammed. Alexa looked over her shoulder and saw her father, coffee cup in hand, cowboy hat on head. He sat down next to her.

"So where did you get hurt this time?" he said.

"What do you mean?"

"You're moving stiffly, and don't tell me you're just tired. I know you're tired, but you got hurt too."

"My Kevlar vest took it. All I got is a hell of a bruise. I went for an x-ray. No fracture."

Alexa decided not to mention that she hadn't gotten an x-ray until after the case was solved and she got back from Mexico. She knew what he'd say and didn't want to hear it.

Dad looked at her, more rather than less concerned for her casual explanation.

"Can I see?"

"No. It's right here," she said, pointing to her middle chest.

"Right between the titties, eh? You should have sued him for sexual harassment."

Alexa laughed. "Dad!"

"Well, I hope you at least roughed him up before you put him in the back of the police car. Give me a minute with him. I'll smack him around a bit too."

"Actually, I never got a chance to arrest him," she said in a quiet voice. "He got killed by his own brother."

Her father didn't say anything for a minute, chewing on this. Malcolm cheered as Stuart took another jump, followed by a warble of fear and a precarious wobble.

"You'll get it eventually!" Malcolm encouraged him.

"You need to stop," her father told her.

"Dad, I—"

"You need to stop. This is wearing you out. Not as bad and as quickly as the BAU did, but you're gonna end up the same. I don't want you stuck on the ranch for a year again, looking off into the distance and barely speaking like some zombie. I almost lost you then, and I don't want to lose you now. And you moping around the ranch all burnt out inside is the best possible outcome. More likely one of these psychos will shoot at you when you aren't wearing a vest, like when that guy stalked you at your house, and what do I do then?"

Alexa gave him a hug, burying her face in his muscular shoulder so as to hide the wetness in her eyes. It wasn't her scrape with death that choked her up. It wasn't the lecture, which she had heard a million times before. It was the slight break, quickly covered up, in that tough old man's voice when he asked what he'd do if his only daughter got killed in the line of duty.

A rancher who never showed any real emotion had almost broken in front of her.

"I can't stop, Dad," she said once she was confident that she could keep her own voice steady. "There's too much to do, and I'm the woman to do it."

"There are others who can do it. You told me yourself Stuart is a way better cop than he is a rider."

That made Alexa chuckle. She shifted a little to rest her head on his shoulder and look out on the corral. Her father slipped an arm around her and gave her a squeeze, more affection than he had shown her since she was a kid.

"I can't, Dad."

"Why the hell not?"

"Could you give up ranching?"

"Of course not. What a dumb question."

"Well, I can't give up policework. It's what I am. You're a rancher and I'm a cop."

"What do you get out of it? Is a commendation from the senator and governor worth risking your life for?"

Alexa shrugged. "That wasn't so much for getting Vicente Pérez as for busting several drug gangs in the Phoenix area, and most of that information came from a gang leader who gave up all that information because he wanted us to hunt the killer down. We did, but it didn't do him much good."

"You talking about that Cortez fellow who was all over the news?"

"Yeah."

"Glad they revoked his bail. Dumb to let him out in the first place."

"The senator wasn't thinking straight. He had just lost his daughter, but yeah, he's back in jail where he belongs, him and all his gang, and most of the big people in all the other gangs."

"New ones will replace the old."

"I know. And I'll be there to knock them down again."

Her father frowned, looking off in the distance toward the rugged mountains past a long stretch of beautiful desert.

"Well, couldn't you work in a CSI lab or do cybercrime or something? Something that keeps you safe?"

"No."

Her dad looked at her.

"I hate it when you say no like that. Because it means you mean it and I'm never going to get your stubborn head to say yes."

"I get that from you," she said, kissing him on the cheek.

Her father grunted and stood. "I'm going to give that partner of yours some riding lessons before he breaks his neck."

Alexa chuckled. After he left, she pulled out a thick journal she kept by her side. The diary of Robert Powers, her former partner, killed when Drake Logan's followers broke him out of custody. It had actually been left to her in Powers's will, and she had been reading an entry every day, as he had obviously wanted her to.

Well, almost every day. She had been so wrapped up in the hunt for Vicente Pérez that she had forgotten for the past few days. That had made her feel guilty and tempted to catch up, but she decided to read them as they had been written—one day at a time.

She opened the journal to where she had bookmarked it. Another day in the life of a man who she thought she knew, but now, from beyond the grave, taught her so much more about himself than she had ever guessed.

She began to read.

"I need to get a grip," Powers began, his handwriting unusually messy and jagged, as if his hand shook as he wrote this blunt statement.

"Been hunting that slasher, the one who cuts people's faces and runs off. Doesn't rob them, doesn't rape them, just goes up to someone passing by on the sidewalk at night and cuts them once across the face. Even if the victim manages to dodge and he only nicks him, he doesn't try a second time. Just walks off. Doesn't run, so it isn't a fear reaction, just walks off.

"How the hell am I supposed to predict a guy like that? I've been losing sleep over it. Olivia says I look tired and distant. I guess I do, but I need to find this guy before he escalates. Assuming he escalates. He hasn't yet. Maybe this is all he wants.

"But why?

"I began to dig into similar cases. Didn't find much until I hit on a guy who committed a series of acid attacks in Miami. Took battery acid and splashed it into random people's faces. Usually that kind of crime is against women, loser types who resent the beauty they can't have, but this guy did it to men and women, and using only a small amount of acid to they would only be partially disfigured.

"Among the evidence was a diary he kept. I requested a scan of it last week and the Miami P.D. sent it to me. Fascinating reading.

"It isn't burning a person's face that matters so much, it's the thrill leading up to it. The idea that this regular guy walking around town has the power, with a flick of a wrist, to traumatize someone. Ruin their day. Ruin their face. Sometimes, he says, he just walked around with the little vial of acid in his pocket and never used it. He smiled at everyone he passed. His mug shot shows he's personable looking. Handsome. No one to worry about if you passed him in the street.

"The slasher must be the same, walking around with a straight razor in his pocket, feeling like the king of the world until the urge gets too much and he has to lash out. It would explain why there's so much time between each attack.

"I needed to get into this guy's head. The journal from Miami helped, but it wasn't enough. So I bought a straight razor, put it in my pocket, and walked around the same areas where he's made his attacks."

Alexa leaned back, looking away from the journal and its terrible insights.

Jesus Christ, don't tell me this.

After a moment, she rubbed the bruise on her chest, took a deep breath, and forced herself to continue.

"It was strange. At first it felt kind of stupid and boring, walking aimlessly around with my hand in my pocket, gripping a straight razor. It wasn't as if I was going to use it, so what was the point?

"But then I began to think—what if I did use it? That thought wheedled into my mind and once it got there it wouldn't get out. I began to look at the people I passed differently, not like they were strangers I'd never meet, but people whose lives I could have a profound influence on. Ruin their day. Ruin their face.

"Then this guy passed by. Young guy. Gym jock. Rugged features. Probably gets lots of girls. And I thought 'I could stop him from getting any girls ever again. I could take that contented smile right off his face.' And I found I had pulled the straight razor out of my pocket."

Jesus Christ. My personal role model was even more screwed up than I am, Alexa thought, feeling sick to her stomach.

"The guy didn't even notice. Off in his own little world. The next second he passed by, leaving me on the sidewalk staring at the straight razor.

"I threw it in a drainage ditch, went straight home, and curled up in bed with my wife. Then I called in for a week off. Personal time. Marshal Hernandez didn't even ask why. I guess everyone could see I was frazzled. Someone else can do the slasher case.

"I've been off for two days now and all I've done is walk in the desert with Olivia breathing fresh desert air and have dinner with friends. The problem with this job is that it puts you on the sidelines of life, keeps you in the dark holes of society. We need to explore those holes, understand them, but we must remember that we cannot dwell in them all the time. If we do, we'll end up being like the people we hunt."

Alexa closed the journal with a shudder. That had hit too close to home.

She looked over to Stuart riding in circles and swaying from side to side as her father cursed him for a "dang city fool" and Malcolm called out encouragement.

They're right, every one of them. I am getting too wrapped up in my work, and I'm getting too wrapped up in this journal too.

So why am I sitting here on the sidelines watching them?

Carefully, Alexa put her partner's journal to the side, stood up, and walked over to the corral. Today she'd help teach Stuart to ride. Tomorrow, all of them would ride out into the desert and breathe in some clean air.

Her phone rang. She almost ignored it, but out of habit pulled it out of her pocket.

Mr. Carpenter? Why is he calling? Oh, maybe Stacy changed her mind!

She answered.

"Hello?" she said.

"Is Stacy with you?" Mr. Carpenter asked.

"Um, no. Why?"

"She's not at your house either. Or at that boy's house."

"What do you mean?" she said, a growing sense of dread rising within her.

"Her wallet and bag are missing. She took some of my money too. She must have run away!"

"Did you call her?" Alexa gasped.

"Her phone is switched off."

"I'm on it."

Oh God, Stacy. What have you done?

Alexa bolted for her truck, stopped after a few steps, and ran for the corral.

She needed Stuart's help. He'd do anything for a kid in trouble.

And Alexa knew with terrible certainty that Stacy was in serious, serious trouble.

NOW AVAILABLE!

THE KILLING FOG
(An Alexa Chase Suspense Thriller—Book 5)

When a fugitive flees the country, U.S. Marshal Alexa Chase is summoned to criss-cross Europe to find him and bring him back. On a wild cat-and-mouse chase, Alexa must venture outside of her comfort zone to stop this killer before he strikes again.

"This is an excellent book… When you start reading, be sure you don't have to wake up early!"
—Reader review for The Killing Game

The Killing Fog (An Alexa Chase Suspense Thriller—Book 5) is book #5 in a new series by mystery and suspense author Kate Bold, which begins with THE KILLING GAME (Book #1).

Alexa Chase, 34, a brilliant profiler in the FBI's Behavioral Analysis Unit, was too good at her job. Haunted by all the serial killers she caught, she left a stunning career behind to join the U.S. Marshals. As a Deputy Marshal, Alexa—fit, and as tough as she is brilliant—could immerse herself in a simple career of hunting down fugitives and bringing them to justice.

But with her recent work a big success, the FBI and the Marshals have decided to make their joint-task force permanent. Alexa, reeling from her own traumatic past and her PTSD of hunting serial killers, has no choice: she will now have to work with an FBI partner she dislikes and hunt down serial killers whose jurisdiction intertwines with that of the U.S. Marshals. Alexa finds herself forced to confront the thing she dreads the most—entering a killer's mind.

Butting heads with local authorities and with a third partner, Alexa is out of her depth and up against a range of obstacles in a

foreign country—all while a diabolical killer is gaining steam. In her toughest case yet, Alexa will need all the strength of her brilliant mind to discover where the killer is hiding—and to bring him to justice before he strikes again.

Unless he finds her first.

A page-turning and harrowing crime thriller featuring a brilliant and tortured Deputy Marshal, the ALEXA CHASE series is a riveting mystery, packed with non-stop action, suspense, twists and turns, revelations, and driven by a breakneck pace that will keep you flipping pages late into the night.

Book #6—THE KILLING PLACE—is also available.

Kate Bold

Bestselling author Kate Bold is author of the ALEXA CHASE SUSPENSE THRILLER series, comprising six books (and counting); the ASHLEY HOPE SUSPENSE THRILLER series, comprising six books (and counting); and the CAMILLE GRACE FBI SUSPENSE THRILLER series, comprising three books (and counting).

An avid reader and lifelong fan of the mystery and thriller genres, Kate loves to hear from you, so please feel free to visit www.kateboldauthor.com to learn more and stay in touch.

BOOKS BY KATE BOLD

ALEXA CHASE SUSPENSE THRILLER
THE KILLING GAME (Book #1)
THE KILLING TIDE (Book #2)
THE KILLING HOUR (Book #3)
THE KILLING POINT (Book #4)
THE KILLING FOG (Book #5)
THE KILLING PLACE (Book #6)

ASHLEY HOPE SUSPENSE THRILLER
LET ME GO (Book #1)
LET ME OUT (Book #2)
LET ME LIVE (Book #3)
LET ME BREATHE (Book #4)
LET ME FORGET (Book #5)
LET ME ESCAPE (Book #6)

CAMILLE GRACE FBI SUSPENSE THRILLER
NOT ME (Book #1)
NOT NOW (Book #2)
NOT WELL (Book #3)

www.ingramcontent.com/pod-product-compliance
Lightning Source LLC
Chambersburg PA
CBHW030618310726
48979CB00003B/767

* 9 7 8 1 0 9 4 3 9 4 5 5 8 *